A Case of Bad Blood?

Gus shifted his focus onto the black case and the contents that had been strewn about. He collected the items and put them in a pile. Even with the scar swelling over his damaged left eye, he could see there was something peculiar about the garments. Just to be sure, he picked them up and took a closer look at each bit of clothing one by one.

"Damn it, Gus, pay attention," Doyle scolded. "Now ain't the time to sniff them bloomers."

"There's blood on these clothes," Gus said.

"So?"

Shifting his eyes to Mason, Gus held up a torn blouse and said, "This is blood and it's on every piece of material in this case."

Ralph Compton

Outlaw's
Reckoning

A Ralph Compton Novel
by Marcus Galloway

A SIGNET BOOK

SIGNET
Published by New American Library, a division of
Penguin Group (USA) Inc., 375 Hudson Street,
New York, New York 10014, USA
Penguin Group (Canada), 90 Eglinton Avenue East, Suite 700, Toronto,
Ontario M4P 2Y3, Canada (a division of Pearson Penguin Canada Inc.)
Penguin Books Ltd., 80 Strand, London WC2R 0RL, England
Penguin Ireland, 25 St. Stephen's Green, Dublin 2,
Ireland (a division of Penguin Books Ltd.)
Penguin Group (Australia), 250 Camberwell Road, Camberwell, Victoria 3124,
Australia (a division of Pearson Australia Group Pty. Ltd.)
Penguin Books India Pvt. Ltd., 11 Community Centre, Panchsheel Park,
New Delhi - 110 017, India
Penguin Group (NZ), 67 Apollo Drive, Rosedale, North Shore 0632,
New Zealand (a division of Pearson New Zealand Ltd.)
Penguin Books (South Africa) (Pty.) Ltd., 24 Sturdee Avenue,
Rosebank, Johannesburg 2196, South Africa

Penguin Books Ltd., Registered Offices:
80 Strand, London WC2R 0RL, England

First published by Signet, an imprint of New American Library,
a division of Penguin Group (USA) Inc.

First Printing, April 2009
10 9 8 7 6 5 4 3 2 1

Copyright © The Estate of Ralph Compton, 2009
All rights reserved

THE IMMORTAL COWBOY

This is respectfully dedicated to the "American Cowboy." His was the saga sparked by the turmoil that followed the Civil War, and the passing of more than a century has by no means diminished the flame.

True, the old days and the old ways are but treasured memories, and the old trails have grown dim with the ravages of time, but the spirit of the cowboy lives on.

In my travels—to Texas, Oklahoma, Kansas, Nebraska, Colorado, Wyoming, New Mexico, and Arizona—I always find something that reminds me of the Old West. While I am walking these plains and mountains for the first time, there is this feeling that a part of me is eternal, that I have known these old trails before. I believe it is the undying spirit of the frontier calling, allowing me, through the mind's eye, to step back into time. What is the appeal of the Old West of the American frontier?

It has been epitomized by some as the dark and bloody period in American history. Its heroes—Crockett, Bowie, Hickok, Earp have been reviled and criticized. Yet the Old West lives on, larger than life.

It has become a symbol of freedom, when there was always another mountain to climb and another river to cross; when a dispute between two men was settled not with expensive lawyers, but with fists, knives, or guns. Barbaric? Maybe. But some things never change. When the cowboy rode into the pages of American history, he left behind a legacy that lives within the hearts of us all.

—*Ralph Compton*

Chapter 1

Gus McCord had lived outside the law for so long that he'd forgotten what it was like to live anywhere else. He carried his victories and losses as scars on his face, wounds on his body and nervous tics that acted up at unexpected noises. Every so often, Gus thought his whole body had gone numb after being put through the wringer too many times. He learned to live with the numbness, just as he'd learned to deal with the pain. It wasn't any harder than learning to live with the use of one good eye.

One of Gus's scars started a few inches above his hairline, cut down perilously close to his left eye and then sliced along the side of his nose to end at his upper lip. The ax blade that had done the damage had also taken out a pair of Gus's teeth in a fight that ended with the wielder of that ax being shot full of more holes than a sieve. Gus never knew that man's name and had left him to rot under a few scoops of dirt somewhere in Oklahoma. It took months for him to see anything out of that eye and even when the wound healed up, the scar was fatter than an oversized caterpillar, which prevented him from opening it all the way again. His aim suffered after that. In fact, it suffered enough for him to find himself a .38 Smith & Wesson to go along with the modified Colt .44 he'd carried since he'd first struck out on his own. Actually, he'd stolen the .38 just as he'd stolen pretty much everything else he'd ever owned.

Gus wasn't an old man, but he looked like someone who'd seen a hell of a lot more than forty-one winters. A thick mustache sprouted from his lip in an effort to cover a bit of the damage done by that ax. His hair sprouted like desert scrub and was colored with just enough gray to make it seem as though ash had taken root in his scalp. Rough yet steady hands were currently wrapped around a fork and knife so he could tear into the steak that had been brought to him. When most men would have sat and enjoyed their meal, Gus looked around to challenge anyone brave enough to try to take it away from him.

The restaurant was in a town near the eastern border of Cochise County that had been built up around a stagecoach platform and the neighboring shed that sold tickets. A telegraph wire hung from a series of poles and threatened to fall to the ground whenever the gentle breezes grew into gusts. It was a clear day and the wind was barely strong enough to push a tumbleweed along, so everything was right in that pathetic excuse for a town.

As he sawed his last hunk of beef in half, Gus looked over to one of the nearby tables. A little boy over there had been staring at him since his arrival.

The young man with the boy could have been the kid's father, but Gus didn't know for certain. When that man shifted around to see what the boy was staring at, he immediately turned the kid's chair around and scolded him.

"It ain't polite to stare at folks," the young man hissed.

"But he looks funny," the kid insisted. "I think he hurt his eye."

"Don't stare. Whatever happened is over and I'm sure it didn't hurt none. Just eat your soup and stop making folks uncomfortable."

Oddly enough, Gus hadn't felt uncomfortable until that moment.

Before the kid could twist around to get another look at the forbidden sight of Gus's beaten face, his attention was drawn to the front door of the little restaurant as it was pulled open with almost enough force to separate it from its hinges. Through that door stomped a man who looked to be on the verge of howling like a coyote. His wild face was covered with thick dark brown whiskers and his jacket was open to display the two pistols hanging at his sides.

Unlike Gus, this man had always carried two guns. Doyle Hill also carried knives and a railroad spike that had been split in two and dented almost beyond recognition. Doyle insisted the spike was a good-luck piece, but Gus knew better. Some men just got bored killing folks the same way too many times in a row.

It didn't take long for Doyle to spot Gus at his table. When he did, Doyle charged through the restaurant as if he intended on knocking a hole clean through the wall. "Order yerself a whiskey, because we need to celebrate!"

Gus bared his teeth a little when he replied, "They don't serve no whiskey here, Doyle. Why don't you just sit down and have some water?"

"No whiskey? What kind of place is this?"

"A place that just serves food," Gus replied. "How about you sit down and stop making so much noise?"

"I don't want to sit down."

"Then just shut the hell up."

Doyle took a look around to find the few others inside the restaurant all glaring nervously back at him. Letting out a sigh, Doyle pulled up a chair, spun it around and sat down in it so his chest was leaning against the back rest. "I got some good—"

Gus raised the hand that was wrapped around his knife. The blade was dented and still covered in juices from his steak, but he brandished it like a weapon. "Quiet. Some folks are trying to eat."

Doyle nodded and leaned across the table until his nose practically touched the steak knife. "I got some good news," he said in a voice that didn't carry through the entire place.

"What's your news?"

"That stage we wanted to catch ain't left yet."

Just then, the woman who'd brought Gus his steak returned to the table to set a glass of water in front of Doyle. "The stage won't leave for another hour," she told him.

Doyle looked up to find the pleasant, somewhat plump face of a woman in her late thirties. Light hair was tied to fall down her back and friendly eyes were framed by deeply etched lines. "That's real nice," he told her. "Thanks for the water."

"Can I get you anything else?"

"Got any whiskey?"

"No," she replied without missing a beat. "But there's a saloon just down the road. They even have a piano that plays loud enough to be heard over the commotion you're making."

Gus smirked and used the last crust of his bread to sop up what remained on his plate. "She's got you there."

Doyle nodded slowly and looked at her closely. His light blue eyes took their time wandering all the way down the front of her body and back up again. By the time they'd reached her face, the woman's expression had changed considerably. Grinning at the way he'd sapped her confidence, Doyle said, "Bring me something sweet. Cake with frosting if you got it."

"We don't," she said as she took a step away from the table.

"Then pie. Just go find something and bring it to me."

The woman wanted to say something else, but she couldn't bring herself to spit out the words. Wincing at the gruff tone in Doyle's voice or perhaps out of frustration with her own squeamishness, she hurried back behind the counter separating the dining room from the kitchen.

After Doyle turned back around, Gus spoke to him in a barely audible snarl. "You know better than to talk about business where others can hear."

"These people ain't nobody. They probably don't even leave this piss bucket of a town."

"You got something to say? Say it so I can finish my meal."

"You ain't finished? There ain't nothin' left but the plate." Seeing the fire that was growing in Gus's eyes, Doyle added, "All right, all right. That stage we wanted to catch won't be loaded when we thought. Seems, they had some difficulties with their team."

"You hobble one of them horses like I told you?"

"Hobbled? I nearly cut one of its legs off."

"For the love of—"

Cutting Gus short with a quick wave of his hand, Doyle said, "I hobbled it just like you told me. Can't you take a joke no more?"

"Maybe you ain't as funny as you used to be," Gus said.

"And maybe you're losing yer nerve. If we ain't ridden together for so long, I might suspect you didn't want to go after this stage at all."

"What's that supposed—" Gus stopped when the woman with the wrinkled eyes came back to the table.

"We don't have any pie," she said. "No cake, either. Nothing sweet."

"Well, ain't this a sorry excuse for a restaurant?" Doyle grumbled.

Before the other man could say anything else, Gus reached out to hand some money over to the woman. "Here you go. This should cover what I ate, plus a bit more for yourself."

"Thank you, sir," she replied. Without so much as looking at Doyle, she turned and rushed away from the table.

When Doyle started to speak again, Gus stood up and walked toward the door. He could hear the other man wrestle out of his chair and stomp behind him as he walked outside and came to a stop along the edge of a crooked street. As soon as he emerged from the restaurant, Doyle circled around to stand toe-to-toe with Gus.

"You know better than to talk to me that way!" Doyle snarled.

"And you know better than to make such an ass of yourself. We don't discuss business where everyone can hear. Did you get a knock to the head or do you just not care that we're wanted men?"

Doyle's eyebrows flickered upward and he glanced from side to side without truly looking around. "You sure you want to say that so loud? There might be a bunch of lawmen hiding behind a spittoon somewhere."

Gus walked along the street toward the portion of town that grew thicker with hastily built shacks and several tents hanging from leaning frames. "How much time you think you bought for us by hobbling that horse?" he asked.

"Another hour or two. The passengers are scattered to Lord knows where and they need to be rounded up. Then the stage has to be loaded. Maybe they need to get a different horse and hitch it up." Looking up to the sky, Doyle added, "That should put the stage at that pass we scouted sometime close to sundown."

Stopping to let a cart roll past him, Gus hooked his thumbs under his gun belt and surveyed the scene in front of him. "We just read about the price on our heads when we passed through Tombstone the other week," Gus said. "Maybe we should just hole up somewhere and wait for the storm to pass."

"Ain't no storm to speak of," Doyle shot back. "Leastways, no more of a storm than usual. Things got a whole lot worse back in Mesa. Of course, that's back when Jake was ridin' with us. I'm surprised that boy didn't get himself shot long before his day finally came."

The day Doyle spoke about was one that Gus thought he'd never live through. He, Doyle and Jake Bannister had caught wind of a payroll shipment being delivered by a single rider who thought a bit too highly of himself. Doyle wounded the rider with a long-range rifle shot, but the man still managed to get away after whipping his horse with every last bit of strength in his body. Help arrived in the form of three men with hunting rifles. Jake rode straight at them with his Colt blazing and caught the brunt of those hunting rifles square in his chest.

"That payroll was meant for a string of silver mines," Gus said.

Doyle chuckled. "That's why it was so much money."

"That's also why that price on our heads won't go away anytime soon. There'll be men looking for us."

"There's always gonna be someone looking for us." As he said that, Doyle tipped his hat to a local who had wandered along to cautiously look the pair over. "All hiding's gonna do is drain our money faster. From what I hear, this stage has something mighty valuable on it that's not the sort of thing that'll come along again anytime soon."

"What is it, exactly?" Gus asked.

Doyle shrugged. "Could be gold. Could be money. Could be another payroll."

"Could be nothing."

"Yeah. That's what makes it exciting."

Gus let out a breath that sounded as if it had been pulled up from his bootheels and dragged over six miles of rough ground before being shoved out of his lungs. "I don't like jobs where I don't know all the angles."

"There ain't no way to know all the angles, Gus. We just gotta think on our feet, and since there ain't nobody else along with us to get in our way, that should be easy enough."

Doyle had a point there. Of all the partners Gus had had throughout the years, he'd never made as much money as when he had Doyle backing him up. Even so, it didn't do any good to let Doyle know just how valuable he was.

"So how do you know there's enough on this stage to make it worth our while?" Gus asked.

"Even if we just rob the passengers, it'll be enough to line our pockets for a ride away from these territories. And—he added with a sly grin—"we can make certain to drop a few hints of where we're supposed to be goin' so the folks on that stage will get the wrong idea when we ride away. I might even let a few of 'em see my face so they can tell the law it's us. Of course, it might stick in their heads better if they saw your face."

Gus curled his lip with a warning growl.

Steering away from the hot water he'd nearly stepped in, Doyle went on to say, "Enough folks spread the word it was us that robbed 'em and that we was headed south or southeast, and the law will charge that way while we ride in the other direction."

"That . . . sounds like a good idea."

"It really hurt to say that, didn't it?"

It did, but rather than admit as much, Gus grumbled, "I still want to know what's on that stage that's so special. How is it you don't know yourself?"

"Because I only heard bits and pieces," Doyle explained. "The man who let it slip was selling tickets when he overheard some of the passengers talkin'. They said they was carrying something valuable. My friend heard it and passed it along."

"Can you trust this friend of yours?" Gus asked.

"He passed along this bit of talk to even a score between me and him. He knows lyin' about a thing under those circumstances wouldn't lead to anything but a whole lot of pain." There was no mistaking the grave tone in Doyle's voice. "He's tellin' the truth. Least, he is as far as he knows." Suddenly, Doyle's face brightened as he dropped an arm across the back of Gus's shoulders. "But if you're still fretting about it, there's one way to get another opinion."

Before Gus could ask for anything more, he was pointed toward a feed store on the opposite side of the street. A young man wearing a frayed vest and dirty britches was walking out of the store carrying a sack of oats on each shoulder. Although he seemed strong enough to keep the oats from hitting the ground, his legs were just wobbly enough to slow him down to something shy of a snail's pace.

Keeping his arm around Gus's shoulders, Doyle led him toward the feed store. Once he was within arm's reach of the man carrying the oats, Doyle asked, "You need some help with them?"

The question had nearly been enough to knock the overburdened man onto his backside. He'd been so intent on watching where he was going that he hadn't even noticed Doyle and Gus approaching him. After regaining his balance, he smiled nervously and said, "No, I've got it. Thank you kindly, though."

Doyle hopped in front of him and nudged the sack of oats on the fellow's left shoulder. He then reached out to narrowly prevent the downfall he'd almost caused. "Looks like you don't have it at all, my friend. Why don't you let us give you a hand?"

Gus didn't help trip the other man up, but he didn't try to help the younger fellow either. Instead, he stood his ground and let his partner carry out his own agenda.

"You're taking them oats over to the stagecoach platform, ain't you?" Doyle asked in a conversational tone. "You work over there, right?"

The younger man tried to look at the two who'd taken such an interest in him, but the effort only robbed him of some more of his balance. "Yeah, I do," he replied. "And I need to get back, so if you wouldn't mind . . ."

Gus placed a hand on top of the oats on the fellow's right shoulder. Now that he saw where Doyle was headed, he decided to help him get there before anyone else decided to lend the fellow a hand. "Nonsense," Gus said in the friendliest voice he could manage. Pushing the oats just enough to rock the other man precariously, he added, "This is about to squash you like a grape. See?"

Between his own momentum sending him one way and the two men nudging him in the other, there simply wasn't anything else the younger fellow could do but keep moving his feet and keep the stagecoach platform in his sight. He sputtered a bit while trying to say something to the men flanking him on either side, but couldn't get out more than a few grunting attempts before he was shoved off the street.

The alley was quiet, for the most part. Most of the activity in town was either at the stagecoach platform or headed in that direction. Even so, Gus stood with his back to the street so Doyle and the stammering fellow could have a moment.

"Wh-what do you want?" the fellow asked.

Doyle slapped his hands against the sack on the other man's shoulder with just enough force to knock him over. Looking over him like a vulture, Doyle said, "I want you to tell me who's on that stage."

"What stage?"

Doyle's leg snapped out to send the side of his boot into the fallen man's ribs. "The stage that's set to leave soon. And don't tell me you don't know anything about it, because I seen you tending to them horses and having words with the driver."

While Gus hadn't seen those things for himself, he trusted Doyle to have his facts straight. It had been Doyle's job to scout the town while Gus was eating, and Doyle was very good at his job.

"I don't know who's on the stage," the fellow on the ground replied. "All I do is feed the horses."

"You unloaded the stage as well," Doyle said. "I saw you doin' that."

"Only on account of one lady getting off here! All I did was climb up to pull her bag down. I don't know what's in it."

Doyle gritted his teeth and reached into one of the pockets of his battered leather jacket. He took the cracked railroad spike from where he kept it, held it like an ice pick and lowered the jagged end to within an inch of the fellow's eye. "I wanna know something good about that stage or who's on it. You tell me anything you know or heard or I'll nail yer head to the ground."

The fellow lay with his arms spread out and his fingers digging into the dirt as if he was afraid of falling off the face of the earth. His mouth gaped open like a trout's and his eyes frantically snapped over to Gus.

Peeling open his duster to show the .44 holstered on his right hip, Gus said, "You'd best do what he says."

Since he saw no hint of a soul in Doyle's eyes and even less in Gus's, the fellow on the ground took the only road left open to him. "I just carried a few bags," he groaned. "I swear."

"Who's on that stage?" Doyle asked.

Gus could feel their time running out. It wouldn't be long before someone happened to look their way or came walking by at the wrong time. The spot Doyle had picked wasn't so much of an alley as it was a footpath that led from the main street, between a few wood-framed tents and to a lot where some horses were tethered. Gus watched for movement in the vicinity, but all he found was a few fidgeting mares.

Once he got to talking, the fellow on the ground couldn't stop. "Besides the lady that's staying here, there's only a few others. One was older than the other and they had a young girl with them. I don't know if the girl was with both of them or not, but she seemed to know the two men. That may be just because they were riding together but—"

Doyle leaned down over the other fellow like a rattlesnake getting ready to sink its fangs in. "Were they carrying anything? Do they have money?"

The fellow on the ground couldn't nod fast enough. "They were dressed real nice. One had a gold pocket watch! I saw it when he was stepping out to stretch his legs. And he asked about a package."

"What package?"

"I don't know what it was, but it seemed important. I offered to move it to a better spot on the top of the stage, but he wouldn't let me touch it. He nearly took my head off for looking at it."

That brought a smile to Doyle's face.

Chapter 2

Gus stood within a dozen paces of the stagecoach platform. From that vantage point, he could turn around and see the entire town laid out in front of him as it spilled along the street. It was a pathetic sight.

The sky was darkening a bit by the time the stage was finally being loaded. Doyle had done such a good job hobbling one of their horses that the drivers had given up on fixing him up for that run and gotten a replacement. Gus didn't know how Doyle had gotten close enough to do the job and he didn't care. Doyle had his ways.

The passengers had been rounded up and were loitering about, chatting to one another and stretching their legs before piling into the stage one more time. Gus stood behind them with a view of the stagecoach that was impeded only when one of the passengers walked directly in front of him. Every so often, the young fellow who'd brought the oats for the horses glanced over to see if Gus was still there. When the passengers stepped aside, he caught sight of Gus and quickly got back to what he was doing.

The young fellow was terrified. Even from where he was standing, Gus could tell that much. There were plenty of chances for the fellow to say something to one of the other workers, but he kept his mouth shut. The threats Doyle had made before letting the fellow go were as cruel as they were creative and served their purpose perfectly. The nervous fellow loading the stage even made a point to climb on top of the coach and hold up a black case while nodding in Gus's direction.

"Hey!" the stagecoach driver shouted. "Put that down!"

The fellow held the case for a few more seconds, giving Gus's good eye a chance to pick up on the fancy silver filigree built around the handles of the bag. Before anyone else followed the nervous fellow's line of sight, Gus scowled and turned away.

Standing up in his seat at the front of the coach, the driver asked, "Are you deaf? I told you to put that down!"

Just then, one of the passengers turned toward the coach. He was a tall man wearing a long black coat; he struck Gus as an up-and-coming gambler. The coat had the look of an expensive garment, but was obviously worn for more than fancy-dress balls or special occasions. The man wore a gun under the coat as well. The weapon might have gone unnoticed to most, but Gus could recognize the telltale lump under the coat the way a horse trader could size up an animal's ailments in a matter of seconds.

"You there!" the man in the black coat said as he impatiently snapped his fingers toward the top of the coach. "Put that down. That's not to be trifled with!"

"Yes, sir, Mr. Mason," the driver replied. "I was just telling him the same thing."

But that wasn't enough for Mason. He'd stopped snapping, but kept his arm extended as if he meant to pluck the nervous fellow right off the top of the coach. "In fact, hand it down to me. I'll carry it in here."

"It'll stay up with the rest of the luggage, Mr. Mason," the driver said. "Like I told you before, we got too many passengers to take up seats with bags and such."

Mason grumbled something and let the matter drop.

Now that Gus had turned his head and stepped aside, the fellow on the coach put the case down and made his way to the footholds that led up the side. Before he could set his boots upon solid ground, he was pulled down by the burly man who'd been hitching the team into its harness. The burly man had the shape of a beer keg and was only slightly taller than the nervous fellow. Gus recognized him as the one who'd ridden shotgun when the stagecoach had rattled into town.

"What were you doin' up there?" the shotgunner asked.

"Nothin', Scott, I swear!" the nervous fellow sputtered.

Scott had ahold of the fellow's shirt with both hands and used his grip to pull the fellow closer and hoist him up onto his tiptoes. "You were skulkin' up there like a damn rodent. Was you the one that hurt my horse?"

"No, Scott! Why would I do that?"

"I don't know. Why would you mess about with folks' bags when they're already loaded?"

Although the fellow tried to speak in his own defense, he was too close to tears to say much of anything. He kept on sputtering, which only ruffled Scott's feathers more. Before Scott could do anything more, the driver came along to swat him on the back of the head.

"Leave him be," the driver scolded. "He ain't the one that hurt ol' Lou."

Gus tried to look busy while keeping his back turned and his face pointed away from the stagecoach. Before he could wonder too long about who Lou was, he heard an answer.

"Lou's been pulling that stage like a champion for years," Scott said. "If someone hurt him on purpose, I'll break him in two with my bare hands."

"Someone hurt him all right," the driver grunted. "It just wasn't Eddie."

Since the nervous fellow's ears perked up at the sound of that name, Gus figured it belonged to him.

"The man I saw pokin' around Lou was a filthy-lookin' mongrel with darker skin."

"An Indian?" Scott asked. "Or a Mexican?"

"Neither, just darker skin like he'd been cooked in the sun too long," the driver said. "And more whiskers on his face. It just wasn't Eddie. Leave him the hell alone so we can pull out of here. I'm sick of this town and I only been here a few hours."

Finally, Gus heard something to which he could wholeheartedly agree. Since the horses were hitched to the stage and the passengers were settling into their seats, Gus walked away before anyone thought to ask why he'd been watching them like a hawk. He didn't have to walk very far before Doyle sidled up beside him.

When Doyle lifted his head to look at him, Gus snapped, "Pull that hat down to cover your face. Them stagecoach drivers are looking for you."

"Aww, those cowboys don't know much. One of 'em thinks I'm an Injun."

"But one saw you fussing about with that horse. What did you do to that animal, anyway?"

Doyle shrugged and told him, "Just wedged a few rocks under a shoe or two. Nothing to cause such a ruckus."

Knowing Doyle as well as he did, Gus figured the horse had more troubling him than a few rocks under its shoes. Since the animal seemed to still be drawing breath, he knew that Doyle hadn't gone too far. "Well you'd best stay out of sight all the same," Gus said. "The driver got a look at you and seems awful sore for having to replace one of his horses."

"He'll be even more sore once we catch up to him again. Did you get a look at what that squirrelly fellow showed us?"

"All I saw was a black case."

"Right," Doyle said with excitement running through his voice like a current. "Now that we know what to go after, we can head straight for it when the time comes."

"What's inside that thing?" Gus asked.

Shrugging his shoulders as he strained his eyes for a better look at the stagecoach, Doyle swayed back and forth more than a tall weed in a strong breeze. "Could be anything. Did you see the way that other man jumped to protect it? That means there's something worth something in that case and I don't give a damn what it is. I just want to get it and sell it."

"Then we lay down a false trail and head north." Not seeing any sort of reaction to his suggestion, Gus slapped Doyle's shoulder and asked, "Right?"

"Yeah, right." Although Doyle said those words, he was barely thinking about them. Gus recognized the faraway look in his partner's eyes after having seen it far too many times before. It was the same look he got when he acknowledged the presence of a lawman, right before shooting him.

"So what's the plan?" Still unable to break through Doyle's glazed expression, Gus grabbed one of his partner's shoulders and turned him away from the stagecoach platform. "The plan, Doyle."

Doyle's eyes flared up with an angry fire. "It's the same as it was before! The same it's been since we followed that stage across these damn territories."

"I want to hear it from you," Gus said as he ignited a spark of his own behind his eyes.

"You're such a mother hen," Doyle said as he shook his head and allowed his anger to dwindle a bit. "We'll follow the stage from here and ambush it. You watch the passengers and I'll watch the driver."

Gus felt a twitch at the corner of his eye as he thought through the possibilities left. There was a shotgunner to worry about as well as the driver, both of whom were much more likely to fight back than a few frightened passengers. "No. You watch the passengers and I'll watch the driver."

"You worried I might drop that shotgunner just for the hell of it?"

"That's been known to happen," Gus replied.

Glancing toward the platform as if he was figuring out what he wanted to have for supper, Doyle finally arrived at a decision. Nodding, he said, "All right. One of them passengers knows what's in that case, so I'd like to have a word with him, anyways."

"If we're taking the case, what do you need to say to him?"

"I don't know just yet," Doyle replied as he narrowed his eyes. "But I'll think of somethin'."

Gus knew that look in Doyle's eyes all too well. It was pretty much even money as to whether that look resulted in a larger bounty placed on their heads or more money in their pockets. Sometimes, it meant both.

At the platform, the passengers had all piled into the coach and the driver was settling in. That only left the shotgunner to fuss with the straps holding the luggage down before swapping a few words with Eddie. The nervous fellow seemed plenty happy to see everyone go, but Gus kept an eye on him just in case there was a chance of him getting pointed out.

"They're about to leave," Gus said. "Why don't you get the horses?"

Doyle slapped him on the back and started walking toward the post where their horses were hitched. "This is gonna be one hell of a job. Mark my words."

"I marked 'em."

"And after this, them law dogs and bounty hunters comin' after us won't be doin' nothin' but chasing their tails and choking on our dust."

"Just go get the horses."

Tossing Gus a quick wave, Doyle turned and rushed to the hitching post.

Gus watched him for a second before turning his gaze back to the stagecoach platform. The driver snapped the reins to get the coach's wheels turning. After a bit of huffing and whining from the team, the coach got moving and the horses fell into an easy gait. When he glanced up and down the street, Gus only saw a few locals watching the stage while the rest just went about their business. A few kids waved to the coach, but one little boy wasn't distracted by the sight.

That little boy stood with his feet planted in a ditch, his arms hanging to his sides and his eyes locked upon Gus. It was the same kid who'd been staring at him back at the restaurant.

Meeting that kid's stare, Gus wanted to shake loose of it any way he could. Old instincts reared up inside of him, bringing some particularly vicious ideas along with them. Rather than give in to such things, Gus bared his teeth and lunged half a step forward.

The kid yelped and spun around to scurry off, but his feet were stuck in the mud. He did, however, manage to bump against the man who'd been watching over him before. Gus still didn't know if the man was the kid's father, uncle or what, but he was glad when the man grabbed the kid and pulled him from the mud.

As soon as the stage rolled out of town, Gus and Doyle rode ahead a ways to scout the trail for themselves. Unless the driver intended on trying his luck on rocky terrain that gave way to steep drop-offs, there was only one way for the stage to go. The trail forked several miles ahead, but that didn't concern Gus in the least. He and Doyle would hit it long before the driver had more than one road to choose from.

The ride to get ahead of the stagecoach was treacherous and had to be made while the sun was blazing directly in their eyes. Gus and Doyle gripped their reins and hunkered down low over their horses' necks. To make matters worse, dust billowed in the winds and grit from the trail pelted against their faces. Just when he'd gotten used to the burning of dust in his eyes, Gus had to figure out which way to steer his horse to get around the occasional gorge that appeared in front of them like a mouth trying to swallow both riders whole.

Things would have been a lot easier if the pair could use the same trail as the stagecoach, but that would have made things too easy for the shotgunner. Surely, the man next to the driver had the skill and the rifle required to pick off any threats from a distance as well as from up close. No, Gus and Doyle needed to blaze a new trail, circle back to the old one and do so with enough time to set up an ambush. The two of them had gone through the motions so many times, they didn't need to say one word to each other. They could convey directions, angles and all manner of details to each other with nothing more than points and nods.

This was why Gus hadn't put a bullet into Doyle a long time ago. Training a replacement would just take too long.

The rumble of hooves churning against the ground filled Gus's ears. He looked to his right and caught a glimpse of jagged hills in the distance, a wide crack in the ground and Doyle spurring his horse to build up enough steam to clear it. Once Doyle had jumped over the crack, he turned to meet Gus's eyes. Gus pointed toward the trail and then held up two fingers.

He wanted to get back to the trail and hit the stagecoach within the next two miles. Doyle nodded and signaled that they would hit the stage within half a mile after meeting up with the main trail. They tapped their heels against their horses' sides and gained some extra speed to tear along a stretch of open land.

Gus had stolen his horse some time ago, so both he and the animal were accustomed to each other. They moved like a single living thing that easily pulled ahead of Doyle. Rather than celebrate winning the race that always seemed to take place between him and his partner, Gus looked around for a good spot to ambush the stage. They'd scouted one or two before, but they'd already passed one and the other was too far away.

There was a ridge in the distance, but it was too far from the main trail to do him any good. Some hills rose a little ways to the north, so he pointed his horse that way and spurred him on. Sure enough, those hills kept on rising until they overlooked the main trail leading to Tombstone. Gus pulled back on his reins and waited for Doyle to thunder up to his side.

"That was damn stupid to go so fast over that

kind of terrain," Doyle scolded. "You coulda been tripped up any number of ways."

"You're just sore because I got ahead of you so easy. Take a look over there."

Doyle looked where Gus was pointing and quickly spotted the cloud of dust being kicked up to the east. "That's got to be them. They're headed this way. How long you think before they get here?"

Slowly shifting his eyes from the cloud to the sky above it, Gus replied, "Less than half an hour. There ain't much daylight left, so they must be hauling that coach as fast as they can. How much farther until the next stop?"

"My guess is they'll make it there after nightfall. It couldn't be much farther than that, since I doubt any driver would want to go too far in the dark."

"Unless he knows this country well enough," Doyle said. "But that don't matter anyhow. I can hear 'em coming."

Gus squinted and shifted his head a bit. When he concentrated hard enough, he could finally pick up the sounds of wheels grinding against unforgiving rock. The ground beneath them had turned into a stone plate covered with a light dusting of gravel, which forced the stagecoach to announce their presence long before it could be seen. The sun was dipping low in the western horizon. Its light wasn't enough to blind anyone, but it could still work in the two men's favor if they put it to use just right.

Pointing toward a low ridge, Gus said, "We should wait there. It's a little ways from the trail, but the sun will be at our backs."

Doyle nodded. "I can take the first shot. You sweep

in after that and we'll go from there." His eyes snapped toward the sound of wagon wheels and a smirk took shape on his face when he caught the first sight of the stagecoach. "Got any last words?"

"Yeah," Gus replied. "Don't be an idiot."

With that, both men snapped their reins and raced for the ridge.

It took less than a minute for Gus to jump down from his saddle and scramble toward the section of the ridge that overlooked the trail. He didn't have to look to see if Doyle was with him. In fact, when he hunkered down and watched the stagecoach round a bend, he knew where his partner was just like he knew where both of his guns were holstered. Doyle inched toward the edge of the ridge, which placed him perilously close to ruining the entire ambush or getting both of them killed. If they were spotted too soon, anyone on that stagecoach could fire at them like they were in a shooting gallery. If they waited too long, the stage would be even tougher to catch.

Sensing Doyle's impatience, Gus stretched out an arm to block the other man's way. The stage skidded on a bit of loose gravel, causing the driver to slow down to keep the coach upright. Gus squinted at the wobbling stagecoach as if his one good eye was strong enough to see the distraction on the driver's face. About a second before Gus gave the order, Doyle fired the rifle he'd brought with him.

Chapter 3

The shot hit the man beside the driver in the chest. It was difficult to say exactly where Doyle's bullet had landed, because the man riding shotgun flopped back and then curled up like a dying worm. The driver looked around frantically, but was fighting with the reins too much to really see much of anything. He had to focus on the horses before they got too wound up, which gave Gus plenty of time to race back to his own horse and ride toward the trail.

Between the low position of the sun in the sky, the dust swirling through the air and the thick scar covering a good portion of his left eye, Gus couldn't see a whole lot. Fortunately, the wheels of the stagecoach, the hollering of its driver and the braying of its horses were more than enough to guide him to the right spot. Gus's horse did a good job of traversing the uneven terrain leading to the stagecoach and responded well when Gus pulled his reins to come up alongside it.

The team of horses pulling the stage had been spooked by the gunshot, and the driver seemed spooked by the kicking and flailing of the man beside him. To make things even worse, the horses were slamming against one another in their frenzy to get loose from the stage altogether. Gus rode beside the team of horses and then snapped his reins again to get in front of the team. From there, he worked to slow the whole team down.

Once it seemed the team was regaining its composure, Gus looked back to the driver of the stagecoach. The man held the team's reins in a tight grip, but seemed more concerned with the wounded man riding shotgun beside him. The shotgunner was alive and howling in pain. As soon as the driver realized the stage was slowing down, he took up the reins in both hands and prepared to give them a snap.

Gus drew his .44, which was modified to be fired with a minimum of movements while also being balanced to sit just right in his hand. That way, the weapon felt more like an extension of his arm. In fact, he felt more off balance when the gun wasn't in his grasp. "Stop right there!" he barked. "Try to snap those reins and my partners will burn you down."

The driver looked around frantically for the other men Gus had mentioned. Even though he only spotted Doyle riding down the ridge, he wasn't about to call Gus's bluff.

"Settle your team," Gus ordered. When the driver didn't move fast enough for his liking, Gus thumbed back the hammer of his pistol and added, "Be real quick about it."

Pulling back on his reins, the driver muttered to his wounded shotgunner. As the stagecoach rattled to a halt, Gus maintained his position beside the front of the team until the animals no longer seemed

ready to bolt. He reached out to pat the closest
horse's ear while keeping a good grip on his .44 with
his other hand.

Doyle approached the stagecoach with a smile
on his face and a Spencer rifle propped against his
hip. Turning his head toward the ridge, he shouted,
"Set your sights on both drivers, but be ready to
pick off anyone who tries to climb out of the coach
as well." Shifting his eyes toward the petrified faces
staring out from the coach, he added, "You'd best
stay put, now."

Gus never liked the way Doyle played up to their
nonexistent partners. It was enough to get folks to
believe there were more gunmen lurking about, but
it wouldn't do to have those same folks look too
hard for whoever else was supposed to be out there.
Sooner or later, someone would realize Gus and
Doyle were the only ones they needed to worry
about. After that, the driver, shotgunner and passengers would figure out they outnumbered the
robbers enough to make a run at them. Before he
thought too far ahead, Gus sighted along the barrel
of his .44 to aim at a spot between the driver's eyes.
"Pick up the shotgun, rifle and whatever other guns
you keep up there and toss them over yonder."

The driver picked up a fairly new Sharps rifle and
started to throw it to the patch of ground Gus had
nodded to.

"Toss that one over here," Doyle said.

Only after he saw a nod from Gus did the driver
shift his arm to toss the Sharps to Doyle. As the rifle
flew through the air, Gus narrowed his eyes and
tensed the muscles in his gun arm. The driver

sensed the subtle change in Gus the way an animal could sense a predator getting ready to lunge.

Doyle caught the Sharps and looked it over with an approving nod. He dropped it into the boot of his saddle and kept his own Spencer at the ready.

"And the shotgun," Gus ordered.

The driver shook his head. "That's all we got, mister."

"Don't lie to me."

No threat was needed. Wincing with a bit of shame, the driver lowered his head and reached under the seat for a double-barreled shotgun. He held it toward Doyle, who refused it with a shake of his head, and then tossed it to the previously mentioned patch of ground away from the stagecoach.

By now the passengers inside the coach were getting restless. Doyle put a stop to that by shifting his rifle so its barrel rested on top of his left forearm and fired a shot that blazed through the window of the coach's door and sped straight through the one on the opposite side.

"Sit tight," Doyle said.

With those two words, the passengers leaned back into their seats and kept their mouths shut. Gus knew the situation wouldn't remain in his favor forever, so he pressed his advantage while he still had one.

"We come for all your valuables," Gus said. Fixing his eyes on the driver, he added, "I want you to climb up top there and throw down whatever you got that's worth anything."

"We're just carrying passengers," the driver protested.

"Don't lie to me!" Doyle snapped.

The sharpness of Doyle's voice caused nearly all the passengers to jump. The driver winced but maintained his composure.

"I ain't lying to you, mister," the driver said to Gus. "Just passengers."

"Then why the shotgunner?"

"He always rides with me."

Gus cocked his head to one side and brought his gun up just enough to better align it with his good eye. The motions barely taxed a muscle, but got some good results.

"All right, don't shoot," the driver spat. "There's a lockbox where we keep ticket money and some more to cover expenses and such."

"Throw it here," Gus said. When he saw the driver's reluctance to leave the wounded man beside him, Gus announced, "He'll be the luckier of you two if you don't get moving."

To his credit, the driver waited to see the shot-gunner's face before he left him. The second man in the driver's seat kept his hand pressed against a blood-soaked section of his vest that was an inch or two in from his right side. Gus estimated Doyle's bullet had caught him in a rib. Any worse than that and the man would be either dead or making a whole lot bigger of a fuss.

"While you're up there," Doyle said, "hand down that black case."

The driver had one foot propped against the edge of the bracket that prevented the luggage from sliding off the coach's roof. A dusty tarp covered the luggage, which the driver was just starting to pull aside.

Doyle's eyes suddenly took on a cold steely glint. "And don't look to Gus no more. I gave the order and you'll do it. You got an objection?"

Slowly, the driver shook his head but was a bit too slow for Doyle.

Firing a shot from his Spencer that hissed through the air a few inches from the driver's head, Doyle barked, "Now! We ain't got all day."

After that, the driver moved as if he was being whipped. His feet scrambled to find purchase atop the stage, even though he could probably climb on it with his eyes shut under normal circumstances. His hands shook so hard that Gus could see the quaking from where he sat.

The first thing the driver found was the black case. Gus recognized it as the one Eddie had shown him back on the platform and knew Doyle was practically drooling at the sight of it. "Throw it to him," Gus said.

The driver complied by gently tossing the case. Catching it without letting his rifle falter in the slightest, Doyle allowed his grin to slip back into place.

"Now for the money," Gus said. "Throw it all to me."

Leaning over to look into the coach, Doyle said, "That goes the same for all of you. Gather up any money or valuables you got and hand 'em over."

It didn't take long for their orders to be carried out. Even so, Gus grew more and more uncomfortable as every second ticked by. He felt as if his skin was shrinking around him, wrapping him up tightly within a constrictive net. A dented iron container about the size of a cigar box was tossed to him by the driver. A few seconds later, a pair of trembling hands emerged from the coach to hand a bundle over to Doyle.

"Wh-what now?" the driver asked.

"I'll tell you what now," Doyle replied. Aiming his rifle into the coach, he said, "That man right there is comin' out here with us. The rest of you can rot in hell for all I care."

"What he means," Gus quickly added, "is that you can all move along. And if anyone so much as throws a rock at us, we'll come back and fill that coach full of blood—you hear me? We caught you once, we can do it again."

The side door of the coach swung open and the man who'd been called Mason leaned outside. He held both hands in front of him. In one hand was his hat and in the other was a pearl-handled .32.

"I forgot I had this," Mason explained.

Doyle smirked and aimed his rifle at him. "Sure you did," he grumbled as he snatched the pistol away and pulled Mason outside. Although the well-dressed man stumbled, he managed to catch himself before falling out of the coach and landing on his face. Once upright again, he quickly dusted himself off.

"You know who we are?" Gus asked the driver, who promptly shook his head. "We're the men that robbed the train bound for San Francisco. The one where all those souls were lost in that fire."

That hadn't been one of Gus's favorite jobs, but it was the most famous.

The driver's eyes widened as if he'd suddenly

realized he was gazing into the soulless face of a demon.

"I see you heard of us," Gus said. "That's good, because I won't need to tell you what could happen if you decide to do anything but get the hell out of here once I give the word."

The shotgunner flopped over and pulled himself up. "We can get rich by bringing these murderers in! Just get their guns away from—"

"Shut up, will you!" the driver snapped. "I don't wanna die and you're already close enough." To Gus, he said, "He's just delirious, is all."

Gus nodded, feeling his grip on the stagecoach loosening despite the fear that kept almost everyone in check. Mason stood outside of the coach with his arms raised up over his head. He looked to be somewhere close to Gus's age, but didn't have nearly the amount of hard lines etched into his face. Side by side, the two men were like two roads: one well tended and smooth, while the other was crooked and nearly too rough to use any longer.

"What do you say, Gus?" Doyle asked. "There's some mighty pretty ladies in there. Should we take one or two of 'em for ourselves?"

"One's enough," Gus said. "Turn this heap around and point that team back the way they came."

"You want us to go back?" the driver asked.

"That's right. That is, unless you want to ride south with us for a bit longer."

The driver couldn't shake his head fast enough and he dropped into his seat to hastily collect the reins. When the wounded shotgunner tried to speak, the driver yelped to the horses and snapped the reins to keep him from being heard.

Gus moved away from the trail to let the driver wrangle his team until the stagecoach was turned around. Doyle had Mason's hands tied behind his back by the time the stage was set to go. The driver looked over to Gus and waited for the nod. When he got it, he snapped his reins to get the wheels turning.

"Oh," Doyle said as he casually aimed his rifle at the coach, "better take this with you." He fired a shot into the coach, which was followed by a frantic cry from within. The gunshot, along with the crack of the reins, got the horses thundering down the trail amid a cloud of dust.

Chapter 4

Gus kept his mouth shut until well past nightfall. Half a moon hung in the sky, its light occasionally dulled by wisps of passing clouds that were pushed along by a lazy breeze. They couldn't afford to ride at full speed in the dark since the terrain grew rockier and more uneven the farther Gus, Doyle and their prisoner got from the trail. Eventually, a tall rock caught Gus's eye and he steered toward it. His partner followed and both horses were reined to a stop within half a second of each other.

Swinging his leg over to drop from the saddle, Gus stomped over to Doyle's horse before the animal had stopped shifting its hooves against the hard ground. As much as he wanted to grab Doyle by the neck, Gus took hold of Mason instead and roughly pulled him down. "What was the meaning of that?" Gus snarled.

Doyle slid down from the saddle, wearing an amused grin. "The meaning of what? I thought the whole thing went nicely."

"It did. Right until you decided to shoot someone in that coach. Sounded to me like you hit a woman."

"That was just a woman screaming," Doyle said in his defense. "I ain't sure if she was the one that was hit." Knowing he was getting dangerously close to Gus's bad side, he quickly added, "I didn't hit nobody. I just got the horses going, that's all."

Gus knew it was pointless to argue with his partner. Doyle could swap words until the cows came home, and if things got any worse, he'd be the first to draw his pistol and put an end to the fight. Since he had other concerns apart from locking horns with Doyle again, Gus shifted his eyes to Mason. The prisoner was composed and sat on the ground like a possum playing dead.

When Mason casually glanced over to him, Gus pounded his boot into his stomach. There wasn't enough force to do any damage, but Mason had a real hard time drawing his next breath. "What are you looking at?" Gus roared.

Latching on to the moment as if he'd been born for it, Doyle pulled his railroad spike from where he kept it and stuck the cold chunk of iron under Mason's chin. "Yeah, what are you lookin' at?"

Mason kept still, closed his eyes and waited.

While there were no outward signs of fear coming from the well-dressed hostage, Gus could smell it better than hot apple pie in a warm kitchen. Before Doyle could get to work with that railroad spike, Gus pulled Mason off the ground and sat him upright. "What did you intend to do with this one?" he asked. "We got that case you were after."

"Sure we got the case," Doyle said. "But he could still come in handy. If not, we can leave him here."

Gus kept his eyes fixed upon Mason while Doyle

picked up the case that hung from his saddle horn. Mason kept still until Doyle dropped down to sit next to him with the case on his lap. When Doyle started to open it, Mason grumbled, "It's locked."

"So it is," Doyle said as he pulled at the case to find it wouldn't even start to come open. Laying the case within inches of Mason's nose, Doyle dropped his fist like a hammer so the railroad spike shattered the little mechanism that kept the handles together. "And now it ain't."

As much as Doyle flustered him, Gus had to chuckle at the sight of his partner enjoying himself so much. "What's inside?" he asked.

Doyle opened the case, glanced to both of the other men and then looked inside. He gnawed his tongue as he fished around in there. When he pulled that hand out again, he was holding something that absorbed the moon's pale light like milk being sopped up by a rag.

"This belong to one of the ladies?" Doyle grumbled. Holding the material to his nose, he sniffed it a few times and scowled as if he'd just caught a whiff of a skunk's tail. "It does, doesn't it?" When he didn't get an answer right away, he threw the material aside and raised the case over his head. "Answer me!" he bellowed.

Gus stepped up to place a hand upon the case. Although he didn't try to take it from Doyle, he kept it from moving long enough for him to say, "I didn't know you insisted on bringing him this far just to cave his head in."

Sucking in a few breaths, Doyle blinked and lowered the case. "You're right."

"Let's just see what we've got here," Gus said as
he reached into the case. Upon first inspection, all
he could see were a few more scraps of material
that resembled the first one Doyle had already
pulled out from there. Gus examined each scrap in
turn, only to find a few lacy bits of stocking as well
as shreds of what might have been a light green
blouse.

Crouching down next to Mason, Doyle grabbed
some of the well-dressed man's hair and forced him
to look directly at him when he asked, "What's the
meaning of this? Why were you so worked up when
this case was being loaded onto the stage?"

Thinking back to how Mason had yelled at Eddie,
Gus looked one more time at the case. He was certain it was the same one. The same silver filigree was
around the handles, but there also hadn't been any
other black cases on the stagecoach. "Yeah," Gus
said as he looked down at Mason, "I think you
should answer that question."

Although Gus had stopped Doyle from shoving
that case down his throat, Mason could tell he no
longer had an ally in the other man. "I-I never got
worked up," he stammered. Since both of the gunmen were scowling at him, Mason was quick to
amend his words. "What I mean is, I just wanted my
baggage treated with the proper—"

"That's it," Doyle said as he drew one of his .45s
and aimed it at Mason's face. "This one's just become more trouble than he's worth."

"Those clothes belong to Abigail Swann!" Mason
sputtered. "They're bound for Dragoon Summit,
where they'll be put on a train and delivered to

Benson. I don't know where they go from there! I swear it!"

Doyle's eyes narrowed even more and he started shaking his head as though he was trying to loosen up something that had gotten lodged in there. "What are you talking about? Gus, do you have any notion of what this fool is saying?"

But Gus had shifted his focus onto the black case and the contents that had been strewn about. He collected the items and put them in a pile. Even with the scar swelling over his damaged left eye, he could see there was something peculiar about the garments. Just to be sure, he picked them up and took a closer look at each bit of clothing one by one.

"Damn it, Gus, pay attention," Doyle scolded. "Now ain't the time to sniff them bloomers."

"There's blood on these clothes," Gus said.

"So?"

Shifting his eyes to Mason, Gus held up a torn blouse and said, "This is blood and it's on every piece of material in this case."

Doyle stepped over to where Gus was crouching and picked up one of the articles he'd so recently tossed away. All the while, he kept his pistol trained upon Mason. "This *is* blood," Doyle said as he examined the dark stains on the clothes. He picked up the rest of the items and looked through them all in a rush. "There's a lot of blood here and it ain't just from nickin' a finger. How'd so much blood get on these lady's frilly things?"

Picking up the blouse, Gus crumpled it up the way it had been when it was inside the case. Although it wasn't perfect, he could tell that gripping the blouse like a rag naturally brought most of the bloodstains together. Holding it up that way, he declared, "The blood was sopped up. Why would you do this?"

When he looked at what Gus was doing, Doyle cocked his head to one side like a dog trying to figure out a peculiar whistle. Turning to the man on the ground, he said, "That's a real good question. Why would you do that?"

Mason was shaking like a leaf and he couldn't force himself to look at the bloody clothes. Sweat beaded upon his brow, and when he heard the metallic click of a hammer being pulled back, Mason curled up and covered his head with his hands.

"Answer the question," Gus said from behind the gun he'd just cocked.

"They'll come find me," Mason whined. "They know where you were headed and they know who you are. My associates will find me."

"Everyone knows who we are," Doyle said proudly. "And as for where we're headed, they only know what we told 'em. Whoever's looking for you won't find you until your carcass is picked clean by the vultures."

Waiting until Mason glanced over to him, Gus nodded. "We left a real good trail that'll lead anyone after us in circles. Unless you want to be lost as well, you should speak up. Why carry around a case of bloody clothes and guard it like it's money?"

"Because it is money," Mason said, sighing in a way that made it sound as though the words leaked out of him. "It's proof that we got Abigail Swann."

"You got her?" Gus asked. "What's that mean?"

"It means she's a hostage," Doyle said with a victorious grin. "Ain't that right?"

Mason nodded. "We're holding her for ransom and have been moving her around. We're about to send our demands and we're sending along those clothes to let her family know we truly have her. My associates and I split up so the plan could continue even if a few of us were caught by the law. We're all moving around even more than she is."

"Those clothes could come from anywhere," Doyle said. "And that could even be your blood for all we know. What good's that stuff supposed to do?"

"There's more arriving at Benson. We sent it over different routes so nobody could track it back to us. Those clothes were specially made for her. You can tell by the stitching on the collar."

Gus examined the blouse to find the word "Abby" stitched in flowing letters. He wasn't an expert on women's clothes, but it looked expensive. At least, it struck him as something a rich lady would wear.

"What's arriving at Benson?" Doyle asked.

"More of her things," Mason said. "There'll be enough to convince anyone who knows that woman that we truly do have her."

When Doyle asked his next question, he was all but licking his lips. "How much is the ransom?"

For the first time since he'd started talking in earnest, Mason stopped himself short. His silence lasted right until he happened to get a look at the cold promise of death written on Gus's face. "Twenty thousand."

"Twenty thousand?" Doyle asked. "You expect to get that much for some woman in fancy clothes?"

"Haven't you ever heard of the Swann family?" Mason asked. "They're old money from the East and Thomas Swann's shipping companies have made them even richer. Abigail is Thomas's youngest daughter. We might have been able to get more for her, but we figured the family could pull together the money fast enough for us to get it and get out."

"And you don't think someone that rich will be able to pay some gunmen to collect his daughter?"

Mason shook his head. "She's moving around almost as much as me and my associates are. She's never even kept anywhere there's a telegraph, so if she's spotted nobody can send quick word out about it."

Gus nodded as he said, "That's a good way to go about it."

"It sure is," Doyle gasped. "Who are you meeting at Benson?"

"My associates," Mason grumbled.

This time, Doyle didn't fool about with harsh words or waving a gun in the other man's face. He dropped to one knee beside Mason and drove a fist straight into the prisoner's gut. "I want names," Doyle growled. "I want to know what they've got and I want to know right now!"

Although it hadn't been said out loud, Gus already knew where Doyle was headed. "We're not getting tangled up in a kidnapping," he said.

Without taking his eyes off of Mason, Doyle asked, "And why not? There's plenty of money to go around. Besides, if whatever is in this case is so important to the operation, my guess is that the folks meeting in Benson will pay to get it back. Ain't that so?"

Reluctantly, Mason nodded.

"They may even pay to get you back."

"Don't get greedy," Gus scolded. "How many times do you need to almost get killed before you'll learn that lesson?"

"That there's my conscience," Doyle said as he nodded toward Gus. "Sometimes he's a real pain in the rump, but other times he makes a good point or two." With that, Doyle eased back and offered a hand to the man on the ground.

Mason was reluctant to accept the help Doyle was offering. In fact, he looked at the outlaw's hand as if it had fangs. "You won't be able to get anything in Benson. Not without me."

"Oh, you're coming to Benson sure enough," Doyle assured him.

"If I'm a prisoner, my associates will know and they'll take steps to free me. If I'm . . . if I'm . . ." Pulling in a deep breath, Mason straightened up and steeled himself before finally saying, "If I'm dead, they'll scatter and you'll never find them. Killing me won't get you anywhere."

"Who said anything about killing you?" Glancing away, Doyle asked, "Gus, did I say I wanted to kill this here fella?"

Gus shook his head.

Mason brightened up a bit but not much. "There might be a way to make this mutually beneficial. We could use men like you in the event things got rough. There could always be entanglements with the law in a situation like this."

"Entanglements, huh?" Doyle mused. "You reckon we know a thing or two about entanglements, Gus?"

Gus nodded. In his years with Doyle, he'd learned more than his share about entanglements. By the looks of things, he was about to get another lesson.

Chapter 5

Benson train depot two days later

The three men rode northwest into Benson as if they had the devil on their tail. Now that he thought he'd won over the two outlaws, Mason was cooperative enough to ride on a horse of his own. Gus stole the animal the morning after their little talk about the kidnapping of Abigail Swann. He rode behind the well-dressed man, prepared to shoot if Mason got it in his head to make a bid for his own freedom.

Not only did Mason ride to Benson without making any waves, but he did so in fairly good spirits. He and Doyle joked at every watering hole along the way and swapped tall tales when they'd made camp. Gus kept his mouth shut and his gun ready. He may not have had full use of both eyes, but he kept them open and on the lookout for a double cross. When he, Doyle and Mason arrived at the train station, Gus was prepared for trouble to be headed his way.

At the station, Gus stood with his back against the

wall of the ticket office and watched the train hiss to a stop. Every time he saw one of those big metal buckets on wheels, Gus felt something grind inside of him. He'd never been fond of trains as a kid and that only got worse as he'd grown older.

There was just nowhere to go inside a train. Even if he stayed close to a door or window, the land outside kept changing too rapidly for him to pick out new places to run or hide. There were too many angles he couldn't figure. Too many things could go wrong. When he pulled his trigger, he couldn't afford to have the floor rocking under his feet.

Doyle gave him no end of trouble for hating trains as much as he did, but Gus didn't care about that. He had his ways of doing things and they'd served him well for plenty of years. Trains were fine to rob, but not so good to ride. After the last few times he and Doyle had robbed a train, Gus was even beginning to think twice about doing that again.

As if hearing the thoughts rushing through his partner's head, Doyle strutted up to him and said, "No need to look so angry, Gus. Nobody's asking you to ride on that thing."

"Shouldn't you be with Mason?"

"I will be once that train comes to a stop. He ain't about to come all this way just to blow this deal now. Didn't you listen to him when we were in camp last night? He's already making plans to spend the money he's set to make."

"I didn't listen to a word he said," Gus told him. "Most of whatever comes out of his mouth is probably a lie."

"You never knew when to accept a piece of good

luck when you found one, Gus. That's always been your problem."

Grumbling under his breath, Gus set his eyes on Mason and kept them there. Although Mason still carried himself like a dandy, his well-tailored suit was showing the strain of being worn for the duration of a two-day ride. Mason shifted on his feet as he stood at the platform and glanced about. So far, the only other folks up there with him were a few old-timers sharing an apple and a small family waving at the approaching train.

"Did you forget about something else?" Gus asked.

Doyle sighed. "Whether I did or didn't, I'm sure you'll tell me anyway."

"We went through the trouble of laying a false trail and telling folks we were headed the other direction. Now that we've changed course, we're drifting close to the same direction as we let on. We should be heading due north. Hell, we shoulda been out of these Territories by now."

"So?"

"So the folks on that stage will have told the law by now and a posse could be on its way to this very station."

"And if they already figured we'd be laying a false trail, this'd be the last thing anyone would expect."

Judging by the look on Gus's face, he was not amused.

"Look, I trust you to sniff out a posse from ten miles away," Doyle said. "I ain't so bad at it either. I also got a good nose for sniffing out a good opportunity when I find one and this is it."

"Why the hell do you want to deal with these kidnappers, anyway? You know I can't abide kidnappers."

"That's mighty righteous talk coming from a known thief and killer," Doyle pointed out.

"Stealing is one thing. I stole plenty and I'm damn good at it. I've killed plenty too, but only when I had to and I never killed a man for money. Assassins are cowards who earn their keep by shooting folks in the back and kidnappers ain't much better. Come to think of it," Gus added as his face twisted into one of his uglier scowls, "this whole thing don't set right with me at all."

"Before you get yourself in a twist, I can tell you for certain that Mason shakes in his boots every time he looks at you. I think it's got to do with that ugly face of yours."

Gus still wasn't amused, but he wasn't as serious as he'd been a moment ago.

Doyle leaned against the wall next to his partner and crossed his arms over his chest. "Since he's scared, he'll do whatever he can to get away from us in one piece. And since he's a kidnapper, he won't go to the law. Since he's close enough to smell this deal of his, he won't want to do anything to spoil it. All of that means he'll want to do whatever he can to get in our good graces as quickly as possible. At the very least, I figure he'll offer to pay us off just to part ways."

"And what's the worst you figure might happen?" Gus asked.

"That we'll be forced to shoot our way out of this station once that dandy's associates arrive. If that happens, I intend on getting everything I can from the pockets of all them fancy suits before we head north. If this kidnapping is half as big as Mason claims, the law will be too busy sifting through them kidnappers instead of worrying about us."

It was a sloppy plan, but Gus didn't expect much more from Doyle. Oddly enough, Doyle had a knack for getting sloppy plans to work in his favor. Most folks, and especially lawmen, expected there to be a rhyme or reason behind a robbery or a killing. Folks looked for why someone got shot or what made gunmen do what they did, just to be plain stumped when faced with the likes of Doyle Hill. Trying to figure him out was like trying to guess which way the wind was about to blow. Besides, turning back now would mean everything up to this point was a stupid waste of time. Gus knew better than anybody that time was not something to be wasted. Since that case only had some frilly things in it, Gus intended on turning that into some sort of profit.

More than that, Gus truly couldn't abide kidnappers. They were all yellow-back shooters and the thought of robbing them seemed mighty nice.

"Maybe," Doyle added in a low voice, "we won't even need them fellas at all."

Looking over to his partner, Gus could almost hear the gears turning inside of Doyle's head. "What's that supposed to mean?" he asked.

Doyle smirked and nodded toward the train that had come to a stop and was steaming from its pistons and whistling like a banshee. "Maybe we could get an introduction to them associates of Mason's and have a talk with them."

"If you think I'll meet with them on their own ground where they can get the jump on us or put a bullet through the backs of our heads, then you've got another think coming."

"I ain't talking about that. I bet we could at least get them thinking it's worth their while to pay us to walk away from their little meeting before our partners burn them all down."

"You and those damn partners. That's a shaky bluff during a robbery and I doubt it'll hold water now."

"It doesn't need to hold up for long. Just long enough for them to fork over some money to cover our traveling expenses. If these fellas are anything like Mason, they'll be willing to part with some cash to keep them out of a fight. At the very least, we can try to add a few dollars to whatever scraps Mason's willing to throw at us to pay for his own worthless life."

As much as he tried to keep his stern expression in place, Gus felt a smirk crack through it all. "You want to hold kidnappers hostage? Is that supposed to be a real plan or are you just trying to think of new ways to get us shot?"

"I never try to get us shot. That just sort of happens all on its own."

"All right." Gus sighed. "I'll make you a wager. If Mason doesn't bolt at the first sight of his friends and tell them to gun us down on the spot, I'll let you see what you can talk them in to."

"How long does he have to hold out?"

"At least until they're meant to head out of this station."

"They gotta wait that long before taking a shot at us?" Doyle asked. Despite all the years Gus had known him, it was still hard to tell whether or not he was kidding. "And what happens if I lose the wager?"

"Then you pay for drinks until we cross the border into Canada. That is, if we get out of this place without getting shot full of holes."

Doyle stuck out his hand. "Done. If kidnappers were any good with guns, they wouldn't need to sneak up on women in a pack. And since you can't handle more than a few sips of whiskey at a time, losing this bet shouldn't take too much out of me."

Before Gus could try to defend himself, Mason waved at him. "Looks like your new friend has found the men he was looking for."

Doyle took his time in looking over there. When he finally acknowledged Mason's wave, the other man seemed ready to jump out of his fancy suit. "You still got that backup thirty-eight?"

"Sure do," Gus said.

"Then keep it where it can't be seen. I'll do the same for one of my forty-fives."

"I know how to handle myself."

"Just try not to embarrass me." As he said that, Doyle swatted Gus's arm and started walking toward the platform.

Gus followed his partner's lead and watched as a group of three men emerged from the train amid a trickle of other travelers. The three stood out from the crowd already, since they were dressed in suits that looked like they were worth more than any of the other passengers could afford. What set them apart even more for Gus was the fact that all those fancy suits looked like they'd come from the same mold as Mason's finery.

One of the three wore spectacles that were barely large enough to cover his eyes. A shade of a smile crossed his face when he saw Mason, but that faded quickly enough when Gus and Doyle approached the group. Not only were the other two new arrivals not smiling, but they reached for the gun belts strapped around their waists under their tailored black coats.

"It's all right," Mason said as he motioned toward Gus and Doyle. "These two are with me."

"Who are they?" the man with the spectacles asked.

"It's a long story and I'll be happy to tell it. Just . . . not here. Where did you intend to discuss our business?"

The eyes behind the man's spectacles darted back and forth between Gus and Doyle and his mouth became a tight line. When he spoke, his lips barely parted enough to let the words out. "The train's not due to leave for half an hour. We'll have the whole dining car to ourselves."

"Sounds fine."

"You never answered my question."

Chuckling nervously, Mason said, "Mr. Smythe, this is Gus and Doyle."

Gus and Doyle tipped their hats when their names were mentioned.

"Gus and Doyle," Mason said as he pointed toward the bespectacled man, "this is Mr. Smythe."

Indicating the remaining pair of well-dressed gentlemen, he said, "Mr. Wade and Mr. Franklin."

Although both of the other two were singled out, Gus could still hardly tell them apart. As far as he was concerned, Wade was the man carrying the Colt Navy and Franklin was the man with the brand-new Smith & Wesson at his hip. If either of those dandies moved in a way Gus didn't like, they'd both just be plain dead.

There weren't many folks getting off of the train, but the three men in the new suits pushed through them as though they were fighting through a crowd. Smythe led the way to the sleeper car and then pulled open the door to the first compartment. Inside, the bunks on either wall were folded up and hooked in place, which left space for two chairs set on either side of a small table. A man sat at that table playing a quiet game of solitaire. Before they could step inside, Gus and Doyle were stopped by Mr. Wade.

"Just wait here a moment," Wade said.

Franklin stepped over to form a wall between Gus, Doyle and the compartment. Both men placed their hands upon the grips of their holstered weapons.

"Where's the case?" Smythe asked. After Gus handed it over, Smythe passed it along to the man in the sleeper compartment. "Have a look inside to make sure everything's there."

"It's there," Mason said. "I didn't go anywhere after she was moved besides directly to the—" He was cut short by a quick, searing look from Smythe.

"I don't know what's going on here or who these

two are," Smythe snapped. "Until I get my explanation, you'll humor me."

Mason nodded obediently and stepped back.

Gus placed the man who took the case as somewhere in his late forties or early fifties. He didn't seem rattled by anything going on and he didn't try to step in on anyone's side. He just took the case, set it on top of the cards and opened it so he could get to work. After a brief look inside, he said, "You men can go on and work things out. I'll need to examine this a bit closer."

Smythe stepped back and shut the door. "Dining car's this way," he said as he continued walking down the aisle that led past all the other compartments. He didn't look back to see if the others were with him. Smythe simply led the way as if the rest of the men had no other choice but to follow in his wake.

When they crossed over to the next car, Mr. Wade once more stopped Gus and Doyle. "I'm gonna have to take your guns," he said.

Doyle stepped right up to the man and stared him in the eyes. "The hell you will."

"You won't step foot inside unless I do."

Doyle put on a good show as he reluctantly handed over one of his two .45s and Gus handed over his Colt. Wade took the guns while Franklin covered him. After that, they let the two outlaws into the compartment and then took positions on either side of the door. When the compartment door shut, Gus was reminded of a coffin lid dropping.

"So who are these men?" Smythe asked as he

sat down at one of the empty tables. "And why are they here?"

Mason sat down at the table across from Smythe, while Gus and Doyle remained standing beside it like hired help. "I met these fellows on the stagecoach. Actually, they robbed the stagecoach."

As anyone would expect, that news ruffled the feathers of all the men in suits.

"As you can see," Mason quickly added, "they haven't done me any harm."

"What about the case?" Smythe asked.

"It's intact, I assure you. As for why these men are here, I believe they could be of some use to us. They have a knack for thinking on their feet and they are quick with a gun. I was thinking they might do well as guards when the final transaction takes place."

"So they already know about our business?"

That question caused Mason to squirm more than when he'd been Gus and Doyle's prisoner. "They do."

"Since we're all on the same side of the fence," Doyle cut in, "we can just all talk plain. You're talking about swapping money for this rich lady you're holding, right?"

Smythe shifted his eyes toward Doyle, but hardly seemed to acknowledge his existence. "That's correct."

Doyle nodded and said, "Fine. Sounds to me like you're worried the law might already be on to you."

"Correct again."

"Then we're your men. Me and Gus have been making the law chase their own tails for years. You men seem to have a good operation here and all them fancy suits tell me you're well funded. Me and Gus will accept a modest fee to scout ahead and find any law dogs sniffing for you. If we find some, we'll give them something else to do for a bit. If we don't find any, you can pick a spot where you want a distraction and we'll be sure to make one for you. That'd be handy at the right time, now wouldn't it?"

Smythe listened with an occasional nod and not much else. "We do have a good operation. That's why we don't need the likes of you mucking it up."

"Then perhaps a finder's fee for returning your case and your little partner there," Doyle snarled. "It's just a neighborly thing to do, especially since *our* partners don't take kindly to dandies like you wasting our time for free. They're probably getting aggravated right now, and when they get aggravated, their trigger fingers get itchy."

The grin that slipped onto Smythe's face was the sort of thing that might be found on a lizard. "If you had such valuable partners lurking about with guns drawn, I'm sure we would have been introduced to them by now." Although Doyle didn't flinch, Smythe obviously knew he'd put him in his place. "Perhaps a distraction might be useful. Let's think about it after I'm done talking to Mr. Mason. That's the best I can do for now."

"That's all I ask," Doyle said.

"Until then, you'll stay where we can see you, and if you step out of line in the slightest, we'll make you sorry you picked that particular stage to rob." Without waiting to see what Doyle had to say to that, Smythe picked up a case similar to the one Mason had been guarding and opened it. When he spoke, it was to Mason. Smythe ignored everyone else in the dining car as if they'd been swept out a window. "Now here's what we've received from our associates in charge of watching over our female guest. I have it on good authority that these items will remove any doubt that may still be lingering in Thomas Swann's mind."

The items Smythe offered to Mason were more personal than the ones Gus had already seen. His good eye was probably keen enough to see more than both of Mason's. The first item was a pearl-encrusted comb that was meant to hold back a rich woman's hair. In fact, there were still strands of hair snagged within the teeth of the comb that dangled like thin tendrils of gold. By Gus's estimation, the comb had to be worth a pretty penny and he would have claimed it for himself if he'd been robbing the lady who'd previously worn it.

The second thing Smythe handed over to Mason was a ring. This caught Gus's eye and held every last bit of his attention. Gus had always had a good sense for jewelry. When it came to jewelry, Doyle would grab anything that sparkled whether it was worth something or not. Gus, on the other hand, had a knack for telling fool's gold from the genuine article. He could tell real diamonds from glass by the way they caught the light. He wasn't accurate every time, but he was close enough to be trusted by every gang he'd ridden with. Sometimes, the pieces that Gus could spot on a lady's finger or around her neck were worth more than the amount they'd stolen from whatever they happened to be robbing at the time.

But it wasn't the diamonds or gold in this particular ring that struck Gus the most. What he saw were nicks in the ring's band. There were flecks marring some of the gems. The overall shape of the ring was bent and distorted.

"Can I see that?" Gus asked.

Everyone in the compartment but Doyle gawked at him.

"I didn't think you could talk," Smythe mused.

"Oh, he can talk," Doyle said. "He can also sniff out trinkets like that in his sleep. Even when ladies try to hide their valuables, Gus can find 'em right quick."

"We already know these items' worth," Smythe protested.

Gus didn't move toward the ring. Instead, he stared at Smythe so the bespectacled man could get a real good look at his bad eye. Gus even let his mouth hang open just enough to display the gaping hole where several of his teeth had once been. When most folks saw him as a wounded old dog, they often figured Gus was as stupid as he was ugly. So far, this didn't seem to be an exception.

Holding on to the ring tightly, Smythe extended his hand and smiled as if he was grinning at a curious child. "Go on and have a look. It's not in the best shape, but it came off of our girl and her family will know it. This, combined with everything else we've got, should convince the family we have her. Pretty, isn't it?"

The ring was anything but pretty. Gus was able to get a bit closer to it, but Franklin stopped him before he could get within arm's length. Even so, that was close enough for Gus to see what he was after.

The flecks upon the ring were dried blood. Gus had seen enough of it to know that much for certain. The nicks in the side of the ring had to have been made by a knife or some sort of blade. They were too clean to be simple wear and were too deep to have been put there by anything blunt. Those things, combined with the squashed oval shape of the ring itself, were more than enough to make something very clear.

That ring had been taken by force.

It had probably been ripped, cut and finally yanked off of its owner after plenty of blood had been spilled and plenty of fighting had been done. If the ring had been taken any other way, it would be in much better condition. Gus could only imagine how that woman had fought to keep from parting with it. No lady liked to part with her sparkling possessions, but they tended to give them up before they got beaten to a bloody pulp. The owner of that ring had fought like hell to keep her kidnappers from getting to it. Either that or it fit so snugly that her finger may have been damn near ripped off for it to come loose. Whichever it was, Gus didn't like it.

He didn't like it one bit.

When he thought about all the blood on those fancy clothes, Gus could hear the echoes of that woman's screams as she'd been put through whatever hell these men in slick suits had decided to put her through. Gus had inflicted plenty of pain in his life. He'd even sent more than his share of men to meet their Maker. He knew how badly someone needed to be hurt to spill so much blood, but even he'd never thought to sop it up and send it to the man's family. Something like that was done by a coward. Every kidnapper he'd ever met had been a coward, and these men in their fancy suits were even worse. They were smug cowards.

Being in the presence of Smythe and the rest of those kidnappers stoked a fire deep inside of Gus McCord. The notion that all that misery had been visited upon a woman turned that fire into an inferno.

As he looked up from the ring and into the smirking face of the man holding it, Gus was only certain of one thing: Nobody deserved what that woman was being forced to endure. All that remained was deciding what he could do about it.

Chapter 6

"Hand it over," Gus said.

The men in the dining car looked at Gus and then looked at one another. Even Doyle seemed perplexed as he studied his partner. In the space of a few long seconds, Wade and Franklin tightened their grips upon their guns and Mason took a step back from the table.

In a low snarl, Smythe asked, "I beg your pardon."

"You heard me," Gus replied. "Hand over that ring."

"If you intend on robbing us, you're in for more trouble than you can handle."

"Mister, I don't believe you know how much trouble I can handle."

As the tension within the room thickened like a cold fog, Doyle lent his voice to the mix. "My partner told you to hand over that ring," he said as he quickly drew the gun stashed under his waistband, which Franklin and Wade had missed. "Do it and be quick about it."

Wade and Franklin were obviously more accustomed to dealing with scared women or lawmen who showed every card they had to play. Even after drawing their guns and aiming at Doyle, they looked at him with scared eyes.

Smythe, on the other hand, stood as if he'd been carved from rock. "You're making a mistake," he said evenly. "Correct it now and we can still work together. Nobody can fault you for making a move that appears to be profitable. In fact, this display proves that you men are exactly the sorts we need."

"Feed that to someone who wants to hear it," Gus said as he pulled up his shirt to show the .38 wedged under his belt in roughly the same spot Doyle had been hiding his. "Just give me that ring."

After calming Wade and Franklin down with a few curt nods, Smythe handed the ring to Gus. He then said, "You won't be leaving this train with that."

"Right there is where you're mistaken," Gus said. "And when we do leave this train, we're gonna go to wherever you're holding that woman."

"What?" Smythe barked.

While the bespectacled man had suddenly become indignant, Doyle put on a smile that nearly lit up the entire car. "Now ZZ *that's* what I call an idea! Tell my partner where she's at and maybe we'll see about cutting you off a sliver of that ransom."

"You men are fools," Smythe said. "Soon you'll be dead fools."

That was all the order the guards needed to hear. Franklin's Smith & Wesson was the first gun to explode inside that dining car and it did so at the same time Doyle dropped and spun toward him. Franklin's shot was a bit off and shattered a stack of dishes several inches to Doyle's right.

Doyle returned fire, but his bullet clipped the brim of Franklin's hat and punched through the wall of the dining car. He was quick to correct himself, however, and put his second shot through Franklin's shoulder.

While Doyle tussled with Franklin, Gus looked over at Wade. As he'd suspected, that man was about to fire at him, so Gus plucked his .38 from its hiding place. Even as Wade pointed his Colt Navy at him and pulled his trigger, Gus didn't flinch. He could see the panic in Wade's eyes and knew that would be enough to affect his aim. Sure enough, Wade's next several shots were wild. Only one came close enough to hiss past Gus's left ear.

Now that he'd had the time to aim properly, Gus squeezed his trigger. The .38 bucked in his hand and set Wade spinning like a top on one foot. Wade staggered back, knocked against a table and fell over amid a downpour of silverware and china cups. Somewhere along the way, his gun hit the floor as well.

Gus knew better than to count Wade out of the fight completely, but he figured he'd bought himself a few seconds to survey the rest of what was going on. Smythe had drawn a pistol of his own and was hiding behind a pair of straight-backed chairs in front of a window a few tables away from where he'd started. Mason huddled on the floor under a window. That left Doyle and Franklin as the two kicking up the most dust.

Franklin was still standing and firing at Doyle. Although he'd backed up a bit, there simply wasn't anything around him with enough bulk to protect him from a bullet. Therefore, the only option left open to Franklin was to plant his feet and fire that Smith & Wesson of his. The wound in his shoulder must have been the only thing that kept him from sending Doyle to meet his Maker.

Doyle let out a gleeful howl as he fired off a few quick shots to cover his retreat. As soon as he reached one of the tables, he kicked it over and ducked behind it. From there, he looked out and found Franklin right where he'd left him. "Is this all you brought with you?" he shouted. "No wonder Gus saw you boys as easy pickin's!"

Just then, the door leading out of the dining car swung open and a conductor poked his head inside. Gus sent him away with a shot fired into the wall a foot or so from the doorframe. "There'll be more coming," he announced.

Smythe chose that moment to stand up and unleash a torrent of lead from his pistol. He fired one shot after another as he backed toward the door that led out the opposite end of the dining car. The moment his back touched against the door, Smythe stopped firing long enough to say, "Finish these men off!" After that, he pulled the door open and ducked outside.

Gus cursed under his breath and rushed straight down the middle of the aisle that led to Smythe's escape route. Along the way, Gus saw some movement to his left. If not for the fat scar that pinched that eye partly shut, he would have noticed Wade a whole lot sooner.

"You're dead now!" Wade snarled as he charged at Gus like a wild animal.

Gus turned on his heels and swung his pistol around in a tight arc that connected with Wade's skull. The .38 bounced off of Wade's head and dropped the man to one knee. Even with that, however, Wade wasn't about to give up. He grabbed at Gus's arm and almost got hold of the .38, but Gus snapped a knee out to knock Wade back.

Wade groaned in pain as blood poured from the wound that Gus had given him earlier. While it wasn't easy to say where Wade had been hit, the front of his shirt was soaked through with blood and every movement brought more pain to his face. Despite all of that, Wade managed to pick his Colt Navy up off the floor.

Acting out of pure instinct, Gus bent his arm at the elbow and fired from the hip. His .38 barked once and put Wade down for good. Gus stepped over the body and continued his march toward the rear door of the car. When he got there, he took a moment to peek through the small square window that looked out to the space between cars. Smythe looked right back at him from the next car.

Gus pulled back and hunkered down as low as he could before the shots came. Three holes were punched through the door in quick succession as Smythe fired at the spot where Gus had been standing. Rather than open the door to provide Smythe with a better target, Gus pulled it shut tight and stepped away.

At the other end of the car, Franklin poked his head up from a table and fired a shot at Doyle. Gus knew his pistol was almost dry, so he took aim and was real careful when he fired. It wasn't much of a gamble, since he had a better angle on Franklin than Doyle was getting. Gus's bullet hit home and caused Franklin to jump when he was hit.

Sensing his opening the way a shark could smell blood in the water, Doyle leapt from behind his cover and emptied his gun into Franklin before the well-dressed gunman could return the favor. Before Franklin had stopped moving, Doyle was already standing over him and stooping down to take away the smoking Smith & Wesson.

"Don't mind if I do," Doyle said. "Let's just see if he's got any ammunition for me."

Reloading his .38 with fresh rounds from his gun belt, Gus stalked down the aisle that cut straight through the middle of the dining car. His eyes snapped toward the window and then to the door at the other end. There was plenty of commotion outside and it was drawing closer.

"We're about to have company," Gus said as he reclaimed his .44 from the man who'd taken it away from him.

Doyle still had his hand in the dead man's pockets as he glanced toward the nearest door. "Yeah, I suppose we did make some noise in here. Did you put down your two?"

"Smythe got away."

Holding his .45 in one hand and Franklin's Smith & Wesson in the other, Doyle grinned and said, "Not for long."

Gus stomped away from the door and said, "Leave him be for now. He's waitin' to pick off whoever comes after him. Collect our guns." As he walked past Mason, Gus extended a hand and grabbed hold of the man's battered, dirty coat and hauled him to his feet. "You're coming with us."

Mason struggled to get away but didn't have much strength left. "What more do you want from me? I tried to get everyone working together, but you went and ruined it! This whole thing is all messed up now!"

Ignoring everything Mason said, Gus shoved him toward the door that led to the sleeper car. He didn't have to look back to know that Doyle was right behind him. "You're going in there and telling whoever's in that compartment that you're on the winning end of the fight."

"But he'll ask me—"

"Just say what I told you," Gus said as he kicked open the door and shoved Mason out of the dining car.

The three of them crossed from one car to another, which gave Gus plenty of time to survey what was happening outside of the train. From between the cars, he saw several armed men in railroad uniforms gingerly approaching the front end of the train. One of them caught sight of Gus, Mason and Doyle and started to shout something, but Gus had already shoved Mason into the sleeper car before he could catch any of it.

Mason muttered to himself while staggering toward the door of Smythe's compartment. Gus reached past him to pull open the door and then stepped aside so Mason could do his part. Pale as a sheet, trembling like a leaf and dripping with sweat,

Mason walked into the compartment and tried to say what he'd been told to say. His first few words were a mess, but Gus stood aside and let Mason go. He was playing his part just fine.

"I heard shooting," the man inside the sleeper compartment said. "What happened? Where's Smythe?"

Mason drew a breath and replied, "Smythe is chasing those two off the train. Franklin and Wade are circling around to help."

"Really? I'll just stay here then and wait for them."

As soon as he heard the first glimmer of hope in the man's voice, Gus stepped in to dash it on the rocks. Sure enough, the man in the sleeper compartment was on the edge of his seat and fully expecting to ride out the storm without having to fire a shot. Seeing Gus shove Mason aside and enter the compartment hit him like a kick in the stomach.

Aiming his Colt at the startled man's face, Gus walked up close enough to tap the gun's barrel against his forehead. That gave Doyle just enough room to squeeze into the compartment and shut the door behind him. Mason would have tripped over his own feet, but fell onto the bunk before he got very far. The older man reflexively tried to jump to his feet.

"Stay right where you are," Gus snarled. "This ain't gonna take long."

"Wh-where's Smythe?" the man asked.

"Dead. They're all dead." When he saw the other man look to Mason for confirmation of that, Gus snapped, "Forget about him. You got us to contend with and we're only offering you one chance to get out of this alive."

The older man had the look of an accountant, from the neatly greased hair right down to the rodentlike eyes. The black case was on the bunk opposite of Mason, but he clutched a satchel to his chest as if it was his firstborn. Somehow, the accountant still managed to grow more of a spine than Mason. At least he wasn't reduced to a shaking, blubbering mess.

"It sounds like you've got some troubles of your own," the accountant said, surely referring to the voices and stomping footsteps that were growing closer every moment.

Gus nodded. "Perhaps we do. And if we need to stay here long enough to fight those men, then we might as well drop you first."

The accountant kept his head up, but lost the defiance in his eyes.

Sensing the change in the accountant, Gus quickly said, "Hand over that satchel."

With both Gus and Doyle aiming pistols at him, the accountant could do nothing but comply.

"Where's the woman being held?" Gus asked.

"Woman?"

"Don't play with me, mister," Gus warned as he allowed every bit of anger in his belly to rise to the surface and twist his face into something even more gruesome than normal. "You're gonna tell me everything I want to know, or by God, I will put you through that window."

The accountant turned to look at the window directly behind him. It was a few feet wide and slightly rectangular, but just large enough to accommodate him.

"Where's the woman being held?" Gus asked.

More angry voices echoed from the hall outside the compartment. Doyle shifted on his feet as he tightened his grip upon his .45 and the Smith & Wesson he'd taken. "We can't lollygag for much longer, Gus," he said. "Them conductors are checking every door."

"You're scared," the accountant said. "Scared and desperate."

Either the accountant was bolder than he looked or he had an ace up his sleeve, because the little man stood his ground without a thing in his favor.

"You haven't convinced me that I should do anything besides wait for help to get here," the accountant said as a way to press his supposed advantage. "By the sound of it, it will be here soon enough, and if you intend on killing me, you'll do it no matter what." Secure in his position, the accountant added, "The woman is ours and there's no way you'll get her back. We'll tear her to shreds before anyone can get close to her. Or, I should say, tear her apart *more*."

Gus lunged at the accountant like a wildcat. Pure animal instinct drove him across the compartment and caused him to forget about his gun for the moment so he could get his free hand around the other man's throat. Once he had ahold of the accountant, Gus lifted him from his chair and slammed him against the window. Knocking the accountant against the window with every word, Gus said, "You'll do no . . . such . . . thing!"

The first couple of times the accountant hit the window, cracks formed in the glass. When his back hit a third time, those cracks stretched all the way out to the frame. On the fourth knock, the glass shattered to allow the accountant's backside to bulge from the train completely.

Gus felt like he'd won the battle of wills between him and the accountant when the other man opened his mouth to let out a frightened squeak. It felt too good for him to end it by pulling the little man back inside the train.

So . . . he didn't.

Chapter 7

Gus leaned with all of his weight against the accountant. Most of the glass had already been knocked out and the accountant's flailing body cleaned out the rest very nicely. A short drop from the train ended with a jarring impact against the ground. Actually, it was less jarring for Gus since he landed partially on the accountant.

Since he knew Doyle would be right behind him, Gus regained his grip upon the accountant's shirt and roared down at him, "Where's the woman being held?"

In stark contrast to the last time the question had been asked, the accountant couldn't answer fast enough. "She was just moved from New Mexico!" he gasped after the wind had been knocked from his lungs. Despite the fact that he could barely suck in any air, he managed to keep talking. "There's . . . a small camp southeast of . . . Ewell's Pass. She's there but . . . you'll never . . . get to—"

"Where in the camp?"

"Bateman Supply Company. That's where she is, but you'll—"

Gus wasn't interested in the accountant's threats before and he was even less interested now. He stood up and tried to clear his head from the fall while the other man prattled on some more. In that time, Doyle jumped through the window amid a loud, glorious howl.

Hitting the ground on both feet, Doyle fired a few shots through the broken window. "They found our room," he said. "Not that you were trying to be sneaky or nothin'."

"Fine. Let's get out of here."

"What about Mason? Did you want him to come along?"

Gus started walking alongside the train. Holding his gun at the ready, he replied, "I've got the satchel and I got what I needed to know from that one there. We don't need Mason. Besides, he's too scared to be of much use."

"What about him?" Doyle asked as he glanced down at the accountant.

"Leave him to explain himself. We don't have time to fool about no more."

Doyle chuckled as he followed Gus along the side of the train. "You know we could have snuck off that train? If you wanted to jump out the window, we coulda done it quieter than that."

"Is that a fact?"

"You realize all that shooting probably made it a lot harder for us to skin out of here?"

"Yeah," Gus replied with more of an edge in his voice. "I also realize your plan wasn't going anywhere."

Holding his hands up, Doyle said, "All right,

then. What's your big plan for leaving this place?"

"Get to our horses. Get on them. Ride away."

"Short and sweet. I like it."

Even if Gus had more to say, he wouldn't have gotten the chance. Whoever had come aboard the train to check on the shots that had been fired looked out the window and caught sight of the two men making their way toward the engine. There was more shouting and soon a few men ran around the front of the engine to point frantically toward Gus and Doyle.

Keeping the accountant's satchel under one arm, Gus raised his pistol and waited for the men up there to poke their heads around before firing a shot that sparked against a piston. "Climb up and run through," he said. "I'll keep them looking this way."

Doyle looked over to find that they'd stopped at a spot between cars. Glancing back and forth between the sleeper and a passenger car, Doyle extended his arms to either side so he could aim at both the front and back of the train. "You go first. I'm better at distractions anyhow."

There was no use in arguing the point, so Gus climbed onto the railing connected to the back of the closest car and then swung over it to drop onto the metal landing. It took two quick steps to reach the other side, where he vaulted over the next railing to drop onto the edge of the platform. All the while, enough gunfire was coming from the other side of the train to make it seem as if war had been declared on the town of Benson.

The war let up a bit once Doyle stopped shooting

long enough to climb onto the landing behind Gus. Rather than jump over the other side, he stopped and quickly reloaded his .45. "You still think this was a good idea, Gus?"

Walking along the edge of the platform, Gus measured a shot and squeezed his trigger. The .38 barked once to place a single round into the edge of the shack that served as a station. The men who'd stuck their noses out to get a look at who'd just emerged from between the cars quickly pulled back behind cover. Rather than answer Doyle's question, Gus looked around for the horses. They were hitched about thirty yards away.

"That's what I thought," Doyle grumbled as he finished reloading. He stuck the gun he'd taken from Franklin under his belt so he could hoist himself up and over the railing. The gun was back out again the moment both of his boots were on the platform. Even though Franklin's gun was still empty, he waved it toward a few passengers who were huddled nearby until they yelped and turned away.

Gus hurried to the hitching post to fetch his and Doyle's horses. As he climbed into his saddle, he said, "To your right."

Hearing that, Doyle looked in that direction and spotted a group of men climbing down from the train a few cars back. Doyle aimed at them, which prompted the men to cut loose with some fire of their own. Bullets whipped through the air, forcing Doyle to quicken his pace toward the horses. All the while, he grinned through the thick whiskers covering most of his face.

Now that he'd hooked the satchel onto his saddle,

Gus switched from using his .38 to the more familiar .44 that he'd reclaimed before leaving the dining car. He sat in his saddle, watching the chaos at the station over the barrel of his gun. Once Doyle had climbed into his own saddle, Gus shifted his eyes toward the rest of Benson.

"Looks like more than just the railroad gunmen heard us," Doyle said.

"Yeah," Gus replied as he counted up the men rushing toward the station. "Remember what we're here for. Let's not dawdle, and if need be, we'll meet up again ten miles north of here."

"Dawdle?" Doyle asked. "I thought we were gonna have a pleasant business meeting. You're the one that went loco and tossed that poor bastard out the window!"

"Like I says, no more dawdling." With that, Gus snapped his reins and bolted away from the station. Doyle stayed close behind him.

Gripping his reins in his left hand, Gus used them to build up some more speed. There were at least eight or nine men rushing to the station, but they hadn't seen enough of what happened to know Gus and Doyle's connection to all the shooting. Working in the two men's favor was the fact that several passengers and locals alike were fleeing from the commotion like a flock of scattered quail. Gus managed to ride among the panicked folks, using the confusion as a dust cloud to cover his and Doyle's escape. Before he and Doyle could get away completely, some of the chaos from the station caught up to them. Thundering hooves rolled in behind them, which were accompanied by the occasional shot.

"That's them, all right," Doyle shouted after glancing over his shoulder. "Too bad there ain't no windows nearby or you could just fix this like you fixed the last mess."

"Just hush up and skin out of here," Gus barked. "You know where to meet up."

"Sure I do. Last one there is a rotten egg!" With that, Doyle tapped his heels against his horse's sides and veered away from Gus while letting out a wild yell.

Gus gave his own reins a snap, pointed the horse's nose to the west and tore out of town at a full gallop.

For a good stretch of time, Gus thought about nothing but maintaining his speed. His horse was well rested, so it was eager for the chance to run. When its enthusiasm waned, there was always a snap of the reins to put some steam into its strides. When he heard the gunshots behind him, Gus turned to look over his shoulder.

There were a few riders behind him, but it looked like they'd gotten snarled up in the panicked crowd before being able to give chase. They struggled to keep Gus in their sights while fighting to gain ground. The shots they'd taken had to have been from rifles, which meant there was the slightest chance that one of those bullets could catch Gus in the back. Considering how fast the horses were going and all the jostling that entailed, Gus wasn't too worried about getting hit. If there was a marksman in Benson with that kind of skill, then this was Gus's day to go.

Gus raced down the trail leading from town and

blazed a few new ones along the way. Just when the men following him made a move, Gus circled around in another direction. The men might have known the terrain better than he did, but that didn't mean they could outguess him. And since Gus was making up his route as he went along, there was no way in creation for anyone to figure out which way he might turn next. Putting his head start to good use, Gus stretched out his lead until the men chasing him dwindled to one or two.

Before long, those men either got turned around or simply gave up the chase. Hopefully, Doyle had the same results. If that fool got it in his head to stop and face off with his pursuers, Gus might just have to waste some time in breaking his partner out of a jailhouse.

It wouldn't be the first time.

Gus rode back just far enough to get his bearings. Once he caught sight of Benson, he pointed himself in the direction he and Doyle had agreed upon and then rode ten miles that way. If he'd been riding with anyone else on any other sort of job, Gus would have insisted on scouting things out and deciding upon a specific spot to meet up if they needed to split apart. Seeing as how it was only Doyle, Gus merely had to pick a spot and come up with a reasonably safe distance. The rest would work itself out.

Gus thought long and hard about the mess he'd made as he settled in at a spot on relatively high ground overlooking a sizable portion of the sunbaked ground outside of Benson. While collect-

ing some firewood, he sifted through everything
that had occurred and played through all the choices
he'd made one at a time. He continued to contem-
plate those things as he piled up the wood and used
a lucifer to set some dried leaves ablaze. The fire became good and high before Gus was able to fully
justify what he'd done.

After mulling that over a bit, he tossed some more
leaves onto the fire and sifted through his thoughts
one more time.

The hours ticked by and the sun dropped below
the horizon. Gus sat in his spot without moving except to swat at something buzzing around his face or
stomp his heel to discourage a snake from getting
any closer. Every now and then, he spit out the sand
that had blown into his mouth.

Gus kept the fire going and continued to pile on
whatever he could find that would cause smoke to
billow up and form a dirty smudge upon the canvas
of the Arizona sky. Doyle shouldn't have any trouble spotting the smoke and Gus would be able to
spot anyone else with the gumption to follow the
marker to its source. But even as he sat and watched
for those men who'd chased him out of Benson, Gus
didn't expect to find them. He'd been chased by
lawmen, posses and a few vigilante mobs, which
gave him a good sense of who was serious and who
wasn't. Those instincts told Gus that the men who'd
chased him weren't interested in going too far from
home. That meant he could stop thinking like a rabbit and more like a wolf.

His arm moved as if only the wind was pushing it
about. His head hung low and his hooded eyes re-

mained fixed upon the horizon. If not for the smoke billowing up to the sky, he might have been over-looked by man and nature alike as just another bump on the landscape.

The truth, however, was that Gus was more like a whirlwind trapped in a bottle. A storm raged behind his scarred face. Even his partially shut left eye was taking in more than most men would ever see. Gus watched the clouds slide along, the dirt swirl and the sky turn a hundred different shades as the sun grew too tired to stay up any longer.

He thought about what he'd done.

He thought about what was in the satchel he'd stolen.

He wondered if that woman was still alive.

He wondered if Doyle had been caught or killed.

He figured how long it would take to ride to Ewell's Pass.

Finally, he thought about the angles required to hit whoever was riding toward the fire he'd built.

There was a spyglass in his saddlebag, but Gus didn't bother getting up for it. Any move he made could potentially give away the fact that he was there beside the source of all that smoke. If he didn't move, the man riding toward him could mistake him for a rock or tree stump. If the man already knew he was there, it was too late for Gus to change his mind.

Gus's eyes narrowed once the horse and rider had moved within rifle range. It would be a difficult shot to knock the man from his saddle, but not an impos-sible one.

When the rider corrected his course to head

straight for him, Gus was fairly certain it was Doyle. Anyone else would have shown a bit more caution, but Doyle tended to ride at a dead run even if he was headed for the edge of a cliff. The light was also shining down just right to show Gus the markings on the horse he'd been looking for. The color of the horse's coat was right and so were the clothes on the rider. Finally, the rider started waving like a blooming idiot.

It was Doyle, all right.

Gus stood up with his hand resting upon his holstered Colt. He trusted his eyes, but never took a chance with anyone. His nerves still jangled and his mind was filled with escape routes. He didn't exactly suspect Doyle would do him harm, but Gus carried too many old wounds that had been given to him by too many old friends to let his guard down now.

Doyle rode up to the fire and asked, "Where do we go from here?"

Standing up, Gus untied his horse from the tree where it had been hitched and replied, "We're heading north. Will anyone else be coming along?"

"Nah. I ran circles around them fellas before they gave up and went home. It just felt good to get some wind in my face."

"So nobody followed you here?"

Doyle looked over his shoulder but was already shaking his head. "I think I winged one right when they chased me out of town. After that, they didn't seem too interested in catching up to me so long as I wasn't about to double back."

Gus hadn't taken anything from his saddlebags

that needed to be put away. He kicked out the fire and then climbed into his saddle. Doyle was itching to give him hell for what had happened in Benson, but Gus rode away before his partner got started. Whatever Doyle wanted to say, it could wait until they made a proper camp.

Chapter 8

If Gus was going to get a wink of sleep, he needed to do more than make another fire and lay out a bedroll. A good spot had to be chosen where they couldn't be ambushed. He had to take a good look around to see if anyone was coming. At least two different paths had to be chosen in the event an escape was needed and then there was the business that came along with merely filling his belly and not freezing during the night.

Doyle, on the other hand, had only to dig some jerked venison from his supplies and find something to lean against when he stretched his legs out. "You gonna tell me what the hell you were thinkin' back there?" he asked as he gnawed on the smoked meat.

Gus poked at the fire and studied the dancing flames. "Same thing you were thinkin' in that feed store back in Wichita."

Although he had to think back a ways, Doyle recalled that day from a few years back. "This ain't the same as deciding to rob a place because the mood struck. Besides, this is you we're talkin' about. You don't squat without plannin' for every possible circumstance."

Nodding slowly, Gus could tell the subject wasn't about to die on its own. "I saw that ring . . . and . . ."

"I knew it! You saw that fine ring and knew we could make a whole lot more money than whatever they were set to give us. I was thinkin' the same thing!"

"No," Gus said as he shook his head, "I didn't just want the ring."

"But . . . you did get it, right?"

Gus didn't need to feel his shirt pocket to make sure the ring was there. He'd tucked it away when the shooting started and he knew it was still in its spot. Even so, he found himself starting to reach up for it. When his callused fingertips brushed against the little circle in his pocket, his thoughts cleared once more. "I got it."

"Good!" Eventually, Doyle frowned. "Then what were you about to say? There was more than the ring? You think we could get something for them clothes?" Snapping his fingers, Doyle added, "That satchel! If they took that ring, there's got to be other stuff in there they didn't even show us. Better stuff! Open it up and let's find out."

"We're going after the woman," Gus announced. He looked over at his partner, only to find Doyle staring expectantly at the satchel resting on the ground near Gus's feet. "You hear me?"

Doyle's eyes snapped up and immediately widened. "Now that is one hell of an idea. You really think we can find her?"

"I know where she is. That squirrelly fellow told me after I shoved him out the window."

"So we ride up there and take her for ourselves. How many men you think they got guarding her?"

"I don't know."

"Did you kill Smythe?"

Gus shifted his eyes back to the fire and replied, "No. He got away."

"That don't matter. Although, if he got away, he probably sent word to whoever is with that rich lady to get some more men. That is, unless he was wounded. But Mason said she wouldn't be near a telegraph, so that should buy us some time. Maybe he bled out somewhere on that train. Or maybe the law got him!" Doyle added excitedly. "He was doing just as much shooting on that train as we were. And it ain't like he's a law-abiding citizen. He's a kidnapper. You think he would tell the law where he's holding that rich lady?"

"Probably not."

For the first time since he'd started running at the mouth, Doyle stopped and took a good look at his partner. "What's the matter with you? Why ain't you the one coming up with ideas? You must have been thinking something when you decided to toss our original plan out the window along with that poor fool and his satchel."

"What do you think they're doing to her?" Gus asked. "For that matter, what do you think they've already done?"

"Done to who?"

Gus looked at Doyle with a fierce anger in his eyes. That anger flared up even higher when he realized Doyle truly didn't know who he was talking about. At the moment, the woman in question was just the reward at the end of the next job. Nothing more.

"The woman being held for ransom," Gus said in a measured tone.

Now it was Doyle's turn to study Gus. "What does it matter what they done to her? Even if she's dead, the family probably don't know it yet."

"All that blood on them clothes had to come from somewhere. That ring looked like it had been ripped off of her hand. It might have even been cut off."

Chuckling as he ripped off another piece of jerky, Doyle asked, "You mean like that mouthy redhead back in Abilene? She had a ring on every finger, and even after we threatened to gun down everyone in that store, she still wouldn't part with a single one of them. You recall that, Gus?"

The knot in Gus's belly cinched tighter. He cast his eyes down as if an unseen hand was shoving his face toward the fire. "Yeah. I recall."

"How long ago was that?" Doyle asked.

"A year and a half." Gus replied. "Give or take."

"Seems like longer. She slapped you plumb in the face when you tried to pull that necklace offa her. I thought you were gonna cut her throat right then and there! I wish you coulda seen the look on yer face."

Rocking back on his heels, Doyle continued as if he was passing the time by telling a bad joke. "Then you went for them rings and she spit in yer face. I remember that like it was yesterday. She spit in yer face and you—"

"Enough!"

Doyle was taken aback by the outburst, but then he started to laugh. "You didn't have to do much before she gave it all up. And you did it with plenty of time for us to skin out of there. That was a hell of a day. I ain't thought about that in a while."

"I said enough, damn it."

At first, Gus figured Doyle was just wrapped up in the story the way he'd been wrapped up in the chase that had brought him to the signal fire. But then he saw the look on Doyle's face as he kept his eyes aimed at him. There was more going on in there. Wheels were turning and Doyle was mulling over more than just a fond recollection.

"I never did mind a good scrap, but I didn't see it coming today. You should let me know the next time you get a burr that big under your saddle."

"It wasn't something I planned," Gus said.

"It was the ring. You went wild when you saw that ring. Why is that?"

Gus pulled in a breath and looked down at the fire. It felt like the darkest part of the night and was growing darker still with every passing minute. He used the stick in his hand to knock away some of the chunks of wood along the side of the fire so the flames would die down a bit. "Those men will kill her and there ain't no cause for it."

"It'll earn someone a whole lot of money. That's the cause."

"The ransom is so the family can get that lady back. They won't get nothing for their money but a corpse and that just ain't right."

"Neither is shooting a man or swearing on Sundays," Doyle said, "but we've done our share of both. You just hate kidnappers. I bet we could've been rich if you weren't so fussy in that regard."

The stick in Gus's hand caught on fire because he'd held it in one place for too long. The flames licked up along the crooked wooden line and flickered against his fingers. Sometimes, the calluses on his hands kept him from feeling such things. This time, however, he felt the heat searing right down to his bones and kept his hand near the flames anyway.

"If they snatched her up and bled her like an animal, they don't think of her as nothin' but an animal," Gus pointed out. "They ripped off her clothes and tore off her jewelry and that ain't nothin' that any lady like that would part with easily. All of that was for a start and it'll only get worse. Men like us know that much for certain."

"What sort of men are you talkin' about?"

"There ain't a need for you to ask that question, Doyle. You know what I mean."

Doyle nodded slowly. "I suppose I do, but we ain't never kidnapped anyone Did you shoot up that train just to put those dandies in their place?"

Guessing games were never his cup of tea, so Gus cut to the quick. "I want to go after her," he announced.

Doyle was still nodding. "You think we can make it before Smythe or any of them other kidnappers get to her first?"

"Like you said, them law dogs that chased after us are probably an even bigger problem for those kidnappers. I doubt Smythe or those others will just ride straightaway to where they got the lady stashed. Since they don't have any better way to contact whoever's watching her, we should be able to get there before word gets out about us."

"And when we get there, we'll have to tussle with whatever's left of them kidnappers."

"That's right."

"There could be a whole lot of 'em. Either that or the ones that are there may be real killers."

"Yeah," Gus said, "I thought of that."

"You did, huh? When did you do all that thinking? In the second or two you was looking at that ring?"

Gus chewed on that for a bit until he decided it was useless to try to paint up his answer too much. Despite all of Doyle's faults, the man had an eye for certain details and he'd be able to sniff out something that was too far from the truth.

"Pretty much," Gus told him.

"So you saw that ring and you realized that woman was awfully rich and that those fellas in that train were serious about ransoming her." Letting his head fall forward so he could rub his eyes, Doyle settled into the spot where he was sitting as if his muscles would no longer hold him up. "Were you gonna tell me about this?"

"That's what I'm doin' right now."

"No. I mean before you started shooting or before you got a whole town to chase us."

"Whole town?" Gus chuckled. "That was hardly a posse and they didn't even intend on missing supper to come after us."

"The men on that train meant business and they were just the messenger boys," Doyle said quickly.

"You can't think that's as bad as it's gonna get. You and I both know that Smythe and those men were just there to collect a few frilly things to be delivered farther down the line. You think goin' right to where they're dug in will be as easy as gettin' off that train?"

Gus looked up from the fire, stared straight into Doyle's eyes and said, "I think it'll be a whole lot tougher than that train and I'd appreciate it if you didn't talk to me like I was some snot-nosed kid who ain't never touched a gun before."

"Then maybe you should stop actin' like one."

The tone in Doyle's voice was a challenge that brought Gus to his feet. Even before Gus's legs were locked beneath him, Doyle had jumped up as well.

"I pulled your foolish hide out of more fires than I can count," Gus snarled. "You owe me."

"I don't owe you a damn thing. In case you been asleep for all these years, I covered your back more than once myself. I also covered you pretty well when you started frothing at the mouth on that train. I coulda caught a bullet on the way out of town, just like I may catch one on account of this new idea of yours."

"You're the one that wanted to have a word with those men," Gus pointed out. "If it was up to you, we'd probably do some dirty work and get paid in table scraps or maybe even get shot in the back before we got paid at all."

"And I suppose you'd prefer we get shot from the front? That's the only reason you might decide to draw your gun when we were already surrounded!

And then, to top it all off, you want to ride straight into the wolf's den after you already tipped your hand that we were comin'! Did you even think to finish off them men in the fancy suits before they got a chance to send word to the others?"

"That's just what we needed, Doyle! Kill some more so we can tack that onto the list of deaths we already got hanging around our necks. You won't be happy until a noose is around there as well."

"That's fine talk comin' from a bloodthirsty son of a—"

Gus snapped his fist out before Doyle had a chance to think about it. His knuckles cracked against the other man's jaw, clipping the insult short while also sending him back a few steps. In the space of a heartbeat, Doyle had regained his senses and thrown himself at Gus with both fists leading the charge.

Although Gus was able to lean away from the first punch, he caught the second against his ear. A powerful ringing echoed through his skull, which wasn't nearly enough to stop him from retaliating. Gritting his teeth, Gus turned his head so his left side could absorb another punch. As Doyle's fist bounced off all that scar tissue, Gus took hold of Doyle's throat and shoved him backward. Even after Doyle tripped on a rock and toppled over, Gus kept his grip and punched his partner in the mouth before Doyle hit the ground.

The two men landed in a heap. Doyle's face was bloody, but there was a wild grin under the crimson mask. His eyes were wide and he leaned his head to one side to expertly avoid the next strike. When

Gus's fist impacted against the ground beside his head, Doyle turned toward it and sank his teeth into Gus's wrist.

Gus let out a pained growl, but choked it back before he made another sound. Steeling himself for the next batch of agony, Gus ripped his hand out from between Doyle's teeth and balled it into a fist so he could take another swing at him. This time, Doyle rolled away from the punch with even more time to spare.

"That's your problem, Gus. When you get riled up, you don't think straight. You make mistakes." With that, Doyle snatched the knife from his boot and swung the blade at Gus's midsection.

Hopping back, Gus allowed the knife to pass by with a hiss. He reached out to grab Doyle's hand but wasn't able to hold on when Doyle pulled it back again.

Doyle snapped the knife toward Gus's chest, but it was a feint. Unfortunately, Gus fell for the ruse out of pure reflex, and before he could correct his mistake, Doyle had already flicked his hand out to slide along the top of Gus's arm so the blade wound up pressed against his throat.

The touch of cold steel on his neck froze Gus in his tracks. Beneath the fire of his anger and everything else in his head, Gus figured a new set of angles that could get him out of his predicament.

Leaning in so some more weight was behind his knife, Doyle asked, "See what I mean? You seen me swing this blade plenty of times and you seen me kill folks using them same tricks. Why the hell would those tricks work on you? I'll tell you why.

You ain't thinkin' straight. In our line of work, that's more than enough to get us both killed."

The fire in Gus's belly dwindled away.

The rush in Gus's head faded enough for him to think about what had just happened.

As much as he wanted to think he had the upper hand and could figure out every move before Doyle made it, the touch of that blade against his throat told him different. Gus straightened up and stood there as if the knife being held to his neck no longer mattered. He reached up and calmly pushed away Doyle's hand.

"You're right," Gus said. "Sorry about that. I should have thought it through, but I didn't. I just got a notion in my head and carried it out."

Despite being the one with the clear advantage, Doyle looked surprised. Allowing his knife to be pushed aside, Doyle slid the weapon back into its scabbard and replied, "That's the Gus McCord I'm used to seein'."

"If you don't want to come along with me, I understand. But I'm heading up to that camp and I intend on getting that lady."

"Why do you want to do somethin' like that?"

"Because the men who got her are damn animals, and if someone were to put them mad dogs out of their misery and bring that lady back to her family in one piece, there's bound to be a reward."

Doyle's eyebrows flicked upward. "You think there's a reward?"

"A rich man's daughter is taken. He's about to get proof that she's hurt and in the hands of some desperate men who mean to do her even more harm. You think there won't be a reward for her safe return?"

"You think the reward could be worth more than the ransom?" Doyle asked.

"Maybe," Gus replied. "But if it isn't, what do you think the odds are of those kidnappers having a price on their heads?"

After a bit of consideration, Doyle said, "This can't be their first dance, so there must already be a bounty offered for them. A job this big would push that bounty up a bit more."

"We know that better than anyone. I also know a few men who might be convinced to collect the bounty money on our behalf. It'll cost us a percentage, but it beats walking into some lawman's office where we might get recognized and strung up right alongside anyone else we bring in."

"Who you got in mind?"

"Mike Halpert. He should still be in Tucson and he's bad enough at cards that he's always desperate for money. He's also too stupid to cheat us too badly on the deal. There's not many ways for him to mess up cashing in a bounty and splitting up the money."

"Halpert," Doyle mused. "I remember him. He's got the pretty little sister that works in a dress shop, don't he?"

"That's the one."

And there was the spark of greed that Gus knew he could depend upon. Doyle may have been a little quicker with a blade, but Gus could always find an angle.

"All we need to do is send these cases along to that family," Gus continued. "They'll get worked up enough to tack a bit more onto the reward so it's nice and plump by the time we get out of this. Getting that lady away from them kidnappers may not be easy, but after that it's smooth waters."

"Nothing good comes easy." The smirk on Doyle's face caused the blood to trickle in different directions along his face. "You came up with all this just by lookin' at that ring?"

"More or less."

"Yeah," Doyle said proudly, "that's the Gus McCord I'm used to."

Chapter 9

Ewell's Pass was due north from where Gus and Doyle had set up their camp. Doyle offered to ride back to the nearest train station and send those things along to the family so they would be convinced Abigail Swann was truly being held hostage, but Gus convinced him otherwise. It took a bit of talking, since Gus was easily more recognizable than his partner. Finally, however, Gus managed to get Doyle set on the task of scouting out that spot where the woman was being held.

Doyle was a faster rider, but Gus couldn't let those stolen possessions out of his sight. More important, he couldn't let that damaged ring get passed around any more than it already had.

After Doyle left that morning, Gus stayed behind to cover their tracks and break down the camp. When he was finished with that, he rode for a ways with Smythe's satchel strapped across his chest. Looking more like a mail courier than an outlaw, Gus sifted through the items to see if there was anything else he could find that might be of any help. All he found was more proof that he was probably too late to do much of anything for Abigail Swann.

Her blood was all over a few more items of ripped clothing and there was even more soaked into the case itself. Besides the ring, the satchel contained a lock of hair, the comb, a letter and a bracelet made from knotted string. Gus held the bracelet in his hand and knew right away that the simple collection of string would carry the most weight with her family. It was obviously something put together by a child. Either she'd made it several years back or a child had made it for her. Either way, it was invaluable.

Gus knew all too well to leave such things alone when he was robbing someone. Folks were more likely to bare their teeth and run straight into the barrel of a gun when they thought they might lose something that had been created by their little ones. He'd never had any kids of his own, but he'd seen plenty of parents willing to step through fire to protect their kin. After tucking those things away into his pockets, Gus opened the letter.

It was a simple ransom note that was filled with the proper mix of threats and promises to put the right amount of fear into any family. There was an address written upon the envelope, which Gus committed to memory. He then dumped the empty satchel like the garbage it was. If Doyle was right and he'd acted a bit too quickly, it was too late to fix that now. No matter how big of a mistake he could be making, Gus rode on.

Rather than go back to Benson, he followed the train tracks to a station that was too small to have a proper platform. It was a little shack propped up by several posts that had been driven into the ground on all sides. It didn't look pretty, but the place was just sturdy enough to withstand the wind. The station was manned by a single young man in a black vest and sweat-stained white shirt who was too busy frying an egg over a little burner to look up when Gus walked in.

"Schedule's on the wall to your right," the clerk recited.

Stepping up to the rickety counter, Gus said, "I need a letter sent on to Prescott."

The clerk glanced up and then looked back down so he could flip his egg. "It needs to be wrapped up and labeled properly and once you do that—"

"I'll need a pencil and paper first," Gus interrupted. "This should cover the expense."

When the clerk looked up again, he found Gus holding out a handful of money. While Gus's face took the younger man aback, the money cushioned the blow. He took the cash and gave him the writing implements in return. "That's plenty to cover shipping. The next delivery bound for Prescott isn't due until tomorrow."

"Fine. I'll have it to you in a second." With that, Gus scribbled out a few words meant for Thomas Swann.

ZZ I KNOW WHERE YOUR DAUGHTER IS AND I MEAN TO BRING HER BACK TO YOU. DON'T TELL ANYONE ABOUT THIS, AS THAT WOULD ONLY MAKE MY JOB HARDER.

He'd thought of more comforting things to say during his ride, but Gus figured it was best to keep things short and sweet. As a way to prove he wasn't just someone with a bad sense of humor, Gus stuck the pearl comb into the envelope with the letter. He thought for a moment before sealing it all up, weighing the different outcomes that could be caused by sending it. His intention was to ease the family's minds a bit, while laying some early groundwork with what had to be a very flustered and powerful man. On the off chance that he found himself in another fight at the end of this whole thing, Gus could tell Mr. Swann about the letter and item he'd sent as proof that he could be trusted, instead of shot on sight.

Setting down the pan as though the egg in it hadn't already been cracked, the clerk wiped his hands on the front of his shirt and reached for the letter. Despite Gus's attempts to fold the paper quickly, the clerk chuckled and asked, "What is that? A ransom letter?"

Gus scowled, but thought once more about what he'd written. Rather than tell the clerk to shut his trap and do his job, Gus conceded the point. "You're right," he said with an uncomfortable grin. He took another piece of paper and wrote something that was just as short, but not as unintentionally sinister as his first go-round. As soon as he was done, Gus lowered his head so the brim of his hat covered most of his ax scar.

"Will that do it?" the clerk asked.

"Yeah. Make sure this gets to Prescott real quick. Otherwise, there's gonna be a problem."

The clerk looked down at the money in his hand and shook his head. "There shouldn't be any problems, sir. I'll even wrap this up some more to make sure everything stays together. This money covers more than the price of shipping and then some." Reluctantly, he asked, "You sure you want to pay so much?"

Oddly enough, Gus felt more than a little peculiar in getting something done so easily. He'd fallen out of the habit of asking for services and paying to get them done. Without any threats or guns in the mix, something just didn't seem right. Even so, Gus nodded and told the clerk to keep all the money. It didn't concern him much, since the money had been stolen, anyhow.

The clerk was pleased with the deal and agreed to see it through.

After that, Gus rode north. When the day neared its end, he steered toward the east. He and Doyle had crossed every trail and ridden every path in the Arizona Territories. That held true for New Mexico, the Dakotas, the Rockies and a good portion of Texas. Between the two of them, they probably even knew dozens of good spots that weren't on any map. Their lives frequently relied on being able to cover a lot of ground in a little amount of time. When they were on their own, Gus and Doyle could move even faster.

The closer he got to the Mogollon Mountains, the slower Gus was forced to ride. There were fewer options where trails were concerned, and fewer still if he wanted to move quickly without risking a nasty fall. In some spots, the trees were too thick to navigate, and at others, the ground was too uneven to cross at any pace faster than a walk. Gus didn't fret about his progress, since it didn't truly matter. He was going as fast as he could and so was Doyle. If that wasn't fast enough, there wasn't anything he could do about it.

When he finally got to Ewell's Pass the next day, Gus was caked in layers of dirt and his eyes had narrowed to intense slits against the sun and wind. His horse's breath had become haggard and its hooves hit the ground heavier and heavier with each step. As he pulled back on the reins, Gus wondered if he would get the animal up to speed again.

Between the pace he'd set and the terrain they'd covered, both of them had taken a powerful beating. Every bone in Gus's body ached. His muscles were strained to their limits and his hands had all but locked up around the reins. Upon getting close enough to see the pass, Gus had to close his eyes and check the map in his head once more.

That was it, all right. The Mogollon Mountains were directly east of him and there was a smaller batch of hills to the west. Tres Alamos lay to the southwest and Benson was at the end of a long stretch in his wake. Although his eyes rattled in their sockets after the long and arduous ride, Gus trusted what they told him. Now all he needed to do was look for the camp.

He was surrounded by rough, rocky terrain that could hide any number of settlements from view. Most folks would have considered themselves lost with only the rocks, scorpions and snakes to keep them company. Gus McCord, on the other hand, felt at home. It was the closest thing to a level battlefield that any man could ask for, and if he was to fall in a place like that, it would suit Gus just fine.

Gus surveyed the land without anything to disturb him. The peace and quiet felt so good that he considered staying put for a while longer. He knew his tuckered horse wouldn't mind having a bit more of a rest. Unfortunately for the weary animal, Gus caught sight of the same kind of signal he'd used to catch Doyle's attention not too long ago. The smoke that rose up had thinned out thanks to the churning winds, but was still enough to let him know there was a settlement nearby.

Gus climbed back into his saddle and rode toward the smudge he'd spotted in the sky. Before long, he happened upon a trail that was marked by signs pointing to a place called Last Chance a mile or so farther down the road. The signs didn't say if it was the name of the camp or merely a warning about what lay beyond it, but Gus figured he'd found the spot the kidnapper had told him about. Even if Last Chance wasn't the place he was after, he could at least get a hot meal there.

Having spent so much time avoiding trails and keeping his head down, Gus felt like he was riding into Last Chance as the prize target in a shooting gallery. He nearly drew his gun on several occasions when folks were simply looking his way to tip their hats or watch him the way they would any other stranger.

The camp was quite larger than Gus had been expecting. It was nestled among a bunch of hills that were covered with trees that spilled down the slope

in a wooden cascade. Last Chance might have gone
unnoticed even if Gus knew it was there in the first
place. Its larger structures backed against the hills
and the smaller ones were scattered among the trees
so the entire place seemed to have sprouted there
right along with the mountains, themselves.

Like most other camps Gus had visited, Last
Chance didn't have particularly organized streets
or boardwalks. There were shops, saloons and carts
selling all manner of items or food. There was even
a fairly good-sized hotel stuck in among it all, making Last Chance appear as if it had been scooped
up and tossed down again like a bucketful of mis-
matched dice.

The farther Gus rode into the camp, the more
closed in he felt. Smells ranging from animal scat all
the way to freshly baked bread assaulted his nose.
He could hear a banjo being played, and when he
looked toward where the sound of the music came
from, Gus found a wide, flat building marked simply as the Cheyenne. That place looked like a saloon,
so he climbed down from the saddle and hitched his
horse in front of it. That was when Gus realized just
how hungry and tired he was. Fortunately, his nose
brought him some encouraging news.

The Cheyenne was a saloon, all right. Either that or
it was the least respectable steak house he'd ever
seen. Scents of cooked beef mingled with smoke from
cheap cigars and even cheaper perfume. Several
warped planks and even a few sections of broken
furniture had been cobbled together to form the bar.
It stretched along a back wall that had holes in it that
were so big, they'd just been fashioned into windows.

The banjo player sat on a stool in the corner closest to the door. He nodded to Gus and then shifted his eyes toward a much prettier sight. Two women stood with their arms draped over some men playing cards. As they worked their way from one gambler to another, they leaned down to display the natural assets showcased by the plunging neckline of their dresses. Gus admired the ladies for a few seconds, as well, but he looked away before he was noticed and singled out by one of them. He didn't have time for that sort of thing. Not right now, anyway.

Cutting as straight a line as he could through the room, Gus had to weave between tables of all different sizes and shapes. By the time he finally made it to the bar, he felt as if he'd walked a mile uphill through timber country.

Knocking on a section of the bar that just happened to be an old door, Gus caught the bartender's attention and said, "I need a drink. What have you got?"

"Beer or whiskey. The owner makes some other sort of liquor from his bathtub, but I don't recommend it."

"Where's the beer from?"

"I brew that myself," the bartender replied as he puffed his chest out proudly.

Against his better judgment, Gus said, "I'll take one of those, with a whiskey to wash it down."

"A popular choice, my friend. You just get to camp?"

"That's right."

The barkeep set a mug and a shot glass down

on the bar. Both were filled with liquid that looked hardly fit for human consumption. "You here to do some mining?"

Gus picked up the beer, which put more of a smile on the other man's face. Since that seemed to be enough to put him in the barkeep's good graces, he replied, "That and a bit of work for the Bates Company. You heard of them?"

Rolling his eyes up and around as if his answers were scribbled upon the canvas ceiling or rickety walls, the barkeep finally shook his head. "Can't say as I have. There's the Bateman Supply Company at the other end of camp, but I think they've been out of business for a while. Is that what you were after?"

When he sipped the beer, Gus couldn't help but wince at the mix of bitter and sour flavors that assaulted his tongue. Swallowing the stuff didn't do him any good, since it left behind something that felt like sandy sludge dredged up from the bottom of a swamp. Playing up his expression, he said, "Damn, I must have gotten turned around somewhere."

"Well, there could still be work for a man like yourself here." Leaning forward to nod at the gun strapped around Gus's waist, the barkeep asked, "If you know how to use that shooting iron, I know some men who might be able to use you. If you need an introduction, let me know."

"I'll do that."

The next few seconds were very important. In that time, Gus would know if he'd tipped his hand by skirting around the subject of the Bateman Supply Company. He'd gotten the information he needed, but he had to be certain he didn't draw any attention to the real reason he was there. If anyone could be relied upon to be the gossip of any town or camp, it was a bartender.

Suddenly, the barkeep turned toward the end of the bar that was a collection of broken chair backs nailed together. A few grizzled old-timers were waving at him, so the barkeep collected the money owed for the drinks and bid a hasty farewell.

As soon as the other man's back was turned, Gus picked up the shot glass and tossed back the whiskey inside. It was only slightly better than the beer, but had enough of a bite to burn away the horrible taste that had collected in the back of his throat. Gus set the glass down and waited for the whiskey to work its way through him like a fiery spark tracing a path down a twisted fuse. The liquor burned like sin, but went a long ways in calming Gus's frayed nerves. He watched the barkeep until he was convinced the other man had gone on to more interesting things than the newest thirsty stranger to ride into camp.

Gus left the Cheyenne and glanced toward the cluster of buildings that were built against the steep face of the nearby hills. Since there wasn't much in the other direction, he guessed he'd find the supply company over there. Before he could give it another thought, Gus felt the touch of iron against his ribs.

Someone had come up behind him with a gun and they'd been real quiet about it.

Chapter 10

"You're gettin' sloppy, Gus," Doyle hissed from a little less than arm's length behind him.

Gus turned around in a flicker of motion to face his partner and snatch the gun from his hand. "Looks like we both are a little off our game."

As always, Doyle looked like the cat that had swallowed the canary. "Just keeping you on your toes," he said. "By the way, if you drank any of the beer from that place, you'll want to know that there are some outhouses right around back."

"I've had worse," Gus replied as he handed back Doyle's gun. He started walking into the denser part of the camp and Doyle fell into step beside him. "How long have you been here?"

"Long enough to get a look at the place we were after. I hope you didn't go around dropping the name of that company where it could be heard."

"I just asked the bartender if—"

"Aww, for Pete's sake," Doyle groaned. "Lord only knows how many of them kidnappers are around here waiting to see if anyone's lookin' for them."

"I thought you were supposed to know that by now. Ain't that why you're here?"

"It sure is, but all my sneakin' about may be for nothing if you just waltz in here and announce your intentions."

Waiting until a group of men walked past them, Gus said, "I'm not stupid. I know how to poke around without making a fool out of myself. That's a skill you might want to practice."

"All right smart-ass, what did you find out?"

"Someone's looking to hire gunmen."

Doyle furrowed his brow and asked, "Is that so? Who's doin' the hiring?"

"Don't know yet. I didn't want to waltz into camp and announce that I was here to start trouble."

"Fair enough," Doyle grumbled.

"The barkeep is the one who brought it up," Gus continued. "He made the offer as soon as he spotted the gun in my holster, so that must mean someone's out to find gun hands as quickly as they can get them. Judging by how eager he was to scout for new men to fit the bill, I'd say there's a good fee being paid to whoever steers candidates their way."

"Either that, or the barkeep needs men to look after his place. Could be any number of things."

"All right then," Gus muttered, "what have you been doing with yourself all this time?"

Doyle rubbed his hands together and replied, "Glad you asked. First of all, I ain't been here very long but it's been long enough for me to get a look at that place you mentioned. See that pile of wood right yonder?" He pointed farther into camp.

Gus looked in that direction to find several larger buildings clustered together. Of all the build-ings, only two of them were three floors high in-stead of just two. One of those taller specimens looked as if it was leaning back against the hill to keep it upright. "You mean that one that looks about ready to fall over?"

"No," Doyle said, "the one right next to it. The shorter one."

Sure enough, there was a smaller building that looked slightly sturdier next to the tall one. The sec-ond floor of that one sagged, but the rest of the building seemed fairly sound. From where he stood, Gus could make out no more than one or two win-dows that actually had enough glass in them to re-flect the sunlight.

"I see it," Gus said.

"That's the Bateman Supply Company. Far as anyone around here knows, it's just another one of the businesses that went under when folks started to leave camp for greener pastures. Some still say there's business being conducted there, but nobody really knows what kind."

Gus turned to look at his partner. "You found out all of that?"

"I haven't been dawdling about in saloons," Doyle replied. "Well, actually I have. Just not the Cheyenne. There's another place called the Broken Spur that serves better liquor. That's also where most of the gambling in town is, and before you get all riled up again, I'll have you know folks say plenty of things when they're sittin' and playin' cards."

"Like what?" Gus asked.

"Like there's been a good number of men comin' and goin' from Bateman Supply as of late. Could be them gun hands you hear about, but I don't know who's doing the hiring."

"Maybe you should find out."

Doyle stopped and crossed his arms. "What if it's just some local matter? You want to waste time with that?" Before Gus could answer, Doyle added, "And what if it is them kidnappers? You want to just stroll on up to them, ask for work and pray they don't know who we are? In case you got your head rattled one too many times, they might just be hiring men to kill whoever threw their operation off track. That'd be us."

"I know. I also know a real quick way to find that out for sure."

The longer Gus kept his eyes on him, the sooner Doyle realized what was on his mind. Finally, Doyle let out a sound that made it seem as if he'd just gotten a nose full of pepper.

"Don't even say it," Doyle snorted. "You want me to go in there and see about taking one of them jobs? That's what you want me to do?"

Slowly, Gus nodded. "Going up to one of the men who've been hiring gun hands would cut right down to the heart of the matter pretty quick. If it's just some local matter, don't accept the job. If it's something to do with why we're here, it might give you a chance to find out how many men they already got working for them. That's something we'll need to know."

"I got a look at the place," Doyle said. "Even in the dead of night, there's armed men near that supply company. There may even be a good number of men inside. If there's any place in this camp where someone could hold a hostage, keep her secret and keep her guarded, that's the place."

"How many men are there?"

Doyle shrugged. "I don't know for certain. I just scouted out what I could without bein' seen. I suppose I could try to get a closer look from the inside, but why's it got to be me that does such a foolish thing?"

"You're better at being foolish than I am," Gus pointed out.

Doyle tried to stay angry, but couldn't hold out for more than a few seconds. Clenching his jaw, Doyle shook his head and muttered, "I shoulda pulled my trigger when I got the drop on you a few minutes ago. I really should have."

"Honestly, Doyle, which one of us do you think will get recognized first? Which one of us always gets picked out first? Which one of us always winds up with a picture on them wanted notices, while the other just gets a name?"

"Folks remember the ugly ones better than the pretty ones, I suppose." After letting out a heavy sigh, Doyle said, "Fine. I suppose I can ask about it at the next game. What's that leave you with?"

"I'll get a closer look at that company, maybe even get inside the place. What I'd really like is to make certain that lady is here at all. If word got back about what happened in Benson—"

"It didn't."

"Pardon me?" Gus asked.

"Take a look for yourself," Doyle replied matter-of-factly. "Do you see any telegraph wires? Do you see any train tracks? There ain't no way for anyone to have gotten here faster than I did."

"And what if they got here while you were playing cards?"

Doyle shrugged and finally admitted, "I suppose that's a possibility."

"Which is why I ought to go into that building and have a look for myself. If word got back, they might have just moved her to somewhere else. Whoever was left behind will know where they went, but it won't be long before the rest of them head out as well."

"And why wouldn't they all leave at once?" Doyle asked.

"Because they wouldn't pass up an opportunity to kill anyone who came looking for them."

Smirking, Doyle said, "You always was the smart one. I got a feeling this could be the biggest job we've had in years."

"What makes you say that?"

"You gotta be right about these kidnappers. There'll be a real nice price on their heads. Bringing this lady home might even earn us some favors from that family and that could come in real handy if they know a judge or a politician or such."

"I guess it could," Gus replied.

Doyle swatted Gus on the shoulder while wearing a wide grin. "Shooting up that train was a hell of a move, my friend. Damn near got us killed and it still might get us killed, but it was a good move. If we work fast enough, we should be able to make the most of it."

"So you'll try to get in with those men looking to hire on gun hands?" Gus asked.

Doyle shrugged as if he was deciding whether he should have cake or pie for dessert. "Sure, why not? I can handle myself well enough to figure out what I need to know. If it leads to Bateman Supply, I'll expect you'll be there to back me up. If not, I can see what I can make of it."

Shaking his head, Gus sincerely hoped the trail did lead to the kidnappers. If it didn't, Doyle would probably keep playing long enough to bilk whoever was hiring gunfighters out of several months' worth of pay. "How quickly do you think you can get a game going?"

"It don't take much to strike up a card game in a saloon," Doyle replied. "The trick will be making sure the right people get there. After that, it's a matter of how soon I can get close to the men we're after."

"Can it be done tonight?"

Without hesitation, Doyle nodded. "I'll get somewhere tonight—that's for certain."

"Well don't get in too deep because I won't be there to back your play."

Doyle scowled and glanced nervously at the darkened building in the more congested section of camp. "If you're gonna creep around that supply company, you might be the one that needs some backing. Why don't we stick together? You can kick your feet up at the Broken Spur while I play. They also serve food there, you know. When that's done, we can both pay that place a visit."

Shaking his head before Doyle had even finished, Gus said, "It'll be easier for me to go on my own."

This time, Doyle was the one to draw in a troubled breath and let it out. His mouth twitched, but he knew how useless it would be to try and talk Gus out of something when his mind was so set on it. Showing those reservations in his eyes, Doyle said, "If that's what you want to do, then go right on ahead. Just remember that getting yerself killed won't put any money in our pockets."

Gus patted Doyle on the shoulder. "I'm sure you'd find some way to turn it to your advantage."

"That's a hell of a thing to say."

"Is it wrong?"

After a second, Doyle muttered, "Probably not."

"Where's this Broken Spur you were talking about?"

"Just take a left at that tent selling the pickaxes. Walk a ways from there and you won't miss it."

Taking in the layout of the camp was like trying to find a pattern in a pile of scattered leaves. There was no rhyme or reason where Last Chance was concerned, which left Gus with no other choice than to try to commit the whole blasted place to memory. Fortunately, he had a knack for such things and soaked in the camp as though he was preparing for any other quick escape. Some landmarks were singled out and the rest were allowed to blend in with the background like different-colored splotches on a painting.

"Give me a few hours," Doyle said. "You think anyone has been watching you since you got here?"

"I doubt it. Still, let's try not to be seen together until we've got something to report. I'll wait for it to get a bit darker and then I'll take a gander at Bateman Supply. Just stay at the Broken Spur until I come for you."

"If I gotta leave, I'll make sure the barkeep knows where I went."

"All right, then. Good luck."

Doyle shook the hand Gus offered and said, "It's poker. I don't need any luck."

When Doyle turned away from him, he left Gus behind as though he'd never met him before. In a matter of seconds, Doyle managed to disappear among the folks who crowded the camp's sorry excuse for a street. Gus did the same by pulling his hat down and matching the pace of everyone around him until the locals enveloped him like water pooling around a rock.

Chapter 11

As night fell upon Last Chance, shadows crept along the crooked paths and slid over the uneven surfaces of all the wood-framed tents. The darkness was especially thick around the section of camp that was more built up than the rest. With the hills adding their shade to the mix, those taller structures quickly took the appearance of something that watched over the camp like a single ominous predator.

Gus had found one shadow for himself and settled into it to wait for his chance to move. His spot was in a nook between two tents that bustled with voices, movement and general commotion. It didn't take long for him to figure out one of those tents was a cathouse. The grunts and laughter from there were unmistakable. The other tent reeked of smoke, some of which had the bitter hint of opium mixed in. Although the smoke didn't do Gus's nose any favors, he stayed put until the last trace of the sun was gone from the sky. Needless to say, the folks in the tents on either side of him were too busy to come out and find him huddled with his back against a pair of wooden support posts.

The Bateman Supply Company was marked by a sign that hung at an odd angle on the front of the building. By the looks of it, the sign had been used more as a target for stray gunfire than for advertising. Most of the lettering was legible, while the rest had been worn away by the elements or simple disrepair. The windows in the place seemed to have suffered the same neglect, except for a few on the upper front corner on the left side.

Those windows caught Gus's eye, mostly because they seemed to have been recently replaced. Someone was maintaining that portion of the building for some reason. Odds were good they were the same folks who were moving inside the building. Gus didn't catch more than a shadow or two moving across the new windows, but someone was definitely inside and looking out at the street.

It was a windy night, which caused the canvas walls of the tents around Gus to swell out and flap against the wooden frames holding them in place. Sometimes, Gus was almost completely wrapped up in the billowing fabric. Even when there was enough dust swirling about to fill his eyes with grit, Gus remained still. Once the shadows moved away from those windows, he got up and spit out the dirt that had found its way into his mouth.

Gus didn't look up at the Bateman Supply building. He didn't even glance in its direction. Instead, he turned to walk past the old place with a stagger in his step so anyone watching him would assume he was just another drunk trying to find his way home.

After going a little ways past the building, Gus

circled back around and studied the road behind
him. Nobody was following him, so he approached
the building from the side with the most broken
windows. Even before he got up close enough to
touch the building, Gus could hear movement from
inside. Boots scraped against dirty floorboards
sharply enough to make themselves known above
the constant rush of the wind. Removing his hat,
Gus pressed against the side of the building and
slowly raised his head to get a look through one of
the windows. At first, he couldn't see anything. Just
as he thought he'd chosen a window that was covered or boarded up, the thing blocking the window
shifted and turned around.

Gus dropped straight down and pressed himself
against the wall. The man who'd been standing on
the other side of the window placed his hands
against the sill and leaned forward to look outside.

Clenching his teeth, Gus looked up to see the
other man's fingertips less than a foot away from his
face. Slowly, the tip of a nose as well as a chin
emerged from the window as the man leaned a bit
farther out. Gus fought the urge to move, even as his
muscles ached from being forced to hold such an
awkward position. His lungs burned since he'd cut
himself short before allowing himself to draw his
next breath. Gus shifted his weight, kept his head
down and stayed quiet while staving off the instinct
to pull in a breath.

As the man inside the building leaned out, Gus allowed his hand to creep toward the gun at his side.
His fingers found the Colt's grip, but he didn't draw
the weapon. Every muscle in that arm was coiled

like a spring, and if the man at the window so much as thought about looking down, Gus would have to do something about it.

Finally, a loud rush of air rolled out of the other man's mouth. He cleared his throat and spat a juicy wad out the window before leaning back in again.

Even after that, Gus refused to move.

Silence fell upon the whole building. After a few more seconds had passed, Gus heard steps shuffling inside before they eventually stomped away from the window. Gus took the breath he'd been putting off for so long and shifted his feet to face the wall. He straightened his legs just enough to peek over the windowsill, which allowed him to see a pair of figures inside.

"See anything?" one of the figures asked.

The man who'd been at the window shook his head and grunted, "Probably just a cat."

"You too jumpy to stay here while I go have a word with Bennett?"

"What's he want?"

"Eh, there's supposed to be some men that might be worth hiring on," the first man said. "I'll go size 'em up and come back to spell you."

Gus grinned when he heard that. Although he couldn't be completely sure the men were referring to Doyle or the other card players, it seemed his partner had caught the right folks' attention in the short time since their plan had been formed.

"Bring me back something to drink," the man from the window said.

"You got it." With that, the first figure turned and stomped toward the back of the building. His boots made enough noise upon the old floorboards for Gus to hoist himself up and over the windowsill without being heard.

The moment he was inside the building, Gus bent his knees and hunkered in the shadows for a few seconds. He was ready to pounce if someone came at him and ready to draw his pistol if someone appeared in one of the other rooms. Before long, Gus straightened up and fought the urge to grunt from the ache in his knees. He walked carefully through the small room, placing any weight slowly upon the floor to test each board for squeaks.

The room he'd entered was empty. The hallway beyond that was empty as well. The back door slammed shut as the first man stepped outside, which meant the other fellow was still somewhere nearby. Unfortunately, Gus wasn't sure where the man had gone. Standing in the darkness, Gus closed his eyes so his other senses could stretch out a bit. It didn't take long before his ears picked up on the very thing he'd been after: footsteps rustling toward the front of the building.

Gus opened his eyes and let them get accustomed to the thick, dusty shadows filling the run-down space. The first floor was a series of small dirty rooms connected by a hallway. He made his way to the front of the building, which had the look of a lobby or someplace where displays might have been set up. Gus recognized the front window after having watched it from across the road. A tall figure stood a few paces back from the smudged glass, just outside the dim glow of a streetlamp.

As Gus crept toward the front room, he moved

his eyes back and forth in search of any hint of movement. So far, it seemed the man at the front window was the only one he needed to worry about. The closer Gus got to that man, the more his fingers flexed and his arms tensed. With his bent back, creeping steps and narrowed eyes, Gus looked more like a ghoul than a man as he crept toward the front window.

When he set his sights upon the other man's back, Gus thought of a dozen ways to put him down.

Unaware of the company he kept, the man scratched his backside and cleared his throat so he could spit on the floor. From there, he turned toward the front door and walked away without casting so much as a glance in Gus's direction.

Gus stalked a few paces behind the man like a cat. At times, he wondered if he was hoping more for the man to walk away or for an excuse to pounce with claws bared. As it turned out, the man walked around the bottom floor of that building in a path that had obviously become ingrained in him after many nights of practice. While tagging along behind the man, Gus spotted a set of stairs leading to the second floor. He stopped and hunkered down to wait for the man to move along.

Oddly enough, it was the absence of Gus's movement that made the other man stop. He cocked his head and looked from side to side.

Standing up straight, Gus pressed his back against the wall a few paces away from a narrow opening that led into a closet. There was no door in the frame, which left a large black space in the wall. The other man was already turning around to look directly at him, which meant Gus wouldn't be able to slip inside without being seen.

Gus's fingers curled around the grip of his Colt.

The man in front of him turned and gazed into the front room, allowing Gus to move his hand along the floor until he found a rusty nail. Before Gus could make another move, the other man looked straight at him.

Gus froze.

The man in front of him squinted and leaned forward. Either he was trying to figure out what the shape in the shadows was or he was trying to decide what to do about it.

The knot in Gus's stomach cinched in a bit tighter. His breath snagged deep in his throat.

Something hissed in the front room, and when the man turned back around to look, Gus tossed the nail in his hand toward the stairway.

The man spun on his heels and took a few steps toward the rattling nail, giving Gus just enough time to duck into the closet and the thick web of shadows inside.

"Damn cats," the man grumbled as he made another lap around the front room. A few seconds later, he stomped past the closet on his way to the back room and the office where Gus had first entered the building.

Gus wasn't the sort who put a lot of faith in luck. When he did get a bit tossed his way, however, he wasn't the sort to pass it by. He hurried into the hall and made his way to the staircase. Although he knew the other man could circle around at any time, he didn't bother looking back. He only had one and a half good eyes, so he kept them facing front, where they could do him the most good.

Gus kept his feet on the edges of the stairs as he worked his way up them. When he got to the second floor, he put his back to a wall and looked around to find a narrow hall branching to the left and right. After he took a moment to get his bearings, Gus realized the newer windows he'd spotted were to his right, so that was the way he decided to go.

Lanterns were fixed to the wall about five paces from the staircase in either direction, but only two were lit. As soon as he stepped within the radius of the closest lantern, the door directly next to Gus swung open. That was the bad thing about luck. When it ran out, it hit a man real hard.

Gus made sure he hit the man who walked through that doorway even harder.

Gus's fist slammed into the man's face dead-on. The impact was so solid that it made a single muffled thump before the man could even yelp in pain. He staggered back a step, pulled in a breath and was silenced before he could let it out. Gus slapped one hand over the man's mouth and placed the other on the back of his head while dragging him into the room. He wrenched the guy's head to one side, stopping just short of breaking anything.

"Do what I say or I snap your neck," Gus hissed. "Hear me?"

The man tried to nod, but couldn't do much considering his predicament.

"How many more of you are up here?"

Once Gus parted his fingers enough for the other man to be heard the guy mumbled, "Two."

"Where?"

"Next room."

"And the lady?"

The guy's eyes widened even more as he strained to get a look at Gus's face. Before he could see much of anything, his head was turned a little more in the wrong direction.

"Just answer me," Gus hissed. "Is she still alive?"

"Yes."

Gus's hand moved away from the back of the other man's head to snatch the pistol from the man's holster and jam its barrel into the man's back. "You're gonna take me to her," Gus ordered. "Anything goes wrong and you're the first to die— understand? Now where is she?"

"Next room."

Pushing the man along using the pistol, Gus kept his hand over the guy's mouth. Fortunately, the guy was too rattled to realize he could just twist his head away from Gus's hand. Either that or he was smart enough to know he wouldn't be able to make a sound before Gus pulled his trigger.

When they walked to the door marked by the second burning lantern, Gus snarled, "Open it."

As soon as the man opened the door, he was shoved inside.

Sure enough, there were two more gunmen in there. They turned to look at who'd opened the door, but weren't expecting a fight. Gus took full advantage of the moment by pushing his hostage into the room ahead of him.

The first gunman in the room reached for the pistol at his hip, but Gus stopped him with a single shot from his Colt. Gus knew there was no turning back now, so he fired a shot at the second gunman. That bullet punched through the wall because the second gunman had lunged for a shotgun propped beside the chair he'd been sitting in.

Gus's hostage turned around to try to reclaim his gun, but didn't make it far before Gus's boot slammed into his knee. As soon as that fellow dropped, Gus had a clear shot at the one with the shotgun. He fired twice in quick succession to knock the shotgunner off his feet and drop him in the corner.

The sound of boots stomping up the stairs echoed down the hall. Gus kicked his former hostage away from the shotgun, which had been dropped, and hauled him up to his feet. Just as the man from downstairs got to the door, Gus's hostage was pushed from the room to meet him in a tangle of arms and legs. All of this confusion bought Gus enough time to put his back to the closest wall.

One quick glance at his surroundings was enough for Gus to realize there was no woman in that room. Apart from a few chairs and some chests set up against another wall, it was just him and the dead gunmen. To make matters worse, it wouldn't be long before the two in the hall got themselves untangled so they could charge at him again. Before that could happen, Gus lowered his shoulder and charged them.

He hit the man from downstairs in the chest, knocking him and the hostage into a wall. The man from downstairs started to bring his gun around, but Gus was able to knock the back of his head against the wall with enough force to drop him to the floor. That only left the hostage to scamper toward the stairs on all fours. The hostage reached the top of the stairs in such a rush that he slipped down the top two steps.

Gus walked toward the man, who now wobbled precariously at the top of the stairs. One strong nudge was all it took to knock the man over. The hostage rolled down a few steps, became wedged with his leg wrapped around a post and started moaning in pain. Since it was obvious that man wasn't going anywhere, Gus left him where he'd landed so he could search the remaining rooms.

The farthest end of the second-floor hallway deteriorated to a mess of collapsed walls that looked like a gaping wound within the structure. Gus kicked in one door to find several bunks, which were probably used by the kidnappers. The room second to the end was smaller than the rest and occupied by one more man wielding a shotgun.

The instant Gus opened the door, that shotgun was aimed directly at him. He hopped away from the door just as the shotgun blasted a chunk from the frame. Dust and splinters filled the air. Gus stepped into that gritty cloud and fired at the spot where the shotgunner had been standing. His aim wasn't perfect, but it was good enough to hit the shotgunner before the second barrel could be emptied.

Gus rushed into the room, ripped the shotgun from the other man's grasp and swung it like a club at his midsection. The other man grunted and doubled over, which provided a perfect target for Gus's knee as it snapped straight up and made contact with the man's chin. Just to be safe, Gus dropped the shotgun's stock onto the man's head.

Now that the shotgunner was unconscious and crumpled on the floor, Gus shifted his eyes toward the second person in there with him.

"Are you Abigail Swann?" he asked.

The woman was sitting in a chair against the wall to the right of the door. Her ankles were tied to the front legs of the chair and her hands were bound behind her back. There was something tied around her mouth, so Gus reached out to pull it away. "I ain't here to hurt you," he said as he removed the gag. "Are you Abigail Swann?"

She nodded as her eyes still darted back and forth to the chaos that had erupted directly in front of her.

"All right, then," Gus told her. "How'd you like to stretch your legs a bit?"

Chapter 12

When he'd first untied Abigail from her chair, Gus thought he might have to carry her out of that building. She was more than willing to work the kinks out of her arms as soon as he cut through those ropes, but her legs were weak and unsteady beneath her. She could hardly stand at first, but wasn't about to stop trying.

"Don't touch me!" she snapped when Gus attempted to reach out for her.

Keeping his hand out despite her swatting at it, Gus said, "I'm only trying to lend you a hand, lady."

"You've already done enough. Just leave me be."

"In case you ain't been looking, I'm the one setting you free."

"Well, you could have fooled me. You almost shot me when you came bursting in here."

"You want us both to be shot?" Gus asked. "Then we could just stand around this place and wait for more gunmen to come along. It shouldn't be much longer before they arrive."

Abigail rubbed her wrists and looked around as if she was seriously considering staying put. Eventually, she announced, "We can go. Just try not to get us both killed."

"Stay behind me."

"Do you know where you're going?"

"It ain't that hard to figure out," Gus replied. "There's some stairs and a front door. I was plannin' on putting both of those to good use."

"Fine. No need to be so—"

"Come on," Gus snapped as he grabbed hold of her arm and dragged her out of the room. "We don't have time for this."

Abigail stumbled along behind him and tried to pull her arm free of his grasp every step of the way. Before they reached the top of the stairs, Gus kicked around the idea of going back for the gag so he could stuff it into her mouth, where it belonged.

"Slow down," she demanded. "We'll break our necks."

"No, we won't."

"I haven't been on my feet for days. My legs feel like straw and they're mostly numb."

"Then I'll carry you," Gus offered.

"You most certainly will not!" Abigail protested in a voice that made it seem as if his proposition had been of a completely different sort. "For all I know you're just a—*Look out!*" Her scream echoed through the entire building and her face was aimed directly at a lump three-quarters of the way down the stairs. That lump happened to be the man Gus had sent tumbling down there. That lump also happened to be lifting a pistol.

Firing his Colt on instinct, Gus put a bullet close enough to the man on the stairs to rattle him. After that, Gus rushed down to where the man had landed and kicked the gun from his hand. He continued down to the first floor and pulled Abigail along with him.

"Don't scream like that again," Gus snarled.

Although she'd eased up on trying to pull her arm from his grasp, Abigail was still a stumbling anchor, making every step twice as difficult as it should have been. "He was going to shoot you," she said. "I just saved your life."

"And I have yet to get you out of here, so keep quiet and do what I say."

"We're not out of here yet. And if I see someone about to shoot you, perhaps I'll just stay quiet and let them do it."

"Good."

Gus couldn't see her face, but he could feel the anger coming from the woman behind him like steam whistling from a kettle. He knew he should let go of her arm to free up that hand, but Gus had already seen enough of Abigail Swann to know she wasn't about to come along easily. He maintained his grip on her and made a sharp turn at the bottom of the stairs.

"Are you the marshal?" she asked. "Or a sheriff? Maybe a Texas Ranger?"

"Texas Ranger?" Gus scoffed. "Do you know where you are?"

"Texas Rangers leave Texas! They track wanted men as far as they need to in order to bring them in."

"I suppose you're just not wanted badly enough."

Abigail sputtered to try to come up with something to say to that. Fortunately for Gus, it kept her busy long enough for them to work their way back to the office where he'd climbed in through the window. "Have you seen anyone else around besides the men I already dealt with?" he asked.

"I would think you'd know that before charging in here like a—"

Letting go of her arm, Gus wheeled around to stare at her. Abigail was stunned to get her hand back, but stayed put so she could glare right back at him.

"Look, lady, if you want to stay here, that's fine with me."

"I didn't—"

Silencing her with a quickly upraised finger, Gus said, "I made it this far and I intend on getting you out. Just so you know, it would make things a lot easier for me if I could toss your carcass over my shoulder and carry you out. How'd that be?"

It didn't take long for Abigail's imagination to run wild. Pretty soon, the defiant scowl on her face gave way to an expression that wasn't much more than a thin, petrified veil. Seeing that she was frightened enough to keep her mouth shut, Gus asked, "You want to help me?"

She nodded.

"How many men did you see in here at any given time?"

"I . . . don't know," she mumbled. "In case you didn't notice—" Stopping herself, Abigail looked away from him and said, "I didn't leave that room, but I heard plenty of men inside."

"Is there anyone watching from the outside?"

"They talked about scouts, but I think a bunch of them left to go somewhere else."

Gus looked outside for any sign that someone

might be waiting for them. As far as he could tell, there wasn't anything beyond that window that hadn't been there when he'd come in. "It should be safe for us to go this way, then," he told her.

"Should be?" Abigail asked. "Don't you know for certain?" Suddenly, the sneer returned to her face and the edge returned to her voice. "Don't you have any partners? Didn't you at least have a plan when you came here?"

"I didn't really intend for all this to happen," Gus said more to himself than to her. "At least, not tonight."

The only thing that kept him from jumping out that window was the fear that came over him when things went too easily. Sure, there'd been shots fired and blood spilled, but Gus had assumed that getting Abigail out of Bateman Supply was going to be a whole lot harder.

"What's taking you so long?" Abigail groused. "Why don't we just go? For that matter, why don't we just go out through the front door?"

"Because that's too easy," Gus snarled. "If there's an ambush, that's where it's bound to be."

"Then what about the back door? I know there's got to be one of those."

As if in answer to her question, a slamming sound came from the rear of the building. That was followed by the thumping of rushed steps and several raised voices.

"That's why we don't go through the back door," Gus hissed. "And that's also what I was hoping to hear. Now that those men are busy by the door, how about you climb outside?"

If she'd been genuinely impressed with Gus's reasoning, she showed it by clenching her mouth into a tight line and glaring at him the way she'd been doing since first laying eyes on him. Rather than say what she was so clearly thinking, Abigail grabbed hold of the windowsill and sat down on it.

"Are you going to help me or not?" she asked.

Fighting back the impulse to help her by shoving her in much the same way he'd shoved that gunman down the stairs, he took her hand while she daintily swung her legs over the sill. After taking her sweet time in turning her back to him, she hopped down and started dusting herself off.

As if to show her how it was done, Gus placed one hand on the sill and climbed through the window. Still able to hear commotion from inside the building, Gus grabbed Abigail's arm and pulled her toward the street.

"The least you could do is take the other arm," she whined.

"Would that make you come along any easier?"

"I'm not in the habit of—"

"Then just keep quiet and keep your feet moving," Gus told her. "There'll be plenty of time to complain later."

Abigail muttered and whined, but Gus didn't pay any attention to her. Instead, he did his level best to concentrate on what he was doing. Dragging Abigail behind him was akin to building a house of cards in a wind storm. More than once, he entertained the thought of knocking her in the head and throwing her over one shoulder. Then again, the thought of how she'd be when she woke up was not a pleasant one.

After winding past a few tents, Gus made a bee-line for the Cheyenne. He recalled there being other saloons in that vicinity, and they should serve his purpose well enough. When he got close enough to hear the music and bawdy laughter that filled that section of camp, Gus was immediately slowed to a snail's pace. The anchor he was towing had dug her feet in and nearly brought him to a stop.

"I'm not going there!" Abigail declared.

Gus turned and glared directly into her eyes. "You're going where I tell you or I can just hand you right back to those kidnappers. Understand me? I risked life and limb to get you out of there and all I've gotten so far is grief! You want to go back and get tied to that chair? Fine with me. You want both of us to catch a bullet? Just keep flappin' your gums and drawin' attention." Pressing a finger against her forehead, he added, "Is steppin' foot inside a saloon worse than gettin' a hole shot through your skull?"

Abigail stared at him as her eyes blinked in a quick series of flutters. Her lips drew tighter together and she was plainly fighting to keep them that way.

"You got something to say?" Gus asked. "Go ahead. It's not like we got anything better to do!"

Finally, Abigail pulled in a breath and told him, "Those men threatened to sell me to one of these places as a whore. They said they'd found someone at one of these saloons who would buy me outright and didn't care where I came from. If I didn't lie down like I was supposed to, I was to be whipped or handed off to someone who could take me somewhere they could do whatever they wanted to me. I don't know which saloon they were talking about, but someone in there might recognize me if we went inside. Ever since they told me all of that," she added, "the thought of stepping foot in any saloon again makes me ill. Perhaps if I close my eyes and you lead me, I can bear it."

Gus couldn't recall the last time he'd felt so bad.

He'd shot men for the change in their pockets.

He'd stabbed some for no reason at all.

He'd even been known to punch people in the face when they tried to play on his sympathies. And yet, somehow or other, Abigail was playing them like a fiddle.

She must have known what she was doing because she closed her eyes and held out her hand as though she didn't expect to get it back. "Well, go on," she said. "Lead me."

"Perhaps it wouldn't be wise to go in there after all," Gus muttered. "More of those gunmen might be inside." A bit farther down, he spotted another place that appeared to have a lantern glowing inside. "Let's try over there. Looks like they serve food."

"You're hungry?" she asked.

"It's a place to keep our heads down for a bit while watching what's going on. If you want something to eat, you can have it."

Gus led the way to a tent that was less than half the size of the saloon. Inside, the place seemed doubly large since the only ones in there were an old man sleeping with his head on a table and a very bored woman perched on a stool. As soon as she saw Gus and Abigail, the woman jumped up and rushed over to them. "Good evening to you both," she said.

"I'm starving," Abigail announced.

"Well, I've got some stew left over from supper service as well as some soup. To be honest, the soup is a lot like the stew. There's also some bread."

"Soup for me." Tossing an offhanded wave to Gus, she added, "I don't know about him."

"If the stew's got meat in it, I'll take it," Gus replied.

"It does, but—"

"Fine. I'll take it."

Abigail rolled her eyes as if she needed to apologize for Gus's behavior. The woman who ran the place looked to be happy just to have some customers and she hurried behind a curtain before they could change their minds. When Abigail tried to sit next to a smaller, window-sized flap in the tent, Gus shook his head and took that seat instead.

"I would like to get some fresh air," Abigail muttered. "But I suppose you know best."

Gus sat upon a chair that creaked loudly as his weight settled onto it. "Yeah," he said, "I do know best. You'll get plenty of fresh air over the next few days."

"I suppose we'll be taking a train back to my father's place. It's in Sacramento, but the smaller place in Prescott is a lot closer. I'm sure we can get a ticket—"

"No trains," Gus said.

The restaurant's owner rushed over to the table to give them both cups of water. "I'm just warming the food up for you. It won't take long." With that, she hurried away.

"What do you mean, no trains?" Abigail asked as if the other woman had never been there.

"The men who're left will be expecting us to ride a train. That's why we can't take one."

"Well, I have something to say about that. Are you listening to me?" She demanded.

Gus smiled pleasantly and replied, "Not at all, but go on."

Abigail crossed her arms and stared at him angrily, which didn't keep him from enjoying his stew. It was delicious.

Chapter 13

Gus watched the street from inside the little restaurant, waiting for the surviving gunmen to come in search of Abigail Swann. When he was done with his stew, Gus stayed and nursed a cup of coffee, but didn't see much of anything outside. Even as they left the place, Gus fully intended on drawing his gun and fighting through a storm of lead at any given second. When none of that came, he wasn't sure what to think.

Some might have been grateful, but Gus knew better than that. It would have been better to have the remaining gunmen charge at him when they were still angry and flailing like rabid dogs. Given time to lick their wounds, they might very well come up with a real plan to track Abigail down and bring her back.

"What's wrong with you?" Abigail asked.

Shaking himself from his thoughts, Gus mumbled, "Huh?"

"You haven't said a word since you paid for all that coffee you drank. Aren't you even going to tell me who you are?"

"Later."

"Where are we going now? Do you even have any notion of what to do after you got me out of there?"

"I'm working on it."

For once, Abigail was speechless. She shook her head as if it had come loose and blinked furiously at him. Under most any other circumstances, it would have been a funny sight.

Gus led her down a few of the many crooked avenues that cut through Last Chance. Along the way, fortune smiled upon him again. Some clothes hung from a line just outside of a little shack and he snagged a few of them without breaking stride. "Wrap this around your head," he told Abigail as he handed over a checked shirt that was still a bit damp after having been washed. "Cover your face."

She took the shirt as though she was appalled by the very sight of it. "This isn't yours. You just stole this."

"Are you joking?"

"We don't need clothes this badly. I can make due with what I've got."

"Fine. Just keep yourself from being seen while I step in there for a moment."

Looking up to where Gus was headed, Abigail pulled in a sharp breath. "The Broken Spur? That's one of the saloons those men were talking about when they threatened to sell me. Oh Lord. You didn't come to rescue me at all. You're one of those slavers!"

"You caught me," Gus said drily. "And rather than deal with those kidnappers, I stormed in and gunned them down because that's so much easier."

Although she picked up on the sarcasm in his voice, Abigail wasn't amused by the joke.

"My partner is in there and I need to meet up with him," Gus explained. "Stay put and keep your head down."

"What if those men do come along?" she asked.

"That's why you stay low. Trust me. Hunker down in a shadow somewhere and keep your face wrapped up. The last thing they'll expect is to find you resting along the side of the street. Odds are they're too busy gathering their forces right now, anyway."

Abigail didn't get a chance to protest any more because Gus had already walked into the saloon. He followed his own advice by pulling his hat down low and tugging the bandanna around his neck up a bit to brush against his chin. That only left a small section of his face to be seen by anyone who was interested enough to look.

"Cold night, mister?" the barkeep asked as Gus walked over to him.

"Lookin' for a card game," he replied.

"Then look over in the back. If you sit down to play, you'd best order a drink. I'm runnin' a business here."

Although Gus hadn't spotted his partner when he'd first arrived, he soon heard the distinctive sound of Doyle's laugh coming from the back of the saloon. It was a small place, but was chock-full of so many folks that only half of them had room to sit down. The other half stood or elbowed their neighbors for more breathing room. A few even threw a punch or two just to claim one of the chairs.

All of the men sitting at the card table in the back of the room were among the fortunate ones. They had chairs and plenty of whiskey to go along with them.

Gus approached the table cautiously. He got close enough to spot Doyle and then waited until his partner glanced his way. When he did, Gus waved toward the door and then turned around to leave. Stepping outside, Gus felt the knot in his belly tighten. Abigail wasn't where he'd left her. Before he could kick himself for leaving her out there, he saw one of the huddled shapes across the street wave at him.

Hurrying over to her, Gus offered his hand and helped Abigail to her feet. "Come on. We're leaving."

"Where are we going?"

"You'll know when we get there."

Gus and Doyle met in the street, but didn't stay put for long. As soon as the two caught sight of each other, they went to where their horses were being kept and rode to the outskirts of the camp. After changing his mind a few times when he didn't like the looks of the first couple spots, Gus settled upon a cluster of tents that looked to have been there since the camp had been founded. Tattered sections of canvas were held up by weathered boards, gnarled sticks or even rope tied between two trees. Most of the tents were empty and the folks residing in the others were content to let the three new arrivals go about their business.

Every step of the way, Gus could feel Doyle simmering like a teakettle that was ready to shriek.

When they finally came to a stop, Doyle jumped down from his horse and stormed over to Gus. "Who the hell is that?" he asked as he stabbed a finger toward Abigail.

Gus helped Abigail down and replied, "This is the lady we were after."

"I have a name, you know," Abigail said.

But neither of the men took notice of her. Although he could now feel her stewing almost as much as Doyle, Gus kept her behind him and his eyes locked upon his partner. Both of them may have had tempers, but Doyle had the guns to back it up.

"You were supposed to go have a look over there," Doyle said. "Just a *look*!"

"She's why we're here," Gus pointed out.

"Why didn't you wait for me? I've been sitting back there, waiting to catch a piece of hot lead in my back while digging for information about them kidnappers. You even stop to think I may have found out something important?"

"What did you find out, Doyle?"

He looked around, but saw nothing other than the wilted tents and a few poor souls forced to live in them. Leaning forward and dropping his voice to a whisper, Doyle said, "It's the kidnappers hiring guns, all right. Either that or Bateman Supply is into more than just snatching up pretty blondes."

Gus had to glance over to Abigail when he heard that. It wasn't until just then that he realized he hadn't taken a real good look at her yet. From the moment he'd first seen her, Gus had only been concerned about who she was and how to get her away from those armed men. Now that things had settled down a little, he could let his eyes take their time in soaking her up.

Abigail was about five and a half feet tall, with thick blond hair streaming down well past her shoulders. Although her hair was a tussled mess, she'd gathered most of it up and tied it behind her head to form a single bushy tail. Her face was a narrow oval shape accentuated by a small mouth and a pert nose. Gus couldn't tell what color her eyes were, but her lashes were almost as long as her fingertips and fluttered like butterfly wings as she blinked and fretted under his scrutiny.

"What is it?" she asked. Getting no reply from Gus, Abigail took it upon herself to look for whatever had captured his attention. She started by fussing with her hair, which kept her busy from then on.

Doyle snapped his fingers in front of Gus's face. "You hear what I just told you?"

"Yeah," Gus replied. "Bateman Supply does more than kidnap pretty blondes."

Doyle's eyes narrowed and he gritted his teeth. "You sure as hell didn't waste any time in getting her, did you? What the hell were you thinkin'?"

"Just tell me the rest of what you found out before we open that can of worms."

"There are gunmen coming in from all over," Doyle continued. "At least, there's supposed to be. One of the bosses over at that supply company was supposed to be at the Broken Spur, but he was tending to other matters. I didn't get a word with him, but the fella seemed awfully upset about something."

"He may have found out what happened in Benson."

"That's right. Seems even the fellas at that card game knew something was brewing. Hired guns are at the top of the wanted list for the folks at Bateman Supply and they're payin' top dollar for them. The fee for steering good men their way ain't too shabby. Supposedly, there's already a dozen or so men who've signed on and are waiting to meet with Mr. Smythe."

"Smythe's on his way?"

"They say he is," Doyle said. "Far as we know, Smythe didn't even make it off that train."

"Why wouldn't he have made it off the train?"

"Not on account of anything you did, but there was a whole lot of law around that station when we left. They could have all killed one another for all we know."

Gus shook his head. "That's hoping for way too much. We were the ones who shot our way out of there and we were the ones to ride off with the posse on our tails. And before you say what you're thinking, yes, I realize I was the one who started all the shooting."

"Just so long as you know it," Doyle grumbled.

"So Smythe ain't here yet. Otherwise you probably would have seen him."

"I would have heard about it," Doyle added. "Those card players sure liked to talk."

"Then it's a good thing I got her when I did."

Doyle started to say something, but stopped as if he'd accidentally swallowed a bug. "What did you just say?"

Gus looked at Abigail and found her still pulling the tangles from her hair. Although she watched them both, she wasn't about to step in between the feuding partners. Lowering his voice so she couldn't hear every last word, Gus said, "I went there with the intention of doing just what I said I was gonna do. I meant to get a look at that place and scout out how many men we'd have to contend with when we went back. When I got there, I was able to get a lot closer than I thought, because there weren't nearly as many men watching the place as we expected. And maybe that's because of what we both already did."

Doyle let out a single snort of a laugh. "All I been doing since I got here is watching and playing cards."

"I'm talkin' about what we did in Benson. Those men on that train were supposed to come back here, but they didn't. For all we know, they could be in jail or bound for this place. Since there ain't no tracks through this camp, that means they got to ride here, and even if they rode like the wind, there wouldn't be as many men with them as they started out with."

"Because of what we did," Doyle said with a grin.

Gus nodded. "Because of what we did. It sounds like Smythe runs this whole show. Those others in the fancy suits were probably high up in the pecking order of this gang, which means them bein' gone forces all the hired hands to sit around and wait for them to get back."

"And," Doyle added, "when hired hands sit around and wait, they get lazy."

"That's the word I'd use to describe the men that

were watching her. Hell, I didn't even spot more than one or two of them from the outside of that building and those looked about ready to fall asleep. What did you want me to do? Wait until they got their second wind?"

Doyle's entire face was scrunched up in thought. If he'd had gears inside of him, they would have been grinding with the effort of trying to see how one thing played off of another. "So that's why you went in to get her without me?" he finally asked.

"Yeah," Gus said. "We couldn't have gotten it all to line up better if we tried. Remember that bank we robbed in Kansas?"

"The one with the twins running the place?"

"No. The one with the diamonds in the safe."

That brought a smile to Doyle's face. "Oh yeah. I remember that."

"We walked in to deposit the money we had stolen from that other job and found the place was nearly empty, so we robbed it. We got to the safe to find there just happened to be diamonds in it."

"And it turned out the bank was so empty because the manager and the staff all went to round up guards and a sheriff's deputy to watch over the diamonds." Doyle chuckled as he recounted the memory. "That was damned perfect."

"It was lucky timing," Gus corrected. "But we took advantage of it. This is what we got here, only we're the ones that put the timing into effect. I may have gone off half-cocked, but it made a big enough mess that it slowed them kidnappers down. Anyone that hadn't known to come to this camp or what to look for once we got here wouldn't have found that lady even if she was sitting by herself in that build-ing. As it turned out, we knew right where she was and even made an opening for us to get there. I just took advantage of it."

"Just like that bank," Doyle mused as if he'd only now put all the pieces together.

Having been the one to set all the pieces directly in front of him, Gus said, "Just like the bank."

Slowly, the devious admiration faded from Doyle's face to be replaced once again by anger. "You still shoulda come and got me."

"I would have, but there wasn't time. I saw a chance and I took it."

Doyle watched Abigail fuss with the last knot in her hair. "However it happened, we got her. That means damn near every man who can use a gun in this camp will be lookin' for us. We should get away from this place."

"My thoughts exactly."

"I'm surprised you didn't just take off on yer own and leave me here. Seems like I ain't no good for anything, anyways."

"Are you going to stay sore about this forever?" Gus asked. "You want me to apologize?"

Doyle looked at him expectantly.

"Well, that's not going to happen," Gus told him. "We came here for that lady and now we got her. You did your job and I did mine. Thanks to you, we know this Bateman Supply organization is more than just some bunch of kidnappers. They're more than a gang, even."

"And you had to go and cross them. Tell me something, Gus. Did you shoot any of their men or do we still have a chance at getting on this gang's good side? They pay a hell of a lot better than most other gangs we worked in."

Gus ground his teeth together before saying, "I shot a few. Pushed another one down some stairs."

"You leave any alive?"

"I think so."

"Well, then," Doyle said, "that's something. We can figure something out on our way to Prescott."

Gus patted Doyle on the shoulder and asked him, "Don't I always figure something out?"

"I suppose you do. The only thing is that I ain't sure how much longer I should listen."

"There ain't a lot to listen to. We skin out of here and watch our backs as always. There's bound to be men ridin' after us, but that ain't nothing new. The price is still on our heads, so we'll watch for bounty hunters and the law."

"And you changed the letter like we agreed?"

"Yep."

"Then that's the ace up our sleeve," Doyle said. "If that lady over there gives us too much grief, we'll collect whatever ransom we can get and call it a day." Doyle stuck out his hand. "Agreed?"

In the years they'd ridden together, Gus had never gone back on a deal after he and Doyle had shaken on it. For both partners, that was a contract that the devil himself couldn't break. Without it, one would have probably killed the other a long time ago.

In the years they'd ridden together, Doyle had also gotten very good at picking up the different types of scowls Gus was known to put on. There was no mistaking the prickly one he wore now. "Fine," Doyle grumbled. "We came this far, so we'll play it your way. There'd better be somethin' at the end of this other than a friendly thank-you."

Gus gripped Doyle's hand, shook it once and said, "Agreed."

Chapter 14

Their first order of business was to ride northwest toward the Salt River. Gus and Doyle didn't ride as quickly as they could have because they had to be alert for an ambush. This would be the time when they would find out whether the kidnappers from Bateman Supply were organized enough to come after them right away. If they weren't, that meant Gus and Doyle had some breathing room to plot their route a bit farther.

Gus was used to riding at a full gallop without being able to see more than a couple paces in front of him. Some folks called that a foolhardy way to go about things, but it was a simple fact of life for a man trying to stay ahead of the law. Posses, bounty hunters and all other sorts of lawmen tended to work on a schedule. Apparently, so did Abigail Swann.

"Where are we going?" she asked from behind Gus.

He shifted in his saddle, which caused her to shift behind him. She rode with her arms wrapped around his chest and her head resting upon the back of his shoulder. Although it may have seemed quaint at first, she treated Gus with as much care as she'd show a lumpy pillow. Every so often, she even poked and prodded him as if that would make his back a little softer.

"Did you hear me?" she groused.

"Yeah, I heard you."

"Then why won't you answer?"

"Because I already answered you," he replied.

"That was this morning and all you said was that we were headed toward the river."

"And we still are."

Sighing impatiently, she asked, "Where's the other one?"

"You mean Doyle?"

"Isn't he the only other one?"

Gus had to grin, but was careful not to let her see. So far, she had yet to acknowledge that Doyle was anything more than an irritating pup that insisted on nipping at her heels. "He rode ahead to scout the trail."

"Scout for what?"

"Those men who kidnapped you were hiring reinforcements, so they're probably after us. Then there's Indians, the law or any number of things that could cost us valuable time."

"Wait. What did you say?"

"The trail may be washed out," Gus explained. "There could have been a rock slide or something else that'd cause us to double back and find another way."

"Not that," Abigail snapped. "The part about the law. You're worried about the law finding you?"

Gus answered that by shrugging enough for her to feel it.

"So you and the other one are both outlaws? Oh my Lord."

"We saved your life," Gus pointed out.

"You did, but that other one wants to ransom me off. I heard you both talking last night. I heard the tone in his voice and I see the way he looks at me. He's no better than the men that snatched me out of the coach."

"What coach?" Gus asked as he reined his horse to a stop.

"What do you care?" For the last few seconds, Abigail's grip around Gus's torso had been tightening. In fact, he could feel her entire body tensing against his back like a coiled spring.

"Look," he said. "You're not tied up anymore. You're free—"

"That's right," she announced. "I'm free and I'll go where I please!" With that, she let go of him and started to pound her fists against Gus's back. When he turned around, she smacked him upside his head with enough force to send his dusty old hat flying through the air.

"What in the hell?" Gus hollered.

"I won't be anyone's prisoner any longer! I'll . . . I'll . . ." Just then, she leaned forward and reached for the pistol holstered on Gus's hip. When he slapped her hand away from the gun, Abigail turned her attention to the Sharps rifle that Doyle had stolen and Gus now carried in the boot hanging from his saddle. "I'll fight my way out if I have to!"

Gus was already twisting around one way, but had to twist around in the other before Abigail got her hands upon his rifle. The Sharps was halfway out of the boot when Gus got to it and he barely managed to keep her from claiming the weapon for herself. Even after he'd pulled the rifle from her fingers, she still clawed for the trigger.

Rather than shove her or do anything that might result in Abigail falling from the horse's back altogether, Gus took hold of her wrist and pulled her hand away from the rifle. He seemed to be making progress when Abigail pulled her arm back and shifted her weight away from the boot. Abigail gave him another smack on the arm and then slid off the other side of the horse.

Gus whipped around and reached back to grab her before she hit the ground, but she hadn't fallen from the saddle as he'd feared. Instead, she'd jumped down of her own volition and hit the sandy ground on both feet.

Once she was off the horse, she looked around in a daze. The expression on her face indicated that she hadn't expected to make it that far. Now that she was on her own, Abigail turned her back to Gus's horse and started running.

All of that kicking and squirming had caused the horse to get its dander up. The big fellow shifted upon its hooves and let out a few snuffing breaths. With a bit of coaxing from Gus, the horse quieted down and came to a rest. Soon it looked toward Abigail with wide confused eyes. Gus was doing pretty much the same thing.

He watched her run for about sixty yards over a

wide stretch of rocky ground that had some scrub bushes sprouting here and there. Beyond that, there were some thirsty-looking trees, a whole lot of open ground and the mountains. "Where do you think you're going?" he asked.

Without looking over her shoulder, Abigail replied, "Away from you! And away from that other one!"

"On foot?"

She stopped and stared at the mountains to the east. Her shoulders rose and fell with a series of deep, panting breaths. Placing her hands upon her hips and keeping her back to him, Abigail asked, "Are you going to give me your horse?"

"No."

"Then it'll have to be on foot."

Sitting with one hand propped upon his saddle horn and the other upon the grip of his Colt, he told her, "I can't just let you walk away."

Abigail turned and stared at him. "What are you going to do? Shoot me?"

"I wasn't planning on it."

"Then why won't you let me go?"

"Because," Gus replied simply, "you'll die."

"Oh, is that a fact?"

"Near as I can tell, yeah. That's a fact."

Crossing her arms, Abigail cocked her head to one side and let a sneer sink into her face like water settling into a perfectly good patch of dirt to create mud. "And what makes you so certain of that? Is it because I'm just some weak little woman? If that's the case, I'll have you know I gave those kidnappers so much of a fight that they stopped coming near

me. And if you don't believe me, I'll give you even
more of a fight."

"That's not why I'm so certain," Gus told her.

"Then why do you think I'll die without some
man and his gun to protect me?"

"Because you don't have a horse or any water."
Holding up his hand, Gus ticked off his fingers one
by one. "You also don't have any shelter, a map,
proper clothes or any weapons to fight off animals
or anyone else that might come along. On top of all
that, I'd wager you don't have the first notion of
where you're headed."

"You're not the only one riding through this
stretch of land, you know. I'm sure there are nicer
men passing through who are willing to treat a lady
like a lady."

"True enough. Is that why you decided to jump
off my horse and run straight onto an Indian burial
ground?"

Abigail hopped up so quickly that both feet cleared
the dirt. She scrambled to gather up her skirts with
both hands and looked frantically at the ground on all
sides. "I'm walking through a burial ground?"

"Hell, I don't know." Gus chuckled. When she
glared up at him, he added, "But neither do you. Do
you even know which way it is to get back to Last
Chance?"

"I wouldn't go there if my life depended on it."

"It's the only town within a day's ride of here.
Since you're walking, better make that three or four
days. Maybe a week."

"Perhaps I'll walk along a set of train tracks." She
perked up at the thought of that and looked around.

"That's a very good idea. If you were any sort of man, you'd let me be on my way. What does an outlaw care what happens to me . . . unless you need to keep me alive for some filthy ransom?"

Gus gave his reins a gentle flick to get his horse moving. His intention had been to draw up a little closer to Abigail, but he only succeeded in driving her away. She whipped around fast enough to send her long blond hair swirling around her head and snapped her skirts with the quick back-and-forth movement of hands that moved like pistons in a steam engine.

"Don't come after me!" she said. "I'm warning you!"

Following behind her, but not moving quickly enough to catch up, Gus replied, "You're not a prisoner."

"The way that partner of yours looks at me, I have a hard time believing that."

"He rubs most folks the wrong way," Gus said.

"When he watches me, he whispers like some sort of fiend."

"A fiend, huh? Doyle will get a kick out of that."

"You go ahead and tell him!" she shouted. "It'll give you two something to say after you've patted each other on the back for killing a defenseless woman."

"Why would we drag you all the way out here to kill you?" Gus asked.

"Maybe you just want to take me somewhere nobody will find me. For all I know, you could be dragging me to another bunch of your friends to do . . . well . . . do Lord only knows what!"

Abigail's voice was so loud, it carried like a bullet and drifted on the air for a good while after her mouth was closed. For a man who lived and died by keeping his head down and staying quiet enough to go unnoticed, such a display went against Gus's grain bad enough to hurt.

Gus tapped his heels against his horse's side and rode around to get in front of Abigail. When she turned on the ball of her foot and stomped in another direction, Gus cut her off again. When she picked yet another direction, he nearly drew his pistol to shoot at her feet. Since that wouldn't have gone over too well, he settled for a sharp "Stop."

Abigail didn't listen.

"Will you stop?"

This time, she grimaced and turned her back to him in a spiteful display of how much she wasn't listening to him.

Gus swung down from his saddle and said, "Please. Stop."

Abigail stopped. Her arms hung down at her sides and she looked up to the light blue sky over her head. "Why should I?" she asked.

"Because of what I mentioned before. You know, about you dying and such?"

Slowly, Abigail turned. She crossed her arms in what had already become a familiar way and tapped her foot against the exposed rock she was standing on. "Who are you?"

"My name is Gus McCord and my partner is Doyle Hill. Have you heard of us?"

Her mouth twisted up a bit and she closed one eye in a contemplative squint. Before long, she replied, "No. Why would I have heard of you? Are you two famous?"

"To some folks, perhaps."

"Are you outlaws?"

Gus nodded. "Yeah, you might say that."

"So you do intend on ransoming me?"

"Actually . . . no. That was never my intent."

"Liar," she spat. "That other one seems just as bad as those kidnappers and he's your partner."

"It may have crossed my mind, but only as a second plan in case the first one doesn't work out." When he saw the appalled expression on her face, Gus smirked. Apparently, she appreciated that as much as she'd appreciated his little joke. "We ain't gonna kill you," he assured her.

"That doesn't make me feel any better."

"Do you know why I bothered doing any of this?" Gus asked as he approached her.

Abigail tensed a bit, but she didn't turn and run. For all intents and purposes, she was the fidgeting rabbit that was fixing to scoot away at its first chance. Her face even twitched as Gus got closer, but Abigail didn't seem to have the strength she'd had only a few scant moments ago.

Gus reached out for her hands, but she pulled away. Rather than try again, he said, "I found some of your things that were taken by those men who had you. Some of your clothes and some jewelry too. There was a ring and a bracelet."

Tears formed in the corner of her eyes, but Abigail swiped them away before they could fall. "Good Lord. When my father sees that . . . he'll know . . . he'll think . . ."

"That was the idea. I saw the blood and it made me think whoever owned them put up a hell of a fight before letting them go. Now I can see I was right."

"I didn't let any of those things go," Abigail said defiantly. "They were taken from me, and yes . . . I put up a fight."

Gus reached out for her and was only able to feel her hair against his fingertips before she turned away and started walking again. "Don't touch me," Abigail warned.

Just then the wound on Gus's face felt twice as deep and the gaping holes in his mouth where some of his teeth should be felt like a hideous crater. Shoving all that aside for the useless drivel it was, he caught up to her and pushed the hair away from where it hung over her neck. Part of him felt victorious for finding the fresh scars there. Most of him was ashamed for looking.

"I knew they hurt you," he said. "I saw the blood and saw what they tore away from you and I couldn't bear it."

Abigail looked ready to pull away from him, but kept from doing so. There was a mix of fear and disgust in her eyes, but now there was also the resignation that came along with defeat. "You're right. There's nowhere for me to go and no way for me to survive out here on my own. I've got no choice but to go along with you, so spare me the sentiments."

Gus kept his eyes level and locked on her as he went on. "I've killed more than my share: lawmen, other killers, men who just looked at me the wrong way. There were women who got on my bad side and maybe even a few young ones who got harmed on account of me and Doyle riding through without giving a damn what we left behind.

"It gets easy after a while you know. Killing, I mean. After so much of it, all that death is like rain fallin' on your head after you're already soaking wet. A little more on top of all the rest don't seem to matter. When I saw them things of yours, it mattered. Even after all the rain that's fallen, this was just too much. Maybe I just tasted so much blood that I'm startin' to choke on it."

"And you thought coming for me would redeem you?"

"No," Gus replied with a definitive shake of his head. "There ain't no redeeming me. I just . . . had enough. When I heard about you and seen those men's eyes, I knew there wasn't no way in Creation you'd get back to your family alive. Instead of be a part of more killing, I thought I'd do something else for a change."

"Like what?" Abigail asked.

Gus dug into his shirt pocket, fished out the ring he'd been keeping and handed it over. "Like return somethin' instead of steal it."

While she took the ring, Abigail studied it as though she'd never seen it before. She held out her right hand and started to slip the ring onto a finger that was bruised, cut and swollen. Wincing a bit, she moved the ring to the finger beside it and cased it on. It wasn't a proper fit, but she extended her arm and gazed upon her hand with a genuine smile. "This . . . is probably one of the sweetest things that's ever happened to me."

"Sweet?"

She shrugged and added, "Don't get a swelled head. It's been a while since I've had more than a few winks of sleep and a proper meal, so I may be delirious. Right now, though . . . yes." She reached up to pat Gus's face and didn't even flinch when her hand brushed against the scar that ran over his eye and down to his mouth. After that, she walked past him toward the waiting horse. "When's the other one coming back?"

"He's expecting us to catch up."

"Then what are we waiting for?"

Gus walked back to the horse and climbed into the saddle. The Abigail Swann in front of him now was a far cry from the one he'd practically dragged from Bateman Supply.

"If you don't mind," Abigail said as she reached up to him.

Gus took her hand and pulled her up to sit behind him.

"Thank you," she chirped.

Gus kept his mouth shut. They had a long ride in front of them and he thought it better to quit while he was ahead.

Chapter 15

By nightfall, Gus and Doyle had covered several miles by leapfrogging the way they always did when on the run. One scouted ahead, waited for the other to catch up and then allowed that man to ride on to do some scouting of his own. A little while later, the first would catch up, ride ahead and then scout. It was a simple system and it worked beautifully. Since it was only broken up by the occasional stop for water or a bite to eat, they tended to go almost as fast as they would if they were able to ride at a gallop without a care in the world.

The spot they'd chosen for a camp was nestled among a group of rocks along a fork of the Salt River. Even though the sound of rushing water made it difficult for them to hear someone creeping up on them, it also allowed them to build their camp and cook their dinner without having to worry too much about keeping quiet. Normally, Gus and Doyle would have shared some whiskey to take the bite from the chill in the air. The moment Doyle took a pull from his whiskey bottle and offered it to Abigail, Gus could tell this wouldn't be a normal circumstance.

"That's disgusting," Abigail said with a sneer etched into her face.

Doyle looked at her and then down at the bottle in his hand. "What's the matter? You don't like whiskey?"

"Not when you've already drooled all over it."

"Pardon me?"

"You heard what I said," she snapped. "I'd rather lick a rock from the bottom of that river than drink from the same bottle as you."

"In case you ain't realized," Doyle snarled, "you're only alive by our good graces. We can just as easily tie you up and drag you from one of the horses than let you ride proper."

She sat up and curtly turned her head away from him. "Gus wouldn't let that happen."

Doyle looked over to Gus, who was prodding a few cuts of salted pork, which sizzled in a dented pan. When he noticed his partner's scrutiny, Gus shrugged and said, "I just wanna cook this and eat it."

Since Abigail was purposely not looking at him, Doyle reached out to grab her face and turn it toward him.

"Easy," Gus snarled.

Hearing that brought a confident smirk to Abigail's face.

Doyle leaned in to hiss, "Just 'cause you're more valuable alive don't give you cause to grin like that. There's plenty we could do that's only made better when you're alive and kickin'."

If there was any fear in her, Abigail hid it well. In fact, she hid it so well that a hint of frustration could be seen on Doyle's face as he let her go.

Glancing over to Gus, Abigail asked, "Is my supper ready?"

"Yeah. Maybe if we get some food in our bellies we can all stop being so cross."

Doyle settled back into the rut he'd made in the dirt. "Maybe it ain't food I need to put a smile on my face."

"Give it a rest, Doyle," Gus said. "Have some beans."

The pot of beans sat on the edge of the fire so the flames could lick the chipped surface. Having sat there while being occasionally stirred by Gus, the beans were hot enough to steam. Doyle spooned some out and dumped them onto a tin plate next to the hunk of pork Gus served him. After that, he sat back so Abigail could come for her own helping.

"Thank you very much," she said.

When she looked at him, Gus saw the contented lady who had made her first appearance after their most recent conversation. To be fair, however, it was obvious that she was pouring it on extra thick just to get under Doyle's skin, and doing a real good job of it, to boot.

Abigail took the fork she was given and examined it carefully. The utensil was missing only one and a half tines, but she held it as though it had just been coughed up by a goat. "Are we going to stop riding in circles tomorrow?" she asked.

"You're a passenger," Doyle told her. "Passengers don't get to say where we go."

"Do I at least get to say who I ride with? Because I'd rather get home bound, gagged or tossed from the saddle than spend any unnecessary time with you."

"You got a real smart mouth on you, lady. Maybe I should—"

"Doyle. Listen," Gus said.

But Doyle didn't take his eyes off of her. Instead, he leaned forward and locked eyes with Abigail. "I already heard more'n enough. She's making me wonder if we're better off ransoming her. Even if we take a loss, I'd be happy to—"

"No!" Gus snapped. "Listen."

Doyle swung his head around to look at his partner. A string of choice words was perched upon the tip of his tongue, but he kept from saying them when he saw that Gus was staring toward the river and straining to hear every little noise being carried upon the passing breeze. Doyle looked in the direction of the river, as well.

"There," Gus said softly. "You hear it?"

"Hear what?" Abigail whispered.

Both men turned to her as if they meant to bite her head off. Doyle gritted his teeth and Gus held out his hand to stop her from saying anything else. As much as she wanted to speak, Abigail bit her tongue.

Seeing that she wasn't about to make another move for a bit, Gus shifted his focus back toward the river. The fire was giving off enough light to see the edges of the small clearing, but there were still too many shadows for him to get a look at the river. Suddenly, a splash that was just loud enough to be heard over the constant flow of water drifted through the air.

The splash might have come from a frog's belly hitting the top of the water. It could have been a stone coming loose and falling in or some critter scampering across to the other side. None of those things would have been so heavy and there was even less of a chance of those sounds drawing steadily closer every time they were heard.

Gus looked over to Doyle and found his partner already nodding at him. He'd heard it too. Without speaking a word, Doyle eased the Smith & Wesson from his holster, tapped its barrel against his chest and waved to the right. Gus nodded, drew his Colt and pointed to the left. Then both men started moving in their chosen directions.

Before he left the camp, Gus turned to Abigail. Rather than say anything out loud, he stabbed a finger downward and mouthed the words, *Stay here*. She must have understood him, because she nodded and huddled against a tree. Just when he thought she would stay put, Gus saw her lean forward again and open her mouth to speak. He hurried over to her before she could make a sound.

"Just stay here," he whispered. "Someone's coming."

"What if I need to defend myself?"

"If they get to you, then it's already too late."

Gus's words had the very effect he'd been hoping for. The color drained from Abigail's face and she suddenly seemed too petrified to move. She gathered up her legs and wrapped her arms around them so she was curled into a tight ball.

As he moved out from the left side of the camp, Gus spotted a subtle hint of movement to the right. The only reason he saw Doyle at all was because he knew exactly what to look for. Since his partner was getting into position, Gus concentrated on doing the same. The river was a little ways off, so he prepared himself by pulling the bandanna up from around his neck to cover his face. Not only did that keep some of the moonlight from being reflected off his skin, but it allowed him to stay low and move through the bushes without catching anything in his mouth or nose. His Colt was held low and out of sight, but Gus was ready to pull his trigger at a moment's notice.

Gus kept moving toward the sounds of rushing water. The Salt River wasn't especially deep at that spot, but there were plenty of rocks and fallen trees for it to splash against. In addition to that splashing, Gus could now hear the distinctive wet slap of boots wading through shallow water.

He was already crouching in the bushes, but Gus bent his knees even more to lower himself deeper into the cover of leaves and spiny branches. The bushes tugged at his clothes and poked at his arms, but Gus hardly felt any of that. Even if he caught a twig in his good eye, he wouldn't have let out a peep. Squinting through the bushes, Gus was able to pick out the shapes of three men crossing a shallow spot in the river.

Doyle was hunkered down in a good spot not too far away, so it was a safe bet that he had spotted the other men too. Doyle looked at Gus and pointed beyond the three men. When Gus looked in that direction, he caught sight of two more approaching the opposite riverbank.

If the men were merely on their way to somewhere else, Gus would have been content to let them pass. Even if they were crossing to try to hook up with a trail, he would have gladly sat in his hiding spot and watched them go. But these men weren't just passing through. They moved in two rows, shoulder to shoulder, carefully surveying their surroundings. If Gus and Doyle hadn't gotten themselves somewhat familiar with the riverbank while collecting firewood and watering the horses, they wouldn't have known exactly where to hide. And if there had been more light than what trickled down from the pale glow of the moon, both outlaws would have been spotted already.

Gus didn't like the way the other men moved or the purpose in their eyes. What he liked even less was the badges pinned to those men's chests. The moonlight glinted off the dented tin just enough to make the badges stand out against the black and browns of the men's jackets, but Gus would have been able to spot them without much more than a single flicker to light the way. His life depended on sniffing out lawmen.

Judging by the hungry snarl on Doyle's face, he saw the badges, as well. The .45 was in his hand and ready to fire, but Gus got him to hold off with a single shake of his head. Doyle wasn't happy about forsaking the first shot, but he eased his gun hand down a bit.

The lawmen were talking among themselves in voices that were just a bit too low for Gus to hear. As long as there was the slightest possibility of those men passing by without incident, Gus meant to let them go. His hopes weren't too high in that regard since the lawmen were headed straight for the camp. After taking a few more steps, the lawman at the front of the group motioned to the others. Those men fanned out a bit farther as if to surround the camp before closing in.

Cursing under his breath, Gus nodded to Doyle and then stood up before his partner could make a move of his own. "Who are you men?" Gus snarled.

The lawmen stopped and brought their guns up. Obviously surprised by Gus's sudden appearance, they pointed their weapons at him. The man at the front of the group proved to be the leader, since he stepped forward to speak for the others. "We're sheriff's deputies from Coolidge, after a couple wanted men." He squinted in the darkness and studied Gus's face a bit too long. "Who might you be?"

"My name's Gerald Whitman," Gus replied, using the false name he'd settled on a few jobs back.

"Gerald, huh?"

One of the other lawmen gripped his rifle tightly and brought it up to his shoulder. "What about him?" he asked anxiously.

The other pair of lawmen crossed the river to stand with the first group of three. They were armed, but couldn't have been half Gus's age and held their guns like they were afraid to pull the triggers.

Sniffing out the younger lawmen's fear the way a dog clung to the scent of fresh meat, Doyle said, "I'm Gerald's cousin. Name's Matt."

.

"Why are you men sneaking about with your guns drawn?" the leader of the lawmen asked.

Gus shrugged and replied, "We could ask you the same thing."

"We're deputized lawmen and you two look an awful lot like the men we're after."

"And who might that be?" Doyle asked.

"A pair of outlaws. One is a fella with a mighty big scar on his face and one good eye. Kind of like you, mister."

Although he withstood the lawman's scrutiny without so much as a flinch, Gus settled his finger against his trigger.

Turning slightly toward Doyle, the head lawman said, "The other fella we're after is about your height, fair features and carries at least two guns at any given time."

"Sounds like plenty of men I've seen," Doyle replied. Nodding toward one of the lawmen at the back of the group, he added, "Sounds like it could be him." Doyle chuckled when a couple of the young men actually turned to get a look at the one who had been singled out.

The lawman at the head of the group wasn't laughing and he wasn't wasting time swapping dumbfounded expressions with his own men. Instead, he narrowed his focus back to Gus and set his feet into a solid shooting stance. "I think you two men better come with us. We've got some questions to ask."

"Why would we do that?" Gus asked.

Doing exactly what Gus hadn't wanted him to do, Doyle squared his shoulders to the men and said,

"We were just stretching our legs and you men are the ones who came stomping up to our camp! Now you demand that we go with you? You got no cause to take us anywhere!"

"The men we're after are killers," the leader said. "They'll answer for what they done and they'll hang for it. We heard from plenty of others that them two outlaws were in these parts. You two sure do look like a couple of killers to me."

Beads of sweat threatened to push from Gus's forehead and trickle down his face. The longer the conversation went on, the more the lawmen could stare at his and Doyle's faces. If they asked Gus to remove his hat and pull his bandanna aside, they wouldn't miss the uncanny resemblance between him and the pictures that were drawn on over a dozen wanted notices across the country. Gus had wanted to avoid a fight if necessary, but wasn't about to let these law dogs get the drop on him if it came down to a shooting contest.

"We ain't the men you're after," Doyle said in something that was a bit too close to a snarl. "Deputies or not, you best make a better argument or be on your way."

After a slight pause, the man to the leader's right asked, "You men passed through Benson lately? There was a shooting there and the folks who saw it described two men who rode away with guns blazing."

"So?" Doyle grunted.

"One of the men threatened someone with a broken railroad tie or something like that. I don't suppose either of you is carrying anything like that?"

Gus frowned and shook his head, knowing that
Doyle hardly even went to an outhouse without taking his good-luck piece along with him. If this conversation went any further along these lines, at least
one of those lawmen would get a real nasty introduction to the gruesome keepsake.

"Why don't you two men indulge us for a second?" the leader asked. When he brought his gun
arm up to sight along the top of his barrel, all the
other men with him followed suit. "Start by taking
off your hats so we can get a better look at you. Bob,
get those wanted notices with them pictures on 'em.
Jory, why don't you go see if either of these men is
carrying anything suspicious like hidden weapons
or something that might pass for a railroad tie?"

Every muscle in Gus's body braced for the gunfight that was quickly approaching. Although he
didn't move just yet, his mind worked out every last
angle. He guessed which of the lawmen would fight
and which would run. He even guessed where the
dead ones would fall after they'd been shot and how
the bodies would trip up the ones who remained. He
knew Doyle well enough to be certain that he was
simply waiting for the first opportunity to skin his
gun and fire a shot. More than likely, he would wait
until a lawman walked up to search him. After that,
all hell would break loose.

"Better toss your gun over here," the lead deputy
said to Doyle.

Doyle grinned and held both hands away from his
sides. "Sure thing, mister," he said as he kept one
hand within easy reach of the spot in his jacket where
the spike was kept. "No need for anything messy."

Gus already knew just how messy it was going to get.

"Did you find my stockings yet?"

That question drifted through the air innocently enough, but stirred up more confusion than a gunshot. Gus, Doyle and all of the lawmen looked toward the sound of the voice to find Abigail working her way toward the river. In fact, they could all see a lot more of Abigail than any of them had seen before.

She wore nothing but her slip, which hung off of one shoulder to give the men a glimpse of her creamy shoulders and the smooth skin along her neck. Her long blond hair fell loosely to cover a good portion of her front, but there was enough exposed to keep the men entranced for another second or two. As soon as she'd stepped all the way into the little clearing next to the riverbed, Abigail pulled in a quick breath and wrapped her arms around herself.

"Oh my Lord," she sputtered. "Gerald, who are these men?"

Even though Gus was used to answering to his assumed name, hearing it coming from Abigail in her current state caught him off his guard. The unsteadiness in his voice wound up helping his cause. "These . . . uh . . . they're lawmen. At least, they say they are."

Abigail's eyes widened and she hopped behind a tree. "What do they want?"

Doyle jumped right into the game by saying, "They think we're outlaws, darlin'. Isn't that a hoot?"

Now that he'd had a moment to collect himself,

the head lawman said, "We're here on official business, ma'am. Are you hurt?"

"No, and I'm certainly not comfortable with so many strangers in my camp. That's why I sent my husband out to check on all the noise. Gerald, could you tell them to leave? They're staring at me."

That got all of the lawmen shuffling their feet and looking anywhere but directly at Abigail. Their guns were still at the ready, but had shifted away from their former targets.

"If you wouldn't mind," Gus said as he made his way over to Abigail, "I'd like to check on her."

"She's fine," the head lawman snapped. "And we're not through with you yet."

Abigail stared at the deputies as if they'd just confessed to setting a torch to a small town. "This is preposterous! You think my husband is . . . Who are these men you're looking for?"

"Outlaws by the name of Gus McCord and Doyle Hill. They're supposed to be loose in these parts and were last seen in—"

"Do those men travel with a woman?" Abigail asked.

All of the deputies froze in their tracks. After looking at one another for a bit, the lawmen stared at their leader, who shifted uncomfortably from one foot to another. "No, ma'am," the leader stammered. "At least—"

"And do most killers you know bring their wives along when they're running to . . . wherever killers are supposed to go?"

"No, ma'am. Not as such."

"Then why are you pointing guns at my husband

and his cousin Matt when they were just out to fetch something I left behind? By the way, darling, look behind you."

Gus hated to take his eyes off of the lawmen, but he glanced down at the spot that Abigail was pointing to. He couldn't keep the grin off his face when he stooped down to pick something up off the ground. The deputies tensed and the hammer of a gun or two were cocked back, but all those tensions eased when Gus held up a frilly stocking that still held the basic shape of Abigail's calf. Gus shrugged and asked, "May I?"

Grudgingly, the deputy nodded. "For God's sake, lower those guns," he said to the deputies around him. The men who'd been aiming anywhere near Abigail didn't just lower their weapons, but nearly tossed them into the river.

"Uncle Eddie is gonna get a real kick out of this," Doyle mused. "Just wait until I tell him that some bunch of sheriff's deputies thought we were known killers."

"I have an uncle as well," Abigail said in an icy tone. "Uncle James Billingsly is a territorial judge who makes the rounds through these parts to settle disputes or hear complaints about dishonest lawmen. Maybe he'd get a kick out of hearing this story as well."

A few moments ago, the leader of the deputies was willing to lower his guard a bit. Now he crumpled like a fish that had just been filleted. "I'm real sorry about this, ma'am. It was an honest mistake."

"Was it?" she asked through tight lips. "Is that why you and your men are still gawking at me?"

The head lawman averted his eyes and some of the others went so far as to actually cover their own eyes with their hands.

Never satisfied until he'd thoroughly pressed his advantage, Doyle asked, "Can we go or did you boys still want to search us? If you'd prefer to turn our camp upside down to see if we're hiding any assassins or such, you're more than—"

"That won't be necessary," the lead deputy quickly said. "We're sorry about the misunderstanding and we'll just be on our way."

"Our camp is right over—"

This time, Gus was the one to interrupt Doyle in midsentence. "I think these men want to move along. They've got important business to tend to."

Doyle shrugged as though he was grudgingly passing up a free meal instead of the possibility of being shot or hung. "Suit yourselves," he grumbled.

As the lawmen turned and walked away, they whispered among themselves. Gus wasn't able to catch all of it, but he heard just enough to let his next several breaths come a whole lot easier.

Doyle stepped up to him and grumbled, "That was too easy. They'll just circle back."

"No, they won't," Gus replied.

"How can you be so sure?"

"Because they're already convinced they followed the wrong trail in getting here. By the looks of it, I'd say they mean yours."

"What's that supposed to mean?" Doyle asked.

"Did you circle around and cross the river from that side when you were out scouting?"

After looking across the river silently for a second or two, Doyle nodded. "Yeah."

"Me and her rode straight up to the camp, so that means we put down enough tracks to make it convincing. If we pack up and leave now, we'll only look like we're trying to hide something."

"And we wouldn't want to give them such a foolish notion as that," Doyle said with a sly grin.

"No," Gus said, "we sure wouldn't. Even so, you might want to follow them for a bit just to make sure of that."

Doyle nodded. "I'll give 'em a head start. Wouldn't want to spook the poor fellas."

When he turned around to face Abigail, Gus found her still huddling behind the tree. "It's all right. They've gone."

Peeking out from behind the tree, she replied, "But you're still there and I'm still indecent. Where's he intending on going?"

"To double-check that your little story worked. I'd say it did just fine, though." He took a step toward her and extended the hand that held the stocking. "You got my thanks."

She snatched the stocking from him and stepped away from the tree. "It was the least I could do. After all, you did save my life once or twice by now."

"I suppose you could hear what we were saying from the camp?" Doyle asked.

She nodded. "I meant to come see what was happening and heard you mention those names."

"And you just happened to have left a stocking over here?"

Abigail shook her head. "I tossed it there right be-

fore I showed myself. I figured that ... well ...
showing myself would fluster some of those boys."

"You sure figured right," Doyle said. Leaning toward Gus, he added, "She's a devious little thing.
Make one hell of a bandito." With that, Doyle eased
his way across the river without making enough
noise to be heard over the normal flow of cold water.

Gus watched as Abigail slowly lowered her arms
to stand in front of him as though her slip was a full
dress. When she looked to the river again, there
wasn't even a hint that Doyle had been there.

"Sorry if I intruded," she said.

"Not at all. You did real good."

Abigail smiled warmly and walked back to the
camp. Gus gave her a few moments before following
her so she'd have enough time to pull the rest of her
clothes on.

Chapter 16

Doyle didn't return for a while after disappearing from the riverbed. Although Abigail didn't have much trouble curling up beneath a blanket and falling asleep, Gus wasn't about to let his eyes close for any longer than it took to blink. If he'd been on his own, he would have ridden out to find Doyle himself. But since Abigail had a tendency to follow him, he remained at the camp to nurse several cups of thick coffee.

When he heard movement from the direction of the riverbed, Gus drew his Colt and snuck that way so quickly that he forgot to put his hat back on. He didn't even consider hiding in the same spot he'd used when watching the deputies close in on the camp. Instead, he picked out a new patch of shadows and prepared for the worst. To his credit, Doyle got a hell of a lot closer than anyone else would have under the circumstances.

"You're losin' yer hair, old man," Doyle chided as he scurried toward Gus's spot. "The moonlight bounces offa yer scalp like a damn mirror."

"Real funny," Gus snarled. "Were you out there

coming up with jokes or did you actually do something useful?"

"Them law dogs followed my old tracks like you said. At least, they did for a while. After that, they got so turned around in the dark they nearly shot one another. It was a real sight."

"You recognize them?"

Doyle pondered that for about half a second before shrugging his shoulders. "We did pull a few jobs around Coolidge. Plus there was that hotel we robbed a few miles north of there. We knew they'd be coming after us sooner or later."

"Them and plenty others," Gus muttered.

Grinning from ear to ear, Doyle said, "Ain't it grand?"

They slept in shifts, with Gus taking first watch. Even though Doyle agreed to keep his eyes open when they traded off, Gus only dozed for a few scant hours before lying on his side and listening carefully to every sound beyond the fading warmth of the campfire. The only thing he heard was the steady rise and fall of Abigail's breathing. When she shifted or rolled over, she mumbled as if she was dreaming of some intricate conversation.

They were all awake and packing up their bedrolls before the sun had fully risen. Gus figured that if the lawmen wanted to pay them another visit, it would be in the light of morning. Therefore, he was certain to clear out of that spot in short order. Abigail fretted a bit, but quieted down once she was given a can of peaches that Doyle had been saving in his saddlebag. It was difficult to tell whether she was happier with the peaches or the fact that she was eating them after Doyle put up such a fuss at the prospect of letting them go.

When Gus rode ahead to scout the trail that lay before them, Abigail kept to herself and slurped at the last of the peaches. Once she'd finally made certain to drain every last drop of juice, she blinked and reached over Doyle's shoulder to hold the empty container under his nose.

"Did you want some?" she asked innocently.

Doyle gritted his teeth and set his eyes upon the rugged landscape in front of him. "You know I did."

She shrugged from her spot behind him and retracted her arm. "Well, you should have said something,"

"I did. I told you I was saving those."

"For what? A special occasion?"

"Yeah, like when we finally traded you in for however much money we could get for you."

Abigail shifted uncomfortably in the narrow strip of saddle she occupied. Unlike when she rode with Gus, she currently perched upon the last bit of leather that would hold her. At times, she seemed ready to fall off the horse's back completely, but grabbed Doyle's jacket or even his collar to hoist herself back up again. "Gus told you to take care of me," she said.

Twisting around to look over his shoulder, Doyle replied, "He told me to keep an eye on you. There's a difference. I can keep an eye on you just fine while doin' any number of things. I could even watch you very carefully as you fall off that cliff right over there."

Abigail drew in a sharp breath and turned to get a quick look at Doyle's cliff. While there were plenty of hills and rocks about, there wasn't any cliff to be seen. She twisted around to take a second look just to be certain, but only found more of the same. "You're a terrible man," she said.

"Then maybe you should watch your tone."

"You won't hurt me. I'm too valuable."

"Dead or alive, honey," Doyle said. "Just like the rest of us."

"Why are you going along with this?" she asked.

"Huh?"

"You don't strike me as the sort who would rescue anyone. You seem more like the men who kidnapped me."

Doyle looked over his shoulder and said, "I resent that! Those men weren't nothing but big talkers in fancy suits. They don't know how to fight someone who ain't some woman."

"All right, fine. But why go along with this?"

"Would you rather I didn't?" Doyle asked.

Abigail shrank back as much as she could without falling off the back of his horse. "No," she squeaked, "I was just curious."

"This brings to mind a whole bunch of old sayings. One's about how curiosity killed a cat. The other is about looking a gift horse in the mouth." Doyle felt her slump against him as she became so quiet that the only thing he could hear was the steady thump of his horse's hooves against the ground. After a bit of that, he said, "Me and Gus have been through a lot. Usually, his ideas are pretty good, so I went along with him on this one."

"But you didn't want to, did you?"

"Actually, no. I wanted to take whatever those men in the fancy suits were guarding, maybe the things they had in their pockets, and skin out of there. I saw that fancy ring and thought Gus was of a mind to rob them fellas, as well. He jumped the gun and took a turn I wasn't expectin' and here we are."

Abigail straightened up and rested her hands upon Doyle's shoulders. She waited for a little while before finally asking, "And then?"

"And then . . . what?"

"Exactly," Abigail prodded. "What happened after that?"

"You been here with us since then," Doyle pointed out impatiently. "You know what happened. Weren't you paying attention?"

"Yes . . . but I was just . . ." She let her words trail off, waiting for Doyle to pick up the conversation from there. When he didn't, she took her hands off him and held on to the saddle wherever she could. Her perch was a bit more precarious, but she seemed to prefer it to hanging on to Doyle directly.

They rode for the next several miles without saying much of anything.

Gus scouted ahead for most of that day. He kept his nose pointed toward the Rio Verde and let his horse run to its heart's content. After going for so long at a more deliberate pace with extra weight on its back, the horse ran with a delight that proved to be infectious. It became downright easy for Gus to forget why he'd ridden ahead in the first place. The simple act of charging forward got his blood racing through his veins and brought a smile to his shattered face.

When it was just him and the horse, Gus didn't need to worry about plotting angles or figuring out one plan after another. He didn't have to worry about fighting with Doyle and there was nobody shooting at him or chasing him at the moment. It was a rare time indeed in the life of Gus McCord.

But that wasn't to say the ride was easy. It was a mountainous stretch of terrain that rose and fell like waves frozen in stone. Trees sprouted in clusters. Fallen rocks gathered in piles or single boulders sat like stubborn pigs in the middle of his chosen course. More than once, Gus was caught unawares by gorges that had been hidden from sight by tall creosote bushes or thick mesquite trees. Gus rose to the challenge by circling around those obstacles and noting them in the back of his head for when Doyle and Abigail passed along that same route. His horse's jumping ability was put to the test every so often when Gus decided to sail over a few jagged holes in the ground instead of skirting them. Hooves skidded against loose rocks and packed dirt, but both horse and rider continued to attempt the next ill-advised leap of faith.

Catching sight of the Rio Verde brought Gus's thoughts back to where they needed to be. The river snaked to the north, where it eventually forked and marked the spot where they'd turn westward and head into Prescott. But no matter how inviting of a path the river was, Gus couldn't follow it all the way to the fork. Fort Verde was along that river as well, just a bit south of the main fork. While Gus had gotten past more than a few Army posts in his time, he wasn't about to push his luck now. He had a bad feeling in his gut about that place and knew they could just as easily circle around than go anywhere near it.

Gus pulled back on the reins, causing his horse to whinny and snort with surprise. It seemed the big fellow had grown accustomed to moving at a full gallop and wasn't ready to slow down. "Easy, now," Gus said as he patted the horse's neck. "Just give me a chance to get my bearings."

Rummaging around in his saddlebag, Gus found the telescope he kept there. He placed his eye to the lens and studied the shape of the river and the formations along its bank. What concerned him the most was if anyone else was following the same waterway.

Just as Gus was ready to make note of what he'd seen and collapse the telescope, something kept him from doing so. He panned the telescope once more along the stretch of river in his view. There wasn't much to look at until he spotted a patch of dust that had recently been kicked up into a dirty little cloud.

The cloud was low enough to the ground that it had to have been stirred up by something moving alongside the river. It was also high enough and dissipated to an extent that made Gus certain the thing that had been moving was gone.

He stood up in his stirrups to look at it from a slightly different angle. Although that allowed him to look over the tops of some trees a ways down the stretch, Gus wasn't able to hold that stance for long before it caused his telescope to waver. Swearing to himself, he settled into his saddle, rested the telescope in both hands and slowly moved it along the river.

After keeping a very fast pace to get to that spot, sitting still was close to impossible. Before long, he felt like a kid wrapped up in his Sunday best, kicking his feet and aching to ditch his pew to go fishing. Just as he was about to dismiss what he'd seen as random movement, Gus caught sight of another cloud.

This one hung even closer to the ground and rose up as he watched. The dust resembled a grittier version of steam billowing from a train's stack as it rolled down the tracks. Like that steam, this cloud formed in a line that traced back to its source as it slowly rose. There was someone riding away from the opposite side of the river, heading to the west. As Gus watched, he saw the dust cloud bend slightly as its source turned to the south.

It could be a herd of animals. It could be a small wagon or a rider making his way to one of the towns or camps along the river.

Pretty soon, a few horses emerged from behind some rocks and into Gus's view. The riders wore dusters and carried rifles from their saddle boots. There weren't any trails in that vicinity, so the riders weren't forging the way for a wagon or stagecoach. Gus looked up toward the north and couldn't see any more dust being kicked up, so he guessed the men he'd spotted were on their own.

The longer he watched them, the more Gus wanted to get a closer look. All he'd need to do was set out toward the river, find a good spot to cross and then catch up with the riders. He may have to track them a ways, but that shouldn't be too difficult. That was, if he even found any tracks.

It was a reasonable course of action so long as he didn't intend on getting back to Doyle and Abigail anytime soon. In the end, Gus had to remind himself of what he was doing out there in the first place. He was a scout, plain and simple. Scouts didn't do anyone any good if they tore off on their own and didn't come back, so Gus stayed put to watch the other side of the river for a little longer. When he didn't even have any more dust clouds to follow, he knew it was time to move on. Lowering the telescope, he took note of the spot, figured out where those other riders might be going and then plotted a course to steer clear of them. Whoever they were, it wouldn't matter so long as he didn't cross their path.

Gus pulled on his reins to bring the horse around until its nose was pointed back toward Doyle and Abigail. He'd scouted ahead well enough to bring the other two this far. If he spotted those other riders again, he and Doyle could figure out what to do. He tapped his heels against his horse's sides, already planning the next few legs of their ride to Prescott.

A rifle shot cracked through the air, announcing the piece of hot lead that tunneled through the upper portion of Gus's left shoulder blade.

The impact hit Gus like a club and knocked him

from his saddle. On his way down, Gus struggled to get his legs or arms beneath him so something other than his back or head hit the ground first.

His landing was hard.

Trying to pull in his next breath was even harder.

Chapter 17

Gus swam through a river of pain, unsure whether he'd been shot, set on fire or left to drown. Part of him ached as if he'd been ripped open. Some pieces of his body burned in a way that sank all the way down to the boiling marrow in his bones. When he tried to gulp for air, he pulled in a mouthful of water that tasted like it had come from the bottom of an old rusty bucket.

Another wave of pain hit him and the contents of his stomach came rushing up. Gus retched and spat until his mouth was clear. It tasted awful, but it gave his muscles something to do other than twitch.

When he tried to lean forward, Gus knocked his forehead against something solid. When he reached out, his hands hit that same obstruction.

The problem was simple: He was lying on his belly.

Flopping onto his back, Gus let his arms fall to his sides and coughed up the last of what clung to the back of his throat. Now that he knew which way was up, he decided to try opening his eyes. As soon as he did, he was hit in the face by another wave of cold rusty water. At least that explained why he'd thought he was drowning.

"Get up, McCord."

Those words went a lot further to bring Gus to his senses than the water in his face. As much as it hurt to do so, Gus peeled his eyes open and pulled in a breath. The moment he moved his shoulders, he was hit with an agonizing jolt that shot through him like another bullet. His hands curled into claws and his fingertips scraped against a splintered floor.

"You weren't shot that badly," the voice said. "And by the looks of you, I'd say you've definitely had worse."

Gus's tongue ran reflexively along his teeth to find the jagged gap where it always was. When he rubbed his face, his hands brushed against the thick scar tissue covering the left side. He tried to sit up, but only made it an inch or so off the floor before he was roughly pushed back down again. When Gus was finally able to see something more than shadows, he realized one of those shadows was stepping on him.

The man who pressed his boot down upon Gus's chest loomed over him like a specter. Large gleaming eyes looked down at him without blinking. Gus coughed up a few more times, filled his lungs, and then blinked away some of the water that had pooled on his face.

It wasn't a specter looking down at him and those weren't large gleaming eyes.

It was a man wearing rounded spectacles.

It was Mr. Smythe.

"Well, now," Smythe said as he gazed down upon Gus like a not so benevolent god, "looks like you've finally decided to join us. Welcome back."

Gus didn't try to banter with the other man. With his body feeling like a trampled piece of meat, his instincts took over. The first thing he did was try to grab the boot shoving him down against the floor. He got ahold of it by the ankle and started to twist. Smythe pulled free, but only because Gus was still a bit weak and unsteady.

Rather than keep his foot out of Gus's reach, Smythe slammed it right back down upon his chest. The back of Gus's head hit the floor with a thump that echoed throughout his entire skull.

"I might have overestimated you," Smythe said. "I thought you would have spotted us long before you did."

"I . . . did spot you," Gus muttered.

"Sure, but only after . . . how long?" Smythe turned away.

Gus followed Smythe's line of sight to find another man standing to his right. The man had an average build, shoulder-length salt-and-pepper hair with a bushy mustache to go along with it. "A few days," he said.

"And how many men were tracking these outlaws?"

"It was up to five by the time we got him."

"Mr. Bennett isn't the sort to boast, but I can't help myself." Leaning down to settle more weight upon the boot that was pressed against Gus's chest, Smythe added, "If I would've known how easily I could have bagged the infamous Gus McCord, I would have done it a long time ago. You're worth a pretty penny, you know."

"Yeah," Gus mumbled, "I heard that once or twice."

As Gus tried to get out from under Smythe's boot, he was shoved back down again. As soon as he was able to use his arms to brace himself, they were kicked out from under him. All the while, Smythe looked down at him and twisted his boot against his chest as if he was grinding out a cigarette.

"Where do you think you're going?" Smythe asked.

"Away."

"Do you know where you are?"

"I'll . . . figure it out."

Looking up to Bennett, Smythe said, "That would be interesting to watch, but not as interesting as what would happen the moment you were discovered."

The cobwebs were starting to clear from Gus's head. Although his movements were sluggish, his blood was pumping to all the vital spots. As he woke up some more, Gus also felt more pain, which kept his muscles moving. The cycle was an arduous one, but it seemed to be working.

Finally, Smythe lifted his boot and stood beside Gus. "All right, then. Since he's so intent on getting up, let's help him."

Bennett stepped up to Gus's other side. Even with the pain of his wounds causing his ears to jangle, Gus took note of the difference in the two men's steps. Bennett was lighter on his feet, which meant he was quicker and probably more of a fighter. He already knew Smythe was a talker and a shooter. Gus would figure out more if need be, but already he could probably distinguish between the two men's steps with his eyes closed.

Smythe and Bennett each took one of Gus's arms and hauled him to his feet. The moment that happened, Gus's senses were awash in a wave of fire that burned from the wound in his shoulder. The pain was enough to blacken his vision around the edges and suck every bit of wind from his lungs. Gus clamped his jaw shut and held on to that pain as if it was a bucking bronco. The pain, even more than either of the two men, got him to his feet and held him there.

"Do you even know how long you were down?" Smythe asked, while wheezing a little from the exertion of carrying his portion of Gus's weight. "More than once, we thought we'd lost you. But you're a stubborn one, aren't you? You made it all the way here and now you're ready to just march out."

They turned Gus toward the right, which shifted his shoulder in a new direction. Gus felt pain similar to the many times he'd been stabbed. This time, however, the phantom blade dug deeply into him and twisted without any intention of getting pulled out again.

"You want to march out of here?" Smythe asked. "March through them." With that, he and Bennett propped Gus up so he could look through a dirty window.

The first thing Gus noticed was that it was early evening. At least he hoped it was early evening. If not, the dull light in the sky was dawn instead of dusk and he'd been knocked out for a lot longer than he'd thought. The next thing Gus noticed was the steady flow of men outside the window. They weren't just locals walking down a street, but were mostly in uniform. Infantry flags were flown in several places and the men wandered between several smaller buildings grouped together in a cluster.

He was in Fort Verde.

Suddenly, Gus knew that being shot was the least of his problems.

"I see the gravity of your situation is finally sinking in," Smythe said. "If you don't want to deal with me, I can surely set you loose so you can deal with them. What's the price on your head by now? Three thousand? Five? Ten?"

Gus didn't answer. He was too busy looking for patterns in the soldiers' movements and the location of possible exits.

"All right, that's enough. You get the idea." Smythe and Bennett dragged Gus away from the window and set him down onto a chair. The moment Gus's back hit the wooden support, Smythe stepped aside so one of the other men could loop rope around Gus's chest.

There were two other men in the room besides Smythe and Bennett. It was an effort to keep his head raised, but Gus got a good look around while he was being tied up. The room was a good size and may have even been a freestanding shed. Three of the four walls had windows, which were covered by sheets of burlap. There were a few cots and stools against the walls, with a table and chairs in the middle of the room. Outside, it sounded as if a heavily loaded wagon was rumbling in amid shouts from a bunch of enthusiastic soldiers.

Gus's senses were quick to come back to him, but his strength was another matter. As much as he willed himself to get moving, he was still feeling the effects of being shot, knocked out and kept down by whatever means Smythe's men had seen fit to use while they'd hauled him to the fort. He was, however, able to keep his wrists apart a bit while his arms were being tied behind his back.

"You must know why you're still alive," Smythe said as he stepped back into Gus's view.

Gus blinked and let his head wobble to maintain the illusion that he was even more out of sorts than he was. "You want to see about getting those pretty clothes back?"

Smythe blinked without emotion and then wrapped his hand around Gus's throat in a surprisingly strong grip. "I don't give a damn about those things," he snarled. "We can send something else to the Swanns, but we need Abigail. Where is she?"

"You mean . . . you lost her too?"

When Gus smiled at him, Smythe smiled right back. He let go of Gus's throat, stepped back and motioned to one of the other men. One of the bigger fellows who'd tied Gus's back to the chair came around and delivered a swift left hook to his face.

Gus's head snapped to one side and he let out a pained grunt. After shaking off the punch, Gus asked, "Is that the best you got?"

Another punch came to either silence Gus or impress Smythe. For the moment, it seemed to accomplish both of those goals.

Nodding approvingly, Smythe said, "You might want to tell me what I need to know. It'll make things a whole lot easier for you."

Gus spat out a wad of blood, but didn't lift his head. "Easier? I'm shot, tied to a chair and in the middle of a fort. From where I'm sitting, I'll either be killed by you or hanged by the Army. None of those things sounds too easy to me."

"That's where you're wrong. You tell me where to find Abigail and I'll consider you one of my employees. You'll be entitled to a cut of the ransom money and then set loose to go about your business."

When Gus's chest started to shake, he felt it in the fresh shoulder wound all the way down to his aching feet. The shake turned into a chuckle, which soon developed into something of a laugh. When he looked up to show the kidnappers his broken grin, Gus could see a few of them recoil. "You must not have knocked me around enough, because I sure don't believe a word of that."

"Why should I lie to you?"

"Why not? Your word don't mean squat. I know you'll say anything to get what you want and then break whatever promises you made as soon as it pleases you."

"I haven't gotten to where I am by not honoring my word," Smythe said. "At this point, it's the only chance you've got."

The grin faded from Gus's face, leaving a snarl on his lips and a gleam in his eye. "I don't believe that, either."

Smythe looked plenty mad when he heard that.

The other men all looked as if they were bracing for one hell of a storm.

But Smythe didn't boil over as everyone was expecting him to. Instead, he folded his hands and began to pace in front of Gus. "All right, so you're not going to believe that I would cut you in. I probably wouldn't believe that either, to be honest. You strike me as a man who's been in this line of work for a good long while."

"I'm not a kidnapper," Gus said. "I can't abide kidnappers."

"I'm talking about stealing. I steal people, and according to the notices with your picture on them, you steal pretty much everything else. It all boils down to money, anyway."

Although Smythe waited for an acknowledgment, Gus wasn't about to give it to him.

Shrugging at the momentary silence, Smythe continued. "You know just as well as I that we can work out a deal. We're both thieves, which means we can come to terms just like . . . well," he said while extending his arms as if to embrace the shed around him, "like generals working out a truce. We could keep fighting the war, but it's always more beneficial for an arrangement to be made."

"An arrangement," Gus snorted. "Sure."

"The fact is that you took what I had and I have every right to take it back. Nobody gets anywhere if we leave things the way they are. Even if your partner decided to cut his losses and let the woman go, she would eventually head back to her family. Don't you think I've got men watching the Swanns? Wouldn't it be foolish of me to let the family do whatever they liked without keeping an eye on them?"

Noticing something in Gus's face, Smythe stooped a bit closer to his level and said, "The moment one of my men sees her with her family, we'll be forced to kill everyone there. If anything, I'd need to do that just to prove I meant business in the first place. After all, I couldn't just allow all my promises and threats to lead nowhere. I'd become a laughingstock and everything I've done thus far will be for nothing. A man like you has got to understand that."

Gus did understand it. That was what stuck in his craw. Any man who didn't follow through on his promises was nothing but a blowhard. For someone who didn't have the law to back him up, his reputation bore even more weight. Men known as fearsome cusses could find good partners and pull off good jobs by just showing their faces and making threats. A blowhard was constantly challenged by men who wanted to be known as the one to kill him or just take whatever was in that man's pockets at the time.

Gus also believed what Smythe was saying about keeping an eye on Abigail's family. That just made good sense. It was something he would do if he was in Smythe's position.

"Here's what I can offer," Smythe said. "You tell me where to find Abigail Swann and I'll let you go. More important, I'll take you out of this fort the same way I brought you in."

"Feetfirst?"

Smythe immediately started to laugh. While two

of the others were too anxious to share the joke, Bennett didn't have any problem cracking a smile.

"You're an amusing sort," Smythe said. "For a man in your position, that's a mighty admirable trait. As for the rest of it, you couldn't be more wrong. Although I do have a few friends at this outpost, they certainly wouldn't be pleased if they knew I was harboring a man of your notoriety without announcing it to the proper federal authorities. Therefore I took it upon myself to wrap you up and bring you in without making anyone the wiser. Folks in uniform aren't the only ones to come and go from this place, but I kept your face from being seen. I can see to it that you are allowed to leave under similar circumstances. You have my word that you will be breathing when we part company."

"How long will that last?" Gus asked.

"Until the next time we cross paths," Smythe replied. "You try to muck up another of my business ventures and I'll put you in the ground. That's a promise."

Gus had heard plenty of threats in his day. He'd made plenty of them as well. All he had to do to put some validity in Smythe's threat was try to move his shoulder. Either Smythe or one of the men in his employ was a good enough marksman to knock him from his saddle without being seen. That was no small feat.

"In return for your freedom," Smythe continued, "I expect you to tell me where I can find Abigail Swann."

"Or," Gus offered, "I could just tell you to go to hell."

Smythe nodded and let out a tired sigh. "I was expecting you might say something like that." He stepped aside and allowed someone else to fill Gus's field of vision.

Bennett stood in front of Gus as a pair of rough hands grabbed Gus's head from behind so someone else could stuff a dirty rag into his mouth. Once that was done, Bennett snapped his fist out to hit Gus with a sharp jab to the nose and followed up with a more solid hit to the stomach. Just as Gus was pulling in a breath, Bennett sent his hardest punch straight to Gus's chest.

Gus felt that last impact move all the way through his heart like a ripple going through a pond. The heavy thump filled his ears from the inside, and when he tried to fill his lungs again, Gus nearly choked on the rag. It took a moment, but he was able to think clearly enough to breathe through his nose and lift his head. Bennett snapped out two more jabs that caught his jaw on either side.

Each time he was hit, Gus felt the pain a little less. He wasn't fading back into the fog that had claimed him after being shot, however. On the contrary, his senses were growing sharper. Each punch added heat to the fire inside of him and it wasn't long before that flame was hot enough to forge one mighty sharp blade. Gus clamped his teeth around the rag in his mouth and set his eyes upon Bennett.

Seeing the spark in the prisoner, Bennett tried to snuff it out by delivering one punch after another. After a while, Bennett stepped back to rub his own bloodied knuckles.

Smythe stepped in front of Gus and asked, "What

about now? Are you feeling a little more open to my suggestion?"

Gus nodded, so Smythe motioned for Bennett to pull the rag from his mouth. After taking a few deep breaths, Gus said, "Maybe you should hire someone else to throw punches for you. These wouldn't even put that smartmouth woman down."

One more subtle motion from Smythe was all it took for Bennett to replace the rag. After that, the punches rained down in a torrent.

Chapter 18

Bennett took a few moments to catch his breath and then one of the other men took his place.

Every piece of Gus's body was starting to wear thin. If he wasn't bruised and battered from the punches themselves, his muscles were tired from tensing in expectation of the next one to land. Blood had soaked all the way through the rag in his mouth to fill it with a foul coppery taste that ran down his throat.

He didn't want the beating to continue, but Gus knew it had to. Instead of writhing in pain like he'd been letting on, Gus rubbed his arms to work some more slack into the ropes around his wrists. That constant motion had been enough to make the ropes slick with some of his own blood, but he'd needed to add sweat to the mix, as well. Since he couldn't just will the stuff from his skin, Gus squirmed and strained while the merciless pummeling continued.

The second of the nameless pair of men took his turn. He started hitting Gus in the same spot on his ribs a few times in a row. It was either very precise aim on his part or very bad luck on Gus's, because one of his ribs was about to snap like a twig.

That realization must have shown upon Gus's face, because Smythe stepped up and pushed the other man aside. "Take that out," he said.

The younger man who'd tenderized Gus's ribs pulled the rag away. When he dropped it, the material hit the floor with a wet slap.

"You look like you've got something to say," Smythe declared.

Gus nodded, but didn't have enough breath to push any words out.

Smythe waited patiently.

"I . . . don't have that case anymore," Gus wheezed.

Bennett and the other men glanced at one another, but none of them seemed to know what to make of that. Smythe, on the other hand, bent at the knees so he could look Gus directly in the face. When he spoke, he measured his words as if he was speaking to a dog. "I want Abigail Swann, not the case. I know you can tell me where to find her. Can you do that, Gus?"

After blinking a few times, Gus nodded. He tried to speak, but was cut short as he coughed up some of the blood that had collected in his mouth. Hanging his head and breathing as deeply as his battered ribs would allow, Gus said, "I can . . . I can tell you, but I won't . . . won't do it here."

"Where would you propose?"

"You say . . . you'll get me out of this fort. Once I'm out . . . I can tell you."

"That can be arranged," Smythe replied.

"And I'll . . . I'll need my guns back."

"Now I know you're rattled. You're not getting your guns back."

"What . . . happens after I tell you?" Gus asked.

Smythe straightened up and replied, "I'll set you free. By that time, we'll be well away from this fort and we can all go about our own affairs. In case you've forgotten what I said before, I most definitely will kill you should our paths cross again. Do we have a deal?"

Slowly, painfully, Gus nodded.

"Good. Bennett, prepare our friend here for his ride."

Bennett stepped forward while pushing aside the thick strands of black and gray hair that had fallen in front of his face. He eyed Gus suspiciously as he asked, "Should I put the gag back in his mouth?"

"I don't think that'll be necessary," Smythe replied. "He'll only be signing his own death warrant if he decides to shout for help in the midst of all these soldiers."

Although Bennett nodded at that, he was reluctant to take his eyes away from Gus. He stretched a hand out toward the younger man who'd punished Gus's ribs. "Fetch them scarves, Dan. The ones we used before."

Dan walked over to the table, which was no more than a few feet from Gus's chair. He pulled several scarves out from a tangled pile, which also included Gus's hat, jacket and gun belt. Before he could tell if his Colt was there, Gus's view of the table was blocked by Dan's wide frame.

"You might want to cover his face up a bit more

than when we brought him in," Smythe said. "It's a bit uglier than normal."

Bennett took the scarves from Dan and waited for the other man to circle around behind Gus's chair. After that, he separated one of the scarves from the tangle and began wrapping them loosely over Gus's eyes.

Smythe started prattling on, but Gus didn't pay any attention to what was being said. The only thing that was of any concern was that Smythe was using fancy words and spewing them out like he didn't have a care in the world. That told Gus the man in the expensive suit was feeling confident. Smythe was the cock of the walk to himself and his men, which suited Gus just fine.

Even though Dan's thick hands pressed down upon his shoulders, Gus didn't concern himself with the pain from his wound or the fact that he could barely move while in the younger man's grasp. He just kept on squirming because he'd been doing it from the moment he was put into that chair. By this time, he felt as slippery as a trout that had been freshly plucked from a stream.

"I shouldn't have to tell you to keep quiet," Smythe went on to say. "You step out of line for so much as an instant and I'll just have to throw you to the wolves. Needless to say, all of these particular wolves are very well armed."

For a man who pointed out how much he didn't need to say things, Smythe sure liked saying them. Although Gus could no longer see much, he could hear Smythe walking away from the table and rustling something. More than likely, he was at the coatrack that was to the left of the door. "There's a wagon across from this shed," Smythe said. "We'll all climb into that and you'll just stay quiet with your head down. If anyone asks, we'll say you're wounded."

Gus's eyes were covered by the scarf that was wrapped around his head. His hat was pulled down low enough to keep the scarf in place while also covering most of it from plain sight.

"You should take all of these precautions as a compliment," Smythe said in a voice that clearly reflected an amused grin. "If you told me exactly where the woman is, I might just let you ride out of here like a man rather than as a lump with his hands bound and his eyes covered. Can you do that for me, Gus?" After a pause, his smug voice drifted through the air again. "That's too much to ask on my part, isn't it? You're probably thinking about how you'll get away once your hands are free and you can see again. Well, think all you want, my friend. If you try anything unexpected, I can gun you down and be rid of you before you even know where the shot's coming from. I could even drag your carcass right back here and hand it in for a reward. Wouldn't that be funny?"

Gus kept his head drooped and his arms trembling, even after he'd managed to work up more than enough slickness between his wrists. One of Dan's hands left his shoulder. Soon the ropes binding his torso to the back of the chair began to loosen. Those were the ropes that he couldn't have gotten to on his own. Now there only remained one more obstacle.

"Help him up," Smythe said.

Dan grabbed his arms and pulled Gus to his feet. Pain lanced through Gus's wounded shoulder, which he played up with a groan. Dan kept hold of one side, while someone else took the other. It wasn't Smythe because that one's voice was still closer to the door when he said, "Stand up, Gus. We don't want to draw too much attention to ourselves."

Gus didn't listen to Smythe. He was too busy listening to everything else in the room. More specifically, he listened to the footsteps knocking against the floor around him. Bennett and the other gunman were lighter than Dan, which meant Dan was still behind him and those other two were on either side. There was no mistaking where Smythe was, which only left that one stubborn obstacle.

When he started to take a step, Gus stumbled and nearly fell. He tried to catch himself, but that only caused his feet to get more tangled up beneath him.

"We should probably just carry him," Bennett said.

There was a pause before Smythe let out a frustrated sigh. "That'll make us stick out like a sore thumb. He can't walk the way he is?"

"His legs are tied together."

"Loosen those ropes. Just give him enough room to walk. If he tries to make a spectacle, we can just drape him over Dan's shoulder and hope too many soldiers don't take too close of a look at him. If they do, well, that's Mr. McCord's fault."

That was obviously meant as a threat, but Gus didn't care. Once he heard the few words he'd been hoping for, the rest was gravy. Maintaining his balance while swaying slightly, Gus drew upon his experience of being drunk to keep up the illusion of a man who could barely stand. It only had to hold up for a few more seconds.

Since the pair of hands on his right side had moved away, Gus figured the third gunman was the one who was now tugging at the ropes around his ankles. The instant those ropes loosened up a bit, that final obstacle in his path was gone.

Everything Gus had done to this point came to fruition. Every punch that had landed brought all those men to the conclusion that he was too weak to fight back. The weakness made them confident enough to give him a bit of slack, since he couldn't use his hands or see what was around him. Fortunately, there wasn't much of anything in that room that Gus hadn't already seen.

The instant he felt some slack in the ropes around his ankles, Gus snapped one leg out toward the man tending to those ropes. His shin knocked solidly against the closest man's jaw, sending him straight to the floor. Before that one's back hit the ground, Gus turned and pulled both arms apart from each other. The ropes around Gus's wrists sliced into his skin, but between the sweat and blood that had soaked into the ropes, Gus was able to slip one hand free of the bindings.

"Get him!" Smythe shouted.

But Gus hadn't stopped moving. He spun on the balls of his feet, grabbed the chair he'd been sitting in and picked it up. Since he didn't have to waste time uncovering his eyes, Gus turned to where he

knew the room's single lantern was hanging and
tossed the chair toward that spot. The chair hit the
post, shattered the lantern and extinguished the faint
light that had illuminated the room. Now everyone
was just as blind as Gus. The only difference was
that nobody other than Gus had bothered to memo-
rize every detail within the shed.

A gun was fired, but the bullet hissed through
empty air. Gus had already moved to another spot
and was keeping low to avoid any wild punches.

Extending both arms out and to the sides, Gus
rushed in the direction where he knew Dan had
previously been, and was able to find the bigger
man fairly quickly. Gus felt his left forearm bump
against something big and solid, so he wrapped
it up in a bear hug and swung it to one side. Dan
let out a surprised grunt as he was nearly taken off
his feet. Gus may not have been strong enough to
toss the big fellow, but he could shove him into
a wall.

Another shot went off, followed by a third.

"Find the bastard before you shoot the wrong
man!" Smythe scolded. By the sound of his voice,
Gus knew Smythe was somewhere near the door.

Dan stumbled and tripped, so Gus punched him
in the face as many times as he could manage. When
his knuckles hit Dan square in the nose without any
resistance from the big man, Gus moved on.

There was commotion coming from outside the
shed. Gus ignored it and circled around to approach
the door from the side. Lowering his shoulder, Gus
put all of his faith in what he could hear as well as
what he could remember. That faith was justified

when he slammed into a body that must have been Smythe.

"Who the hell?" Smythe growled as he reflexively pounded his fist against Gus's back.

The grip of Smythe's pistol hit Gus a few times, but he shook off the pain. Since he knew this was his only chance to escape, sheer desperation kept Gus moving. He dug his feet into the floor and pushed until Smythe's shoulders hit the wall. Then Gus pulled back and slammed Smythe into the wall again. When he felt Smythe start to move, Gus snapped his head up and caught Smythe on the chin or on the side of his face. Either way, Smythe let out a painful yelp.

Gus reached out quickly to find both of Smythe's arms. There was a struggle, but Smythe was still reeling from getting the wind knocked out of him and Gus was able to pry the gun from Smythe's grasp. As soon as Gus's finger found the trigger, he had a choice to make. He could either start shooting or he could just get out of there before the other men in that room got their bearings. The decision was easy to make once Gus heard the sounds of voices and commotion directly on the other side of the door. The next thing he heard was the pounding of a very angry fist with the voice to match.

"What's going on in there?" someone shouted from outside the shack.

Using noise to refigure his position within the darkened space, Gus pointed Smythe's gun at the door and pulled his trigger. Gunshots filled the room to put a powerful ringing in his ears and the stench of burned powder in his nose.

As Gus had expected, those bullets punching through the door were enough to kick the commotion outside into a frenzy. He slammed his elbow against Smythe and then turned away from the door. On his way across the room, Gus finally bothered to pull the scarf away from his eyes. By the time he reached the window at the other end of the room, he could finally see the dull glow of moonlight and torches through the dusty glass.

The scant light drifting through the window was like a beacon to Gus. It wasn't a large opening, but it was just big enough to accommodate him as he climbed outside.

Behind him, angry voices filled the shack. Smythe hollered for his men. The men shouted as they swung at each other in the dark. Outside, soldiers barked orders and demanded to know what was going on. Before long, the door was kicked in and both groups of armed men were introduced to one another.

As all this went on, Gus hurried away from the shack as quickly as he could. The shooting had drawn plenty of attention to the little structure, but focused it upon the front door. The soldiers formed a firing line and sent a few men to go inside. Gus had to grin at the predictable clockwork nature of military men, which allowed him to slip away before the soldiers surrounded the building.

There were a few more sheds nearby and several tents beyond those. Gus barely made it to the closest of the sheds before soldiers rushed past him to get to the shack. He almost didn't want to look back, out of fear that he'd be recaptured. All it would take was one man who'd seen the wanted notices to recognize his face. For that matter, Smythe had only to point Gus out and it would all end with a noose around his neck.

Gus took a quick look over his shoulder, only to find soldiers armed with rifles surrounding Smythe's shed. Folks outside were trying to get a look at the commotion, but Gus was able to ease his way through them. A few of the people were chattering excitedly, but Gus kept his head down and kept moving.

Once he'd made it to the tents set up a ways from the shed, Gus made the one move he knew Smythe wouldn't be expecting: He went to get a drink.

Chapter 19

It didn't take long to find a bottle of whiskey in Fort Verde. Gus wouldn't exactly call the place a saloon, but it was a large tent where drinks were served to off-duty soldiers and anyone else who happened to be passing through. There were a few men outside, but they were craning their necks toward the commotion that Gus had just left behind.

"What's going on over there?" one of the men asked. "Was that shooting I heard?"

"I think so," Gus said as he kept his head down and his feet moving.

Inside, the saloon was filled with a collection of crooked chairs and cracked tables that looked to have been tossed out from somewhere else. Gus pulled his hat down low over his eyes and leaned against the bar so he wasn't looking anyone directly in the eyes. Fortunately, there weren't many other people in there to worry about.

"What'll it be, mister?" the barkeep asked.

Suddenly, Gus froze. He patted his pockets and realized that Smythe had been more concerned with knocking him out and taking his weapons than with stealing his money. Taking the few coins he had and setting them onto the bar, Gus asked, "This enough for a whiskey?"

The barkeep squinted and stared hard at him. "You a friend of Colonel Riley?"

"Can't say that I am."

"Good," the barkeep said with a smirk. "Then I won't charge you extra."

A glass was set in front of him and filled with a healthy splash of liquor. Gus took the drink and sipped, rather than toss it all down. The whiskey burned in a dozen or so places that had been cut or bruised during the last few hours. He gritted his teeth and waited until the pain dulled and the liquor trickled down his throat.

"You look like hell," the barkeep said. "I bet you've got some stories to tell."

"Not really."

"All right then, let me know when you want another dose." With that, the barkeep let Gus be.

Standing still in the middle of that fort was putting a strain on every one of Gus's nerves. Despite the cold expression on his face and the steadiness of his hands, he couldn't stop thinking of all the different sorts of trouble that would be stirred up if he was discovered for who he truly was. He and Doyle had stolen enough Army money over the years to put them on the top of several different generals' most-wanted lists. Forts like this were also spots where lawmen stopped to resupply or just sleep somewhere other than a camp of their own making.

Of all the places for Gus to be, Fort Verde was not even close to a good choice. For that reason, Gus settled in and took another sip of whiskey. Right about now, Smythe and his men were explaining what had happened. Since there had been shooting, one or two of his men might even be hurt. All of them could be headed for the stockade. At the very least, Smythe would be dragged in front of one of those important friends he'd mentioned to do some explaining.

In that time, Gus continued to reason, Smythe would probably spout some story about how he'd captured an outlaw and brought him back. He would concoct a tall tale about how that outlaw had made his escape and bolted amid a hail of gunfire. The word might be spread, and if there was a reward notice with Gus's picture on it, that would surely be passed around as well.

Sitting in the eye of that storm seemed like a better idea than running for the hills like a madman. Gus wasn't foolish enough to shoot his way out of Fort Verde, but he also couldn't stay for much longer. He needed to get out, he needed to be quiet about it and he needed to go soon. There were already men examining him a bit too closely.

One of those men was a tall, slender man with short, dark brown hair. The man had been sitting toward the back of the saloon when Gus had first walked in, but was now standing. More than that, he'd moved up from the back of the room to the middle. Since it wasn't too big of a place to begin with, the difference meant a lot to someone who couldn't afford to stay in anyone's sight for very long.

Gus not only felt like he was backed into a corner, but was starting to feel like he'd made a fatal mistake in not trying to bust his way out when he had momentum on his side. Since there wasn't a way to reverse what had come before, Gus finished his drink and took a moment to allow the whiskey to burn down to his gullet. When he shifted his eyes toward the other part of the room, that tall fellow had taken another step closer.

"Sounds like someone's in trouble," announced a portly sergeant whose uniform shirt was only partly buttoned. "A bunch of rowdies are getting hauled in to see the colonel. If they wake ol' Riley up, there'll be hell to pay."

"Wouldn't be the first time," the barkeep chimed in.

As those two men talked back and forth, Gus set his glass down and left. Keeping his head down and his eyes pointed straight ahead, he watched from the edge of his vision to see if anyone was following him. By the looks of it, talking about the commotion was more important to the men in that saloon than actually doing anything about it. Those soldiers were off duty and the rest were too drunk to care. Still, Gus wasn't about to celebrate a clean getaway just yet.

He stepped outside of the saloon and walked with purpose in his steps. Even though he was scouting as he went, he moved as though he knew exactly where he was going and had no time to waste in getting there. Only when he turned to walk between a pair of the more solid buildings in Fort Verde did Gus take a look over his shoulder.

The path behind him looked clear, but something still nagged at him.

Gus stopped and leaned against one of the darkened buildings. The whiskey was having its effect on him and his heart wasn't slamming quite so hard within his ribs. There was still a commotion going on, but all Gus could hear was a bunch of angry voices coming from the vicinity of Smythe's shed. Since there weren't soldiers searching the area in force, Gus figured Smythe was busy explaining the shots that had been fired through the door. Smythe was a smooth talker, to be certain, but even he would have a rough time making a story about an escaped outlaw seem like anything more than a diversion. Gus hoped to figure a way out of there before Smythe got some breathing room.

After watching for a few more seconds, Gus was confident that he could move a little farther toward some horses that were hitched to an unwatched post nearby. When Gus looked around to make certain he could steal one without being spotted, he saw the tall man from the saloon step outside. Rather than take a gander at the ruckus by the shed or get a breath of night air, the man looked around quickly to find Gus. He kept his hands down by his holster and started walking.

The tall man didn't come at Gus straightaway. Then again, Gus didn't expect he would. Instead, Gus knew the man would walk in a slightly different direction before circling back to approach him from another angle. That was how bounty hunters worked.

It had only been a hunch at first, but now Gus was fairly certain of it. The tall man had the eyes of a bounty hunter: sharp and narrow like a hungry rat's.

He carried himself like he wasn't just ready for a fight, but looking for one. And when he'd spotted Gus back at the saloon, there had been the slightest hint of smug victory in the tall man's beady eyes. Those were all things common to most bounty hunters and Gus McCord definitely had plenty of experience where those bastards were concerned.

Before the tall man could circle back, Gus ducked around the other side of the building he'd been leaning against. It didn't take long for him to find a perfect section of wall that was busted out and covered by a flap of canvas. All Gus had to do was take half a step back into the canvas for the shadows to fall over him as though he was just another section of the wall.

Gus stayed put, even when his instincts told him to run. If that man really was a bounty hunter who was good enough to track him this far, he'd be good enough to track him a bit farther.

Fort Verde was full of sounds that night. They came from the saloon as well as the group gathering around Smythe's shed. Horses' hooves crunched against the ground. Wagon wheels turned and a subtle set of footsteps approached the spot where Gus was waiting.

Gus's heart skipped a beat when he saw the shadowy figure walk around the corner. Seeing it up close, he wasn't immediately sure if that was the man he was after or not. Once that figure turned toward him, Gus was able to catch a glimpse of those narrowed piglike eyes.

The man looked at the shadows where Gus hid and studied them. Before he could be fully discovered, Gus lunged out with both arms extended. One hand grabbed the man's jacket and the other reached for his gun belt. As he pivoted his entire body to swing the man around, Gus found the holster at the man's side. It was empty.

The man's boots scrambled to find purchase in the dirt as Gus shifted his weight and pulled him around with even more force. Acting reflexively, the man swung both arms out to regain his balance or try to get free of Gus's grip. Once Gus saw the gun in the man's hand, he grabbed hold of it and twisted. The man let out a yelp as his finger was caught within the trigger guard. Gus thought he heard a snap, but twisted a little harder just to be sure. When he pulled the gun away, Gus didn't feel any resistance.

"You a bounty hunter?" Gus snarled as he pointed the gun at its owner's face.

The other man was too flustered to answer right away. He was also too busy reaching for a weapon with his other hand. By the time Gus picked up on that, he was almost too late to stop him. Rather than pull his trigger, Gus turned the gun sideways and smashed the shooting iron flat against the man's face. That took the fight out of him while Gus flipped open the man's coat to find the backup pistol.

Holding an Army model .44 in one hand and a smaller .32 in the other, Gus nodded and said, "Much obliged. I've been in the market for some of these. Now you'd do well to answer my question."

The other man wasn't inclined to say a word until he found himself staring down the barrels of both of his guns. "Yeah, yeah," he said quickly. "But I ain't after you."

"You know who I am?"

The bounty hunter nodded. "You're Gus McCord, but I wanted to have a word with you."

"A word, huh?" Gus snarled. "What's your name?"

The bounty hunter blinked in confusion, but replied, "Jacob. Jacob Hawes."

"Now that I know what to scratch on yer grave marker, I don't think I'll give you a chance to have that word with me."

"I ain't after—" Jacob stopped short when he saw the warning glare on Gus's face. Lowering his voice to a whisper, he said, "I ain't after you. I'm after those men that dragged you into that shed. That's what I wanted to speak to you about."

"Go on."

"They're wanted for kidnapping a rich man's daughter. The father is putting up a good reward for the girl's return. If you know anything that can help me, I'd be willing to—" Stopping short when he saw the glare on Gus's face, Jacob added, "Or, if you'd rather, we can just part ways without any hard feelings."

Gus nodded slowly as his eyes darted about. It seemed he'd chosen a nice, quiet spot to lure the bounty hunter to. Despite the voices he heard from other places, nobody seemed too interested in poking their noses behind that particular structure. "You'd like that, wouldn't you?" he snarled. "What were you planning on doing once you got the drop on me? Would you have bothered making this offer or were you just gonna shoot me in the back?"

Now that Gus was so close, he could see the bounty hunter carried plenty of scars upon his narrow face. Compared to Gus's own collection, however, Jacob had barely cut his teeth. "I was tracking those kidnappers when they shot you and dragged you here," Jacob said. "It wasn't until I saw you at that saloon that I knew who you were. I came after you to see if you might know if those men still had the girl I'm after."

Gus couldn't tell if the bounty hunter was being honest or merely trying to talk himself out of getting shot. "What girl might that be?" he asked.

"The one that was kidnapped. This one right here." When Jacob moved his hands to reach for one of his pockets, the barrels of his own guns were nearly shoved down his throat. Looking at Gus with wide eyes, he said, "There's a picture of her in my pocket."

"Get it . . . real slow."

Jacob eased his hand into his shirt pocket and removed a small picture. Seeing as how it had been cut down to an oval smaller than Gus's thumb, he figured the picture had previously been in a locket. One glance at the picture was all it took for him to see it was a photograph of Abigail's face.

"This is her," Jacob said. "Have you seen this woman?"

"Maybe, but I ain't about to just tell you what you want and let you go. I need something in return."

A flicker of a smile crossed Jacob's face. "I suppose you'll want a way out of here. Am I right?"

"For a start."

"You were smart not to run straightaway. The man with the spectacles who brought you here has got some soldiers working for him. Either that or he's on friendly terms with a few of the federals. I saw him talking to a few men in uniform after you were hauled in here. How'd you get away, anyhow?"

"How many soldiers?" Gus asked as his brow furrowed with an angry sneer.

Jacob immediately started to squirm. "Three but the man with the spectacles was only really talking to one. I don't know the soldier's name, but he was the highest ranking of the bunch. Could be that he just paid the soldiers off to have some peace and quiet. Judging by the ruckus going on over at that shed, I'd say their deal is off."

Gus backed off so the guns weren't touching Jacob's face. Although that seemed to ease the bounty hunter's nerves for a moment, being able to look clearly down those barrels didn't do him any good. After stepping back a little more, Gus dropped the .44 into his empty holster and said, "You're helping me get out of here, but it'll be on my terms. I shouldn't have to tell you to keep quiet."

Jacob eyed him cautiously. "You kill me and my partners will come after you. Let me go and I can just tell them to chase after someone else."

"If you had partners, they would have come to find you by now," Gus pointed out. "But you did a good job of saying that with a straight face. How long have you been tracking these kidnappers?"

"The one with the spectacles led me all the way to

a train station in Silver City. They were to meet up with someone in Benson, but things went to hell there on account of some robbery or something. I caught up with them again about half a day before they caught up with you."

"Think you can find someone else for me?"

Although he hesitated, Jacob seemed more than confident when he said, "Yeah, but I already told you we can part ways here and now. Just let me go and—"

"Let you go?" Gus asked with a gleam in his eye. "After you hear the deal I've got for you, that'll be the last thing you'll want me to do."

Chapter 20

Gus wasn't about to let Jacob out of his sight, so he talked while helping himself to a few of the horses that were tied up behind the saloon. Those animals must have belonged to customers or hired help, because soldiers wouldn't have left their animals unattended in such a way. After procuring them both some transportation, Gus and Jacob rode away from Fort Verde, using a narrow trail that led to some nearby houses. After skirting around a few of those little homes, Gus snapped his reins and motioned for Jacob to follow him. Since those motions were made with a gun, Jacob was inclined to do what he'd been told.

It was black as pitch once they'd ridden clear of the flickering lights that emanated from Fort Verde. All the while, he kept the .32 in an easy grip that was loosely pointed in Jacob's direction. Between the gun in Gus's hand and the words Gus had spoken a while ago, the bounty hunter came along without much fuss.

Finally, Jacob had had enough. "All right," he said as he pulled back on his reins to bring his horse to a stop, "the least you can do is tell me where we're going."

"No," Gus replied, "that ain't the least I could do."

Jacob's eyes drifted down toward the .32, which had now come up to a proper firing position. Swallowing hard, he said, "If you're going to shoot me, go on and do it."

"I just might."

"But you mentioned something about a deal," Jacob pointed out. "Then you said it was something I could profit from. You made it sound like a genuine offer. If it was just a way to get me out in the middle of nowhere, I don't see the point in wasting so much—"

"I wasn't wasting anyone's time," Gus snapped. "That's 'cause I don't have any to waste. You and me were lucky to cross each other's path back there."

"We were?"

Lowering the gun so it rested upon his lap, Gus said, "Them soldiers were out lookin' for a man on his own bolting out of there like his life depended on it. I was lucky to weather that storm and find someone to accompany me this far like we was just out for a breath of air. I'm also lucky this ain't one of them properly closed-in forts with only one or two ways in or out. With no walls closing me in and all them soldiers looking for a lone thief, getting out of there was easier than I could've hoped. As for you . . . you're real lucky you found me without Doyle. If you know anything about my partner, you'd know that he's killed a few bounty hunters in his time and would've been plenty happy to add you to his list."

Holding his chin up, Jacob replied, "You mean Doyle Hill. I heard as much about him."

"Good. That way you'll be able to appreciate this." When he said that, Gus held up the .32 so Jacob could see it. Then he lowered the gun and tucked it under his belt. "Now we're just two fellows having a talk."

"What's the deal you're offering?" Jacob asked.

Although he wouldn't have admitted as much out loud, Gus had to admire the bounty hunter's pluck. He'd seen plenty of other men blubber like little girls under similar circumstances. Others might have taken a run at Gus, even though they knew it was a fatal mistake. This one kept a level head. As long as he kept that up, Jacob Hawes might actually live through the next couple of hours.

"The deal depends on how good of a tracker you are," Gus said. "And I'm not talking about hanging back to watch a speck through a telescope. I'm asking if you're good enough to hunt someone down in a hurry."

"Who am I tracking?"

"My partner."

Even in the near-total darkness, Gus could see the confused squint on Jacob's face. Finally, the bounty hunter asked, "You mean Doyle Hill?"

"Yep."

"What's the catch?"

"No catch," Gus said. "I need to find Doyle and I need to find him quick. We weren't supposed to get separated and I don't think he's about to come after me, since I doubt he knows where I'm at or when I went missing. Even if he did know, there's too much at stake for him to come charging into a place like that."

"But he's your partner. From what I hear, you two have been riding together for a good long while. Surely you've been forced to part ways."

"Sure, but when we get split up, we usually got things worked out so we can meet up again. Other times, we put a quick plan together with a few words. This time is different. Doyle would have moved on, and even if he did know where to find me, he's got someone with him to keep him from doing what he pleases. At least, he'd damn well better have someone with him. We're on a schedule. He can't afford to wait or track me down and I can't afford to poke about looking for smoke signals."

Jacob was reluctant to take his eyes away from Gus. He watched and waited to hear more, and when Gus didn't say anything further, Jacob seemed even more confused. At present, the bounty hunter would probably have been more comfortable if Gus was trying to kill him. At least he would have expected that much from the outlaw.

"All right," Jacob said reluctantly, "after I find Doyle, I suppose you'll let me go."

"There's more to it than that."

"Well, so far this doesn't sound like much of a deal," Jacob said.

Gus had intended on spelling it all out in a timely manner. Every second counted, especially since he'd already wasted too much time already. But when it came time for him to show his cards to a bounty hunter, Gus felt as if he was forcing himself to take a nice deep breath while his head was being held in a bucket of water. Finally, he said, "You find Doyle quick enough, and I'll put you on the trail of someone worth a hell of a lot more than me."

"I don't know," Jacob blurted. "You're worth quite a bit."

Gus fixed his eyes upon the bounty hunter and felt his hand twitch toward the guns he'd so recently acquired. "The men I'm talking about are the kidnappers you'd tracked to Fort Verde. If that one with the spectacles ain't worth as much as my scalp or Doyle's, the lot of them should put you way over that sum."

"I took the job of tracking Abigail Swann. I can't just switch."

"I know where to find her too."

Jacob blinked and then blinked some more. For the next few seconds that seemed to be all he was capable of doing. "What are you talking about? If you want my help in finding Doyle, I can do it. All I want is to call it even between you and me. Just set me free afterward and we can call it square."

Now Jacob was bargaining for his life. Although that may have been good enough on some occasions, Gus couldn't afford to settle for it now. A desperate man would only be doing the bare minimum to save his skin. Gus wouldn't be able to blink or rest for a second, since Jacob would try to get away or kill him the first chance he got.

Gus was a fair enough tracker. He could find Doyle. He sure knew what to look for, but he needed to find Doyle quickly. He knew his partner well enough to know that Abigail was treading on thin ice every moment she was with him without anyone to speak on her behalf. If she spoke up at the wrong time or overstepped a boundary somewhere, Abigail was likely to wind up in a very bad way.

Most women like her could wrap a man around their fingers or even take them by surprise with a sharp tongue. But Doyle wasn't like any man she'd ever dealt with. He was used to solving problems the quickest way possible and he didn't have much of a conscience to get in his way.

"I'm serious about Abigail Swann," Gus said.

Jacob blinked yet again.

"My partner and I have her," Gus continued. "We intend on taking her back to her family, but things are going to get rough."

"How rough?"

"First of all, if I don't find my partner quick enough, Abigail might not make it to Prescott. Even if Doyle behaves like a gentleman, he probably doesn't know that the man with the spectacles and—"

"You mean Smythe?"

Gus grinned and nodded. The simple fact that Jacob knew that much was a comfort. "Right. The last time we checked, Smythe and those others were wrapped up in Benson. I didn't figure on them catching up to us this quickly, so there's no way Doyle would know any better. I know the direction he's headed, but I could use someone with a genuine tracker's nose."

"There's got to be more to it than that," Jacob said cautiously.

"There is. If Smythe got this close already, he's

bound to get closer. You were able to hunt him
down once, so you know how they operate. Surely
you saw how they scout the trail or how they got to
me. Someone who knows that could be just as useful
helping us steer clear of Smythe and his men as he
was in tailing those same fellas."

Jacob's eyes narrowed with thought. "I suppose so."

Since the bounty hunter didn't seem to be on
board with the proposition and time was running
short already, Gus laid his final card on the table. "I
intend on meeting Mr. Smythe's men again sooner
or later. Even if we get all the way to Prescott without a hitch, Smythe's got men keeping an eye on the
Swanns. There's only me and my partner at present,
but there's bound to be a lot more of Smythe's men
already in Prescott."

"I don't know what I could do about that. I didn't
even know there was anyone watching the family."

Gus wanted to call Jacob out for being a fool, but
had to remind himself that the bounty hunter
thought more like regular folks. Gus may not be on
the same page as Smythe, but they were both outlaws and that meant they understood each other the
way one predator understood another. Forcing his
voice to remain calm, Gus explained things with
more patience than he would show a child. "There
are men watching the Swann family. There's got to
be. Otherwise, how would Smythe know when
things had gone too far in the wrong direction? A
man's got to be able to know when to cut and run,
especially when hostages are involved."

"I suppose that makes sense."

"You know it makes sense," Gus announced. "The look in your eyes tells me as much."

Jacob turned his head as if he was trying to hide a twitch that he knew was giving away the hand he was holding in a poker game. "So why should I believe this is a genuine offer? I mean, I know who you are. I've even tried tracking you down a few times."

"I'm away from Fort Verde. Why would I waste time flappin' my gums when I could just as easily put a bullet through your head and be on my way?"

"How do I know you won't do that once you catch up with your partner?"

"Because we need to work together to get this whole thing to work. I won't get into it all, but I didn't exactly plan everything out too good when I got ahold of Abigail. It just sort of happened and now I need to scramble to try to make it work. You've already started working with Thomas Swann, so he trusts you. If his daughter comes back with the likes of me and Doyle, that rich fella might just think we're a couple of the sons of bitches who stole her. Even if she speaks up for us, me and my partner might get strung up. But if he sees me bring his girl home alongside one of the men he sent out to find her, we stand a chance of walking away from this."

Jacob raised an eyebrow and said, "You could just let me bring her in myself. I could see to it you got a portion of the reward. Thomas Swann is throwing enough money around to make us all rich a couple times over."

Meeting the bounty hunter's stare, Gus told him, "Whether it was a wise decision or not, I brought her this far and I'll see to it she gets where she needs to go. If you want the job, we need to get started right now. Otherwise, I might as well do it myself and I sure as hell won't need you dogging my tail." Gus waited for a few seconds and then brought up the .32. "A man who can't make up his mind ain't no good to anyone."

"I can make up my mind," Jacob quickly sputtered, "but . . . haven't you killed a few bounty hunters?"

"More than a few."

"So you can see why I'm a little slow to accept any deal you're offering."

"I suppose," Gus said.

"So you really have Abigail Swann?"

Gus nodded.

"And you're just taking her home?"

Letting out a tired, aggravated breath, Gus replied, "No, I'm really one of the kidnappers and they shot me from my saddle as a little joke. Now I'm wasting my night going back and forth with you to amuse myself."

Despite the darkness, the way Jacob rolled his eyes was more than easy to see. "You made your point. How many ways will that reward be split?"

"You'll get a cut, but me and my partner get the lion's share." Before Jacob could protest, Gus held up a finger and added, "Smythe and his men will be coming for us, and if you back up me and my partner when they do, you'll get the reward for those men all to yourself. Smythe's got to have a price on his head almost as big as mine."

"He does and I meant to get it at the end of this job, anyway."

"Then since me and my partner have Abigail and you wouldn't have gotten her on your own, anyway, any piece of the reward for her return is icing on the cake as far as you're concerned."

Jacob took a moment to think about that. Finally, he nodded and said, "I guess you're right. That is . . . if you do have her."

"My partner's got her. I need to get to my partner in a damn hurry and that brings me right around to you. Take my offer and you'll meet Abigail yourself once we catch up with Doyle. If we dawdle for too long, Doyle will either drag his feet waiting for me or will get ambushed by Smythe, because he don't know how close them kidnappers are. If any of those things happen, Abigail's as good as dead."

"Fine. I'll do it," Jacob said. "But as a show of good faith, you should give me one of my guns back." If Jacob didn't see the scowl on Gus's face, he may very well have felt the chill that rolled off of him like a stiff breeze coming from a graveyard. Therefore, he was quick to add, "We may run into any manner of things out there. Maybe even snakes or Indians or—"

"Indians won't be able to pick us out in the dark and we'll be riding too fast for a snake to catch up."

"But," Jacob said as he glanced around at the open inky blackness surrounding them both, "you can't be thinking of riding any farther tonight."

"Don't tell me you ain't never tracked a man in the dark," Gus chided. "Maybe you ain't any use to me after all."

Jacob stood up in his stirrups as if he could suddenly see for miles in every direction. "Where was the last place you saw Doyle?"

"He would've made it to the spot where I got ambushed since he knew I was headed that way. Since he ain't charged into Fort Verde with guns blazing, we know he struck out on his own. That's where I need you to work your magic."

"We should start riding that way, but it'd be foolish to go for too long," Jacob said. "There's a hundred different ways for a horse to snap its leg out here, you know."

"I know," Gus said. "Now get moving."

Chapter 21

They rode through a good portion of that night with Jacob leading the way back to where Gus had been shot. Gus's shoulder hurt like the devil, but the bullet that had knocked him from his saddle had only torn through the clothes and skin before glancing off the bone. Stitches would be a good idea, but until he got them, Gus made the best of it by wrapping a scarf around the upper section of that arm. Every breath caused his battered ribs to scream for mercy, but Gus was able to push the pain from his thoughts with some good old-fashioned stubbornness. Once they'd put some distance between themselves and Fort Verde, Gus was content to slow their pace to avoid recklessly charging into a gorge or tripping over one of the hundreds of rocks that blended in so well with all the shadows. Pale moonlight trickled down from the inky night sky, but wasn't nearly enough to make riding anything less than a harrowing experience.

Jacob rode steadily onward, only stopping every so often to squint into the darkness and get his bearings. For the most part, he was merely retracing the same path that had brought him to Fort Verde.

While Gus wasn't about to put every bit of faith he had into the bounty hunter, he knew Jacob was leading him in more or less the proper direction. He allowed his gun hand to relax a bit, but kept the pistol ready to fire at the first sign of anything suspicious.

Pulling back on his reins, Jacob turned to Gus and announced, "This is as far as we're going to get in the dead of night. Riding for a stretch under these conditions may be acceptable in small doses, but it's plain loco for any more than that."

"You got to find Doyle's trail," Gus snarled.

"What do you expect me to do? Crawl on all fours with a lantern held to the ground?"

Gus raised his eyebrows and glared at Jacob intently.

The bounty hunter shook his head emphatically and groaned, "Not on your life. I am not about to do that. Searching for a needle in a haystack is one thing, but trying to fumble about for that needle at night is just asking too much."

"I suppose you're right," Gus said reluctantly. "Wherever Doyle's at, he probably made camp a while ago. We might as well do the same."

"Oh," Jacob with genuine relief in his voice. "I can make a fire and—"

"No fire," Gus interrupted.

"But it's a cold night and it's bound to get colder before it's over."

Gus shook his head. "No fire. There'll be men out looking for us before long and I'm not about to make their job any easier. And before you get any ideas, you should remember that Smythe and his men aren't exactly partial to bounty hunters, either."

"We should probably keep watch, then. You want to take a rest first?"

"No. You get your rest. You're gonna need it."

Jacob wasn't of a mind to argue, so he got settled into a spot with his back nestled between a few large rocks. It was just as well that they hadn't gotten their hopes up for a warm camp, since they didn't have much by way of supplies. The horses Gus had stolen were carrying saddlebags, but they were mostly cleaned out. Gus's was also carrying a bedroll, but its owner had left it strapped to the saddle for a reason. The thing nearly fell apart when Jacob unrolled it and every square inch of it was full of rips, tears and holes. Even so, Jacob put it to use and was resting on his side before long.

Gus spent a good portion of that night sitting against a rock that was slightly higher than Jacob's. Due to the constant throbbing in his ribs and the aches that filled the rest of his body, just making that short climb to higher ground was a chore. Gus would never have admitted to anyone that he was too old or in too much pain to do anything. Even when the evidence pounded through his body in time to his own tired heart, Gus refused to give in to it.

He wasn't an old man, but every wound from a bullet, blade or fist tended to add up and tack some years onto his battered hide. He'd ridden through hell so many times that it had burned away anything close to youth in his face or eyes, leaving him tired and sore. The truth rested in the back of his mind like a rock. He needed help tracking Doyle because the pain from being shot and beaten was causing his vision to fade. He'd wobbled in his saddle during the ride from Fort Verde, but covered it up so Jacob didn't think him weak.

Now that he'd gotten to somewhat higher ground, Gus strained his eyes to stare at the northern horizon. He wished he still had his telescope, but didn't know if it would truly be much of a help. If Doyle was trying to signal to him, Gus had almost as good a chance of spotting it with his naked eye as he would with a spyglass. Unless he was a whole lot closer to anything Doyle might use as a signal, it would just be swallowed up by the miles upon miles of blackened terrain.

Gus didn't spot anything, but he wasn't about to stop looking. He also wasn't about to get any sleep. Jacob may have agreed to work with him, but that didn't mean Gus was inclined to offer the bounty hunter a clear shot.

Gus was still awake to watch the sunrise. Jacob's snoring stopped at about that same time. The bounty hunter kicked the bedroll away as if it had tried to bite him. "The only reason to keep that thing is for kindling," Jacob grumbled.

"You'll take it with you," Gus said. "We both know better than to leave behind things like that."

"You think someone might be tracking us while we track Doyle? That's an awful lot to worry about."

"I like worrying," Gus said. "It keeps me alive. How long for you to pick up on Doyle's tracks?"

Jacob stretched his arms, craned his neck and took a few slow steps to work the kinks from his legs. He looked toward the rising sun and then slowly let his eyes drift toward the south. "I'll need to do some searching to find the tracks and that's assuming he came by here at all."

Resting his hand upon the Army model .44, Gus said, "If you need to waste so much time getting to it, I might as well do the tracking myself."

"Then again," Jacob quickly added, "it shouldn't really take that long. I should be able to pick up the tracks pretty quick."

"See that you do," Gus snarled as he started walking to his stolen horse.

Jacob rode to the spot where Gus had been shot and shook his head after looking around for all of three seconds. He moved on to another spot and Gus followed.

Upon reaching the next place, Jacob looked around for about ten seconds before shaking his head and moving on.

Gus gritted his teeth and followed.

By the time they reached the fourth spot, Gus was ready to draw the .44 if the bounty hunter so much as started to shake his head again. To his surprise, Jacob climbed down from his saddle to get a closer look at the dusty ground.

"They were here," Jacob announced.

"You sure about that?" Gus asked.

"As sure as I can be. Come see for yourself."

Wary of a double cross, Gus swung down from his saddle and walked over to get a look at what had caught Jacob's eye. He kept his hand on the .44 as he studied the ground for himself. Sure enough, there were telltale signs that someone had ridden past there not too long ago.

"There's only tracks from two horses, but one of 'em's got to be yours. The fresher tracks are deep, though. It looks like there were two people in one saddle." Turning to look at Gus, Jacob asked, "Does that sound right?"

Gus didn't give a hint one way or another. When he looked at Jacob, he wore less expression than the rocks that cropped up around them.

Jacob shrugged and said, "Anyway, these here tracks were made by a single horse carrying more weight than just a single rider. See how these scrapes in the ground are so deep?" Following them for a few yards, Jacob stopped and crouched again. "This horse was running pretty good and they were headed north."

Gus could see the tracks for himself, but the pain rolling through his head might have caused him to pass them by if he was on his own. It seemed he'd made the right decision in asking for help, but Gus wasn't happy about it. "Just follow those tracks as quick as you can," he said. "Doyle should be headed north, all right."

"Good. That gives me something to work with. Anything else you can tell me?"

Gus settled into his saddle and stared blankly down at Jacob.

This time, the bounty hunter wasn't about to just do what he was told. "Look," he said as he angrily pulled himself up onto his own horse's back, "I know I'm supposed to be the one doing the tracking, but it's not all just some trick of looking at the ground and such."

"You hunt men, so get to hunting."

For the first time since Gus had laid eyes on the man, Jacob had a look about him that made it seem he was truly ready to lock horns. He set his jaw into a firm line, straightened up and even lifted his chin a bit so he looked down his nose at Gus when he said, "For a man who earns his money by stealing it, you say those words like I'm the crooked one. Every man I track is running from the law."

"Is that so?" Gus snarled. "At least the law is doing their job by trying to enforce some bunch of rules. Bounty hunters just go about licking up what's left behind like dogs beggin' for scraps."

"Then why the hell did you bother trying to work with me when you could have just—"

"Could have what?" Gus asked as he drew the .44 in a quick snapping motion of his arm. The draw wasn't as fluid as it would have been before his shoulder wound, but it got the job done. The pistol was in his grasp and it was soon pointed at Jacob. "If you're thinking I should have just put a bullet through you, that sounds like a hell of a good idea to me!"

Jacob didn't flinch. Normally, Gus didn't like to make threats without backing them up and this was the reason why. Anyone with a backbone could grow accustomed to seeing a gun pointed at him and would figure out sooner or later that the trigger wouldn't get pulled. In Jacob's case, however, it was a case of one man finally deciding to make a stand.

"Look here, old man," Jacob said. "If you're going to shoot that gun, then do it. I know I'm probably living on borrowed time, but if these are the last few hours I got on this earth, I ain't about to spend them flinching every time you reach for that holster."

Gus squinted over the top of his barrel. Suddenly, it seemed he was looking at a new man.

"I can follow these tracks and find Doyle quick enough," Jacob continued. "You want me to track him like I was hunting him? Fine. If I was hunting him, I wouldn't just go off of what's left on the ground. I'd go by what I know and what I seen and what I'd heard along the way. I go by instinct, and if that ain't enough, I look back to the ground. You think it'll make things go smoother if I get my nose shoved into the dirt?"

Slowly, the scowl framing Gus's eyes loosened a bit.

Jacob obviously feared he may have gone too far, but held his ground.

As he lowered the .44, Gus felt a reluctant grin creep onto his face. "You got sand, Jacob, I'll give you that much. Most bounty hunters I seen would be content to grovel and crawl until they had a chance to run. Some would even rather beg for their lives than strike a fair deal with a man like me. Not you, though." Resting the pistol across his knee, but keeping it in his grasp, he said, "Just don't get lippy with me and don't call me old man again."

Knowing he'd been granted a reprieve, Jacob nodded and said, "Sure thing. Is there anything else I should know?"

"If there's anything that might help in finding Doyle, I'll tell you. Other than that, you should know that Doyle will be looking for someone dogging him by now. I've been missing for too long, so he'll move on but he'll be keeping an eye open for me. If he spots you, he's likely to take a shot at you before doing anything else."

"Won't he see you along with me?"

"Maybe, maybe not," Gus said with a shrug. "Even if he does spot me, he may figure he's doing me a favor by knocking you out of that saddle."

"We can't have him thinking that."

Gus bared his teeth just enough to form half a grin and half a snarl as he eased the .44 back into his holster. "Yeah," he said, "we wouldn't want him thinking that."

The little bit of confidence that Jacob had shown evaporated quicker than a drop of water on a desert rock. He held on to it for as long as he could, but Gus's ugly scowl didn't make it easy. "Yeah . . . well . . . the tracks head off in that direction," he said as he pointed toward a slope to the northeast. "If your partner slowed up at all in the hopes of you catching up to him, we should be able to find him sooner rather than later."

Gus didn't say anything to that. He merely nodded and watched the bounty hunter ride on. Despite his better judgment, Gus was actually starting to like the younger fellow. His hand stayed close to his holster, however, and the scowl remained carved onto his face. No need for the younger man to be too pleased with himself.

Chapter 22

It was a hard day's ride. Jacob remained in front and practically kept his nose to the ground the entire time. If he wasn't studying a piece of land, he was jumping down from his horse to examine a set of scrapes on the side of a rock. Every so often, he would stop and think for a moment before pressing on. Other times, he would simply pull on the reins to steer in another direction without so much as a wave to let Gus know what he was doing.

By the middle of the day, Gus didn't fret about those sudden changes in direction. If Jacob was trying to get away, he was doing too bad of a job to be of much concern. Since he knew all too well what it was like to make up a plan as he went along, Gus did one thing he never thought he'd do: He put his faith in a bounty hunter.

Jacob picked up on the same tracks that Gus would have found if he was at his best, only he did it a lot faster. He led the way north for a bit until he met up with the Rio Verde. He stopped there and studied the northern horizon before looking to the west. As Gus came to a stop beside him, Jacob looked to the north once more before his eyes were inevitably drawn westward.

"You said Doyle would be heading west?" Jacob asked.

"That's right."

"I think this is the spot where he turned that way and tried to make up for lost time. The tracks are spreading out and getting harder to spot, so it's just a hunch. We'll have to go a ways before I know I'm right or not."

Gus made a show of thinking it over, but didn't have to think for long. Now that he was in that spot, he could tell this was where Doyle would strike out to the west. The river was running quicker in that stretch and Doyle always preferred to avoid crossing whitewater if at all possible. Also, Gus could see the remains of a signal fire not far from the spot where Jacob had been circling and studying the ground. There weren't enough tracks or other signs to mark the spot as a camp, but the scorched pile of wood was easy enough to see.

Rather than let Jacob know how good of a job he was doing, Gus said, "Follow your hunch, then. Just don't be wrong."

The bounty hunter mumbled something and started riding again.

As the day wore on, Gus figured he was moving at close to double the pace with the bounty hunter's help than without it.

As one last test, Gus allowed Jacob's horse to pull away farther than he'd been able to get since they'd left Fort Verde. Gus knew Jacob was aware of the distance between them and gave the bounty hunter credit for being able to do something with that distance, but nothing came of it. Jacob kept leading the way toward Prescott and picking up speed as the sun drifted toward the western horizon.

The sky was taking on a dark orange hue when Jacob pulled back on his reins and signaled for Gus to stop. The sudden halt brought Gus's hand reflexively toward his holster even though he'd become accustomed to following the bounty hunter's lead.

"What is it?" Gus asked.

Rather than say anything, Jacob gave him a sharp wave that was a none too subtle request for Gus to shut his mouth. Ignoring the deathly glare he got from the older man, Jacob stood up in his stirrups and focused his attention on a spot in the distance. "I think I see a campfire."

Gus's nerves were still jangling when he leaned forward. The pain lancing from his shoulder had spread throughout his entire upper body like daggers being slowly pushed through his neck and shoulder. That, combined with the constant pain from his battered ribs, made it difficult for him to focus his eyes. Following the bounty hunter's lead, he stood up and squinted in the same general direction. Finally, he grumbled, "I don't see anything."

"Right there," Jacob said as he pointed. "Can't you see the smoke?"

Already shaking his head at the very notion that his eyes might have missed something like that, Gus leaned toward Jacob as though he could sight down the other man's arm like the barrel of a rifle. After a second or so, Gus spotted a flicker of light. From where he was, it looked more like a spark on the faraway ground. When he spotted the black-and-gray smudge in the sky over that flicker, Gus knew the younger man's eyes had been correct.

What irked Gus even more was that Jacob had been quicker to spot the very thing Gus had been looking for all day long.

"Yeah," Gus said in a casual voice, "that's a campfire. I couldn't see it 'cause you were right in front of me before."

"Oh, is that why?"

"Must have been." Noticing the wry smirk on Jacob's face, Gus added, "Either that or it was the damn sun. It's setting over that way."

"I would have gone with that second excuse before the other one. Seems more plausible."

"Just 'cause I haven't shot you yet doesn't mean I won't," Gus warned.

"And just because we spotted a campfire doesn't mean Doyle is the one who built it."

"It's Doyle, all right," Gus said. "It's placed up high and smoking enough to draw attention."

"Well . . . it drew one person's attention."

"You sass an awful lot for someone who's so outgunned, boy."

When they arrived at the fire, Jacob was obviously disappointed. Seeing the empty space upon the flat rock brought a scowl to his face that was almost as ugly as one of Gus's. The bounty hunter jumped down from his saddle and started to approach the fire. He stopped a few paces shy, however, as his hand reflexively dropped to the empty holster at his hip. "Where'd they go?" he asked.

Gus reined his horse to a stop and draped the leather straps over his knee. "You sure this is the right spot?" he chided.

"Yes! The damn fire is right there!"

Sure enough, the fire sputtered and crackled less than five yards away. The wood was piled even higher than it had appeared when they'd first spotted it, which caused the flames to stretch up into a column of smoke billowing into the sky. The air was thick with the gritty, smoldering fog and Jacob cleared it away from his face as if he was swatting a swarm of insects.

Jacob looked at Gus, but only got a slight shrug in return.

After being shown up in spotting the campfire in the first place, Gus took no small amount of pleasure in watching the bounty hunter fret now. What made it even better was the knowledge that it was about to get a lot more interesting real soon.

Crouching down on one knee, Jacob ran his fingertips along the ground. "These are the tracks I've been following, all right. The horse that put them down was here not long ago. Why the hell would they just set up a fire and leave it burning—"

"State yer business, kid, or the next thing getting tossed into that fire is your worthless hide."

Jacob stood and turned toward the sound of that voice. Every muscle in his body tensed.

"Jacob Hawes," Gus announced, "I'd like you to meet Doyle Hill."

Doyle stepped forward from a hiding spot that was so good, he might as well have emerged from the ground itself. He carried his Schofield, which was aimed at Jacob despite the friendly introduction. Without taking his eyes from the bounty hunter, Doyle said, "I was about to give up on you, Gus."

Swinging down from his saddle, Gus stepped forward to clap his partner on the shoulder. "I'm glad you didn't."

"So is this one with you or was he just attracted by the signal fire?" Doyle asked as he looked over to Jacob.

"He's with me."

"He's got the look of a lawman about him. Should I bother showing him back to my camp or just bury him here?"

Gus fixed his eyes upon Jacob to find the bounty hunter staring back at him expectantly. Both of them knew this was a crucial moment in Jacob's life. If a few of the wrong words were spoken here, it would most likely be the final moment of that life.

"Jacob's a tracker," Gus said.

"How do you know him?"

"He was looking for work in Fort Verde and managed to help me out of there when some folks were too lazy to bother."

For the first time since he'd made his presence known, Doyle looked away from Jacob. "After you left me with that blasted woman for this long, serving some time in a stockade would suit you well. So what happened to your face, Gus?"

"It's not as bad as it looks."

"I was gonna say it's an improvement," Doyle replied. "It's good to see it anyway, I suppose. Come on with me. The camp's tucked away not too far from here."

Gus gave Jacob a reassuring pat on the back, which turned into a gentle shove to get him moving after Doyle. "Watch your step from now on," he warned under his breath. "Step out of line with Doyle and you'll be deader than a goose on Christmas morning."

For the time being, Jacob kept his mouth shut and followed the other two.

"I see you brought some company with you," Doyle said as he navigated down a gravel-covered slope that led along the back side of the hill where the fire had been built. "I take it them horses ain't yours?"

"They are now," Gus replied. "I found them back at the fort."

Being accustomed to evaluating horseflesh on the run, Doyle quickly nodded and turned his attention back to the path ahead of him. "Anyone lookin' for them?"

"By now, more than likely. Might even be soldiers."

Doyle let out a sharp, quick laugh. "All the better. Sows in uniforms always keep the best for themselves, don't they?"

Gus nodded and Jacob chuckled uncomfortably. Fortunately, the matter was allowed to rest and the group made their way to Doyle's camp without much more conversation.

The spot Doyle picked was perfect. It was surrounded on all sides by just enough rocks, bushes and trees to keep the camp from being spotted from a distance and provide enough cover to allow them to build a small cooking fire. By the time the three of them had dismounted to walk their horses toward the campfire, Gus could smell the bacon that was being cooked over it.

Doyle approached the camp first. He pushed aside a couple of sickly trees and kept his hands held up in front of him. "It's all right," he said. "I brought company for supper."

Jacob stepped through the trees and Gus followed. The moment his face cleared the dry leaves that hung like a tattered curtain around that section of the camp, Gus was treated to the sight of a blond woman pointing a gun at him. Oddly enough, the sight brought a smile to his face.

"Gus!" Abigail shouted as she rushed toward him without bothering to lower the gun she was holding. "Where have you been? We were so worried! This one might not say so, but he was and I was too and it's so good to see you!" She may have said a few more things, but all the words blended into a mush once she'd wrapped her arms around Gus and squeezed him.

After disentangling himself from Abigail's embrace, Gus took the gun away from her before someone got hurt. "Good to see you too, Abigail. It truly is." Although he spoke to her, Gus looked over at Doyle.

Gus didn't need to ask if she'd been hard to handle. Doyle knew what was drifting through his partner's mind and grumbled, "You don't know how close I came."

"And who's this?" Abigail asked.

Gus waited for Jacob to introduce himself, but the bounty hunter was silent. In fact, he was utterly speechless. "This is Jacob Hawes," he said. "Jacob, this is Abigail Swann."

Abigail smiled and daintily extended a hand as if she was arriving at a cotillion. Jacob shook her hand and let out what sounded like a breath he'd been holding for days.

"Very nice to meet you, Abigail," Jacob said.

While it wasn't hard to figure out why Jacob was so happy, Gus hadn't been expecting Abigail to respond in kind. In fact, she was positively beaming.

Chapter 23

Jacob didn't regain his ability to talk for some time. He tried to mumble a few times when questions were directed right at him, but was grateful when Gus stepped in to speak on his behalf. All the while, the bounty hunter couldn't take his eyes away from Abigail. Although she wasn't inclined to stare back at him, she was clearly intrigued by the new arrival.

"So you said his name's Jake?" Abigail asked as she scooped some more bacon onto one of the dented tin platters Doyle carried with him.

Since he was the one who insisted on carrying more bacon than any other kind of food, Doyle took the plate from her and stuffed some of the food into his mouth as he spoke. "Jacob Hawes," he said. "He helped Gus get back to us. Ain't that right?"

Finding himself under Doyle's scrutiny didn't rattle the bounty hunter nearly as much as being studied by Abigail. Jacob nodded quickly and replied, "That's right."

"Is he a friend of yours, Gus?" Abigail asked.

"After getting me out of Fort Verde, he's a friend now," Gus said.

Her eyes lit up and she turned toward Jacob. "I want to hear all about it!"

"Yeah," Doyle said as he shifted so he could sit, eat and watch Jacob at the same time. "I want to hear it too."

Gus leaned forward to take the next plate Abigail filled. "We don't got time to swap stories," he said gruffly. "We still got a ways to go before Prescott and there's plenty of men that'll be looking for us."

"But I like stories," Doyle said with a snarl. "And I bet this one's a beaut."

"All right," Gus said, "you want to hear a story? Why don't I tell you about the beating I took while I was waiting for my partner to come and get me after I was shot?"

"You were shot?" Abigail gasped.

Doyle hunkered down to focus upon his supper and snarled, "You're still walkin', so it couldn't have been too bad."

"Didn't you wonder where I went?" Gus asked. "Didn't it strike you as somewhat peculiar when I didn't come back?"

"What did you want me to do?" Doyle snapped. "I rode along the route you were scouting and found your horse grazing all by his lonesome. Farther up a ways, there were more tracks, but they was a damn mess and I ain't some Injun who can just put my ear to the ground and figure out where you got off to."

"He tried, Gus," Abigail said. "Doyle really did try."

More than anything, what caught Gus's ear was the fact that Abigail actually used Doyle's proper name instead of just referring to him as "that other one." The sound of that particular word coming from her seemed to have caught Doyle by surprise as well, because both partners merely glared at each other without taking the fight any further.

A cold wind ripped through the camp that made the fire sputter and the trees rustle.

"This bacon is really good," Jacob said timidly. "Is there anything else to go with it?"

Abigail let out a sigh and told him, "That one there doesn't carry much, but there were a few cans at the bottom of a saddlebag he didn't want me to see. Why don't I dig them up for you?"

Doyle set his plate down and stomped across the camp, but it wasn't to keep Abigail from rooting through his things. Instead, he motioned for Gus to follow him away from the feeble glow of the fire.

Standing up, Gus walked over to Abigail and asked, "Where's that gun of yours?"

"Actually, it's not mine."

"Where is it?"

Abigail blinked and took the pistol from a pocket in her skirt. The gun was one of Doyle's holdout weapons, which was usually kept in his boot. In her hands, the pistol looked twice as large. "Here," she said. "Go on and take it. He just let me carry it in case someone came along while he was gone."

Gus snatched the gun away from her and checked the cylinder. It was loaded, so Doyle must have been somewhat concerned for her safety.

"I mean what I said," she told him. "He really did try to find you. After he brought back your horse, he was worried sick. He didn't say as much, but I could tell. He barely got a wink of sleep this whole time and I've been so concerned that I barely know what day it is." Gus was still tucking the gun away when she wrapped her arms around him. "I'm glad you're alive. How did you get hurt?"

"Never mind that. Do you have any other weapons?"

"No."

"If Jacob asks for a gun, you let me know all right?"

"Sure, but why? Can't you trust him?"

"I'm just not taking any chances is all," Gus assured her. "We made it this far by being careful, so I'm not about to let up now. Just keep your eye on that other one and let me know if he does or says anything that strikes you as peculiar."

"You mean Doyle?"

Half a grin drifted across Gus's face as he said, "No. The other other one."

Abigail nodded and then leaned to one side, which was all she needed to do to get a look at Jacob. The bounty hunter had been eating the whole time and was about to lick his plate clean. "He's handsome."

"I'll just take your word on that one." After saying that, Gus walked around the perimeter of the little camp to where Doyle was waiting. As soon as he got close enough to Doyle, Gus thought his partner was going to take a swing at him.

Doyle's fist stopped just short of knocking against Gus's jaw, but not before Gus's hand snapped up to block it. Doyle grinned and said, "Nothin' wrong with your speed, Gus. Looks like that hurt, though."

"I was shot in the shoulder."

"Bad?"

"Just a cut." Wincing as he worked out some of the pain that had flared up, Gus added, "A deep cut."

"So what the hell happened to you anyway? You got shot and then what?"

Gus swiped at his head and pushed back the hair that had become a matted, tangled mess. So much dust and grit fell out that he felt as if he'd been dragged from the back of a horse rather than ridden one. He gave Doyle a quick account of what happened after he was shot, including everything right up to the moment when he caught sight of Jacob.

"So he just happened to be there when you escaped?" Doyle asked.

"Yeah. What's bothering you now?"

Dropping his voice to a harsh whisper, Doyle said, "Whoever that fella is over there, I don't trust him. He's got a bad look about him."

"What's that mean?"

"It means he still smells like he's got a star pinned to his chest. He ain't comin' with us any farther. I ain't about to risk getting caught with that woman. Unless we do this the right way, we'll be gunned down and planted in a shallow hole before anyone stops to ask why we brought her back. I doubt that woman would even speak on our account."

"She won't let anyone shoot us without trying to explain things," Gus said.

"You sure about that?"

"Has she tried to run away?"

Doyle clenched his jaw, even though he obviously didn't have to think about his answer. Finally, he grumbled, "No, but—"

"And has she tried to knock you in the head to get away? Seems like she had plenty of opportunities while you were riding. Speaking of that, why'd you let her sit behind you if you were so worried?"

"I was testin' her."

"And?" Gus asked.

"She didn't try anything, but that only means she doesn't want to be left out here all on her lonesome."

"You figured that out all for yourself, huh?" Gus draped an arm around Doyle's shoulder and guided him a bit farther from the camp. He spoke even softer on the off chance that Jacob's ears were as good as his eyes. "I put him through a test or two of my own and he did just fine. He had plenty of chances to double-cross me and he didn't."

"I thought you trusted him so much," Doyle growled. When he saw the stern glare on Gus's face, he shrugged. "Fine, so maybe I ain't one to talk about being suspicious. But tell me, if you trust him so much and he passed all them tests, why'd you take his gun?"

"What kind of question is that?"

"A pretty reasonable one," Doyle replied, "especially since you got a gun that you didn't have before and your friend is wearin' an empty holster."

At that moment, Gus realized just how tired he was. Everything over the past day or so weighed down upon him like a set of lead weights. Under normal circumstances, he would have been able to whip up a lie to fit any occasion and tell it in a way that would have convinced his own mother he was quoting the Gospel. Now Gus could barely keep his eyes open and could hardly think straight, thanks to the pain that had soaked into every last one of his joints as well as the wound in his shoulder that had still hardly been tended.

"I was tryin' to keep my head down until Smythe and his men either rode off to try to find me or were stuck trying to explain all that shooting," Gus said. "The last thing I needed was for someone like Jacob to mention my name in the wrong company or even attract a bit of attention at the wrong time. I pulled him aside and that's when I found out he was a bounty hunter."

"He's a what?"

The gears in Gus's head were starting to turn again, but it was just easier to come clean. "Jacob's after the reward being offered by Abigail's father. He heard the shot that took me down, followed it to its source and saw the men hauling me off to Fort Verde. Since he seems to know a lot about Smythe and the rest of those kidnappers, I figured it might be better to keep him close than to leave him be."

"So," Doyle said in a surprisingly controlled tone, "he's a bounty hunter?"

Gus's eyes snapped toward the campfire. Although he and Doyle were far enough away to talk with a bit of privacy, they suddenly didn't seem far enough. "Yeah," he finally replied, "that's what he told me."

"Is he anything like that bounty hunter you talked into helping us root out the Swillen brothers?"

"You remember that, huh?"

Doyle grinned and nodded. "Hell, yes, I remember. That was a fine piece of work. You got that bounty hunter convinced to track down them Swillen boys so's we could kill 'em and he could drag in their sorry hides for the reward. You just forgot to mention Roy and Jack Swillen were sittin' on a strongbox full of cash that was worth ten times that reward."

"In some regards I suppose this is a bit like that time," Gus admitted.

"Why didn't you just say so?"

"Because you nearly killed that bounty hunter three times before he could get the job done. I didn't want to take a risk on the same thing happening here. We've come this far and everything nearly got ruined by me getting bushwhacked. I needed to track you down quick and I . . . I couldn't. . . ." Gus gritted his teeth as if pulling out his next words was akin to pulling an arrow out of his leg. Looking Doyle in the eye, he spoke in a rumbling voice that barely caused his lips to move. "I was in a condition where I could barely ride. Lord only knows if I could have caught up to you without someone leading the way. I was in a hurry to get away from that place, so I had to take what I could get. Jacob was the first likely prospect I could find."

"In case you forgot, that bounty hunter woulda shot us both in the back if he had half the chance," Doyle reminded him.

"Which is why we won't give this one half a chance. And, in case you forgot, that letter I sent to Thomas Swann said we'd be bringing his daughter back in one piece to that little town southeast of Prescott. If we make him wait too long, the rest of his hired guns may just burn down the two known outlaws with his daughter before we get a chance to explain ourselves."

Doyle's face took on the qualities of frozen rock. "This idea of yours just gets worse and worse, Gus. How many different sets of hired guns are gonna be after us when it's all said and done?"

"That's why we could use someone else on our side. After tangling with us twice already, Smythe will think he's got us all figured out. Just one more man on our side could tip the balance back in our direction."

"Sure, but only if you know he's on our side."

"He is," Gus assured him. "He came this far to find Abigail and now he knows we're all working to that same end."

Doyle looked toward the campfire to see Abigail and Jacob talking to each other. "Looks like he's doin' his best to get awful close to her awful fast."

"Which is fine by me," Gus replied. "That just means he'll do his best to make sure she stays safe. He ain't stupid, so he's got to know that he'll do better with partners than on his own. How else will he pull down the bounties on Smythe and them others?"

"Just as long as he don't expect a piece of the reward money bein' offered by Abigail's father." The silence coming from Gus along with the look on his face wasn't encouraging in the slightest. "He doesn't think he's gonna get any of that reward does he?"

"If he works with us and holds up his end, he should get a cut."

Although Doyle may have been suspicious before, hearing that made him mad enough to spit. "You can't promise money that ain't yours."

"Yeah? Well Smythe's got more hired guns work-

ing for him and they'll all be comin' straight for
us. We'll need the help and there ain't no reason
why Jacob won't step up. We're all workin' to the
same end."

Doyle ground his teeth together as if he was liter-
ally chewing on what he'd heard. Finally, he glanced
over to the camp and said, "He may earn his keep
just by keeping the lady occupied."

Gus looked over there as well and found Abigail
still sitting beside Jacob, talking in hushed tones.
Every so often, Abigail would reach over to pat
Jacob's arm. Each time she did so, she kept her hand
on him for a little longer.

"Say what you want about that bounty hunter,"
Doyle said, "but I don't know him from Adam. He
ain't getting a weapon until he proves himself
to me."

"I've got no problem with that."

"That's funny. You don't have problems with a
lot of things anymore."

"What's that supposed to mean?" Gus asked.

"Last time I checked, you were the sort of man
who'd string a man like Jacob along until you
got out of that fort and then put a bullet through
his head."

"So what would you suggest?" Gus asked. "You
wanna shoot him?"

"Not straightaway," Doyle said, "though I might
have done that if I'd been the one to meet him first.
What bothers me is why you would take a chance
like that, Gus. Why would you risk trusting a
bounty hunter when you're trying to escape with
your life?"

"I didn't know how long I been knocked out or how far ahead you might have gotten. I knew he'd set his sights on me and the last thing I wanted was to allow Jacob to follow me, so I got to him first."

"But you didn't kill him," Doyle mused. "Ain't that peculiar? I seen you kill a man with yer bare hands because he *may* have been a lawman. Remember that?"

"Yeah. I was drunk."

"But you were the Gus McCord I known for all these years. Now you ain't. Maybe yer gettin' soft."

The more Doyle spoke, the more his voice resembled an animal's growl. "After you got close enough to spot the signal fire, you could have killed that kid and left him for the coyotes," Doyle said. "Why didn't you? Would that be one death too many?"

Gus must have had a nervous twitch or two of his own, because Doyle's eyebrows perked up as if he'd spotted a tell on the face of a rich man sitting across from him at a card table. Doyle nodded and said, "Abigail told me all about how noble you become and how you're sick of all the killin' and such. I wanted to tell her all about the blood you spilled and all the lead you've thrown all these years, but thought it might just break her little heart."

For a strange reason, Gus felt a tighter knot in his belly than when he'd been forced to rely upon Jacob to catch up to his partner.

"I didn't tell her none of that, though," Doyle continued. "That make you feel better, noble man?"

Gus straightened his back until he could glare defiantly into his partner's eyes. "I'm through with fretting about why I do what I do. If I wanted to an-

swer to someone, I'd earn my daily bread doin'
chores for some man in a suit or farming someone
else's ground. I don't answer to anyone and that in-
cludes you!"

Gus's voice quickly rose above the whisper he'd
used to keep from being heard by the couple near
the fire. Because he made sure to keep the other two
in the corner of his eye, he knew Abigail and Jacob
had halted their own conversation. He could feel
their eyes on him, which didn't slow him down in
the least.

"So maybe he is a bounty hunter," Gus said.
"And maybe I didn't kill him when I got my first
chance. Maybe I am sick of getting blood on my
hands. What the hell is that to you?"

"I'll tell you what it is to me!" Doyle snapped. "It
could be the difference between me havin' a lily-
livered tenderfoot for a partner or havin' the old Gus
McCord. Havin' one of those men at my side could
get me rich and the other could get me killed. You
know what happens to tenderfeet in our line of
work, Gus? They catch bullets and they catch them
right quick!"

Stepping up to Doyle until he was nose to nose
with the other man, Gus snarled, "Who's gonna
send that bullet my way, Doyle? You? If you think
I don't have the sand to kill you no more, then
go ahead and reach for that gun at yer side. You
think I've gone soft? Make a move and see what
happens."

For a moment, Gus was certain Doyle would take
him up on that offer. In his mind, Gus was thinking
about every possible thing Doyle might do to put an

end to him and every possible thing he could do to prevent it. He didn't show any of that to his partner, however. Gus's face may as well have been a solid unreadable slab of stone.

In a matter of seconds, Doyle backed down. "I don't wanna fight you, Gus," he said as he relaxed the arm that had previously been drifting toward his gun. "Things are bound to get ugly before they get better and I just wanna make certain I ain't goin' into it alone."

"Smythe nearly killed me and the only reason he didn't was because he took too much time enjoying himself while beating me to a pulp. Nobody does that to me," Gus vowed. "I may be getting tired of killin', but I ain't about to let Smythe and the bastards workin' for him get away with what they done."

"So the lady wasn't lying?" Doyle asked. "You really had your fill of all of this?"

"Every man's got his limit. I suppose I reached mine."

Doyle stared at Gus as if he couldn't decide whether he was going to shoot him or shake his hand. In the end, he did neither. "I suppose some extra help on this job could do us some good. But if he steps out of line," Doyle said as he jabbed a finger toward Jacob, "he'll be dead where he stands. Agreed?"

"Agreed. And after this job is done, I'm through."

"You really think we stand to make enough money to retire on?"

"It should hold us over for a while," Gus replied. "Maybe a good, long while."

"Then I'm still in," Doyle announced. He extended a hand, and when Gus accepted it, Doyle added, "Think long and hard before you try to be all respectable, Gus. It may not be as easy as you think."

"I know."

With that, Doyle reached out with his free hand to pluck the .32 that had been tucked beneath Gus's gun belt. "Here you go, bounty hunter," Doyle said as he walked toward the campfire and tossed the gun to Jacob. "You'll need this if yer ridin' with us to Prescott. But if I think you're about to aim that pistol at the wrong man, I'll see to it you die real slow."

Although Doyle grinned when he spoke, the warning didn't lose one bit of its sharpness. It was plain to see he would have been just as happy for an excuse to put the bounty hunter down. For the moment, Jacob merely held the gun in both hands as if the iron was burning his skin.

Abigail looked at Doyle for a moment and then looked at Gus. Her eyes inevitably returned to Jacob, and when they did, they were wide and eager. "You're a bounty hunter?" she gasped. "How interesting!"

Chapter 24

Twenty miles southeast of Prescott

With the two horses Gus had stolen in Fort Verde, there were enough for each member of the group to have his own. Even so, Abigail stayed so close to Jacob that she might as well have shared a saddle with him. There was no mistaking the way she looked at him. Her blond hair may have been matted from too many days without being properly washed, but she'd fussed with it enough to keep it presentable. Every time they'd stopped to water the horses, she'd used the opportunity to splash her face and clear away as much trail dust as possible. When they finally made it to a spot where they could spend the night at a hotel, she'd practically jumped for joy. The town's name was Killebrew.

"I've never heard of it," Abigail said as the other three led the way down the street.

"I'm not surprised," Gus grumbled. Ignoring the well-practiced scowl she showed him, he added, "But we can still rent a room here. That is, if there's one to be had."

"Of course there's one to be had. I can see the hotel from here."

"I can see the whole town from here," Doyle said as he nodded toward the battered collection of weathered buildings that was overshadowed by a single structure that had a second floor. "That's why it's perfect."

Jacob and Abigail looked down to the sign that bore the name of the town, along with several bullet holes, a few knots and splintered edges that had been chipped away by too many birds using it as a perch. Actually, from what they could see, the rest of Killebrew wasn't a whole lot better.

"Why are we even stopping here?" Abigail asked. "We aren't that far from Prescott, are we?"

"Probably a day's ride or less," Jacob said.

Abigail's eyes lit up even more than usual when Jacob spoke. "There you go! We can be in Prescott today!"

"That's a day's ride from here," Doyle corrected. "Most of the day's gone already."

Although she obviously wasn't happy with the situation, Abigail knew all too well that it was useless to argue with the two outlaws. Rather than try her luck, she declared, "Then I'm going to that hotel and I'm having a bath. I won't spend one more day smelling just as bad as the rest of you." With that, she snapped her reins and was off.

In the time he'd spent riding with the two outlaws, Jacob had learned to keep his mouth shut and his head down. So far, that had served him well enough to get this far without more than a few cross words passing between him and Doyle every so often. This time, Jacob merely flicked his reins and rode through the cloud of dust Abigail had left behind.

Killebrew felt like a settlement through and through. Some folks had settled for that spot and were too lazy or too tired to find a better one. Even the couple of mangy dogs hunkering along the sides of the street seemed to have settled for that spot as a place to catch their breath until they could find a better place to go.

Upon reaching the hotel, Gus found a register lying open upon a spotless desk. The last name scrawled upon that page had been put there nearly a month ago. For that reason, the clerk tried to charge them triple the normal rate of any other hotel. The skinny fellow in the dark brown vest didn't hold up long under the angry stares of the three filthy men standing in front of him. Even Abigail looked at him as if she was about to cut his throat.

"You folks seem like good sorts," the clerk sputtered. "Why don't we make that the price for two rooms instead of just one?" When the silence grew even heavier, the clerk quickly added, "And breakfast! It'll include breakfast as well. Will that do?"

"That'll do nicely," Abigail said as she replaced her sneer with an angelic smile. "I'll need a bath as well."

"That'l . . . ummm . . . that'll be extra, I'm afraid."

"Perfectly reasonable," Abigail chirped. She looked to her three companions and waited. Jacob was the one to step forward and give the clerk an extra few coins, which pleased her to no end. As soon as the fee was paid, she all but skipped toward a staircase that looked like it could barely hold her weight.

"We'll settle the rest of the bill when we leave," Doyle said.

Squirming under the cold gazes from the outlaws, the clerk nodded and replied, "As the lady said . . . perfectly reasonable."

Gus may have been through with being a murderer, but he wasn't above stealing a free night and breakfast from some scrap heap of a hotel. When Doyle promised to settle up a bill that way, it meant skipping out of town before the clerk had a chance to corner them for his money. Right now, all Gus wanted was to sit down on something other than a saddle and kick his feet up. If Doyle wanted to save a few dollars the old-fashioned way, that was just fine.

Killebrew's stables were even sorrier than its hotel, so the horses were watered, fed and hitched to a shady spot under an old tree. Gus got the rest he was after once he found a rocker on the hotel's front porch that looked as weathered as the rest of the town. When he sat in it and felt the creaky wooden slats bend to conform to his backside, Gus thought he'd died and gone to heaven.

Doyle and Jacob were chatting like old friends as they stepped onto the porch. While Jacob seemed relieved to be treated as something close to a partner, Gus knew that was only Doyle's way of keeping the bounty hunter close enough to watch him. All things considered, the situation could be a whole lot worse.

"I suppose we should ride in to Prescott sooner

rather than later," Jacob said. "We might want to pay Mr. Swann a visit before we just waltz up with Abigail at our side. Since Smythe's probably got someone watching the family, it might be better if I—"

"We won't need to pay him a visit," Gus muttered. "He'll be comin' here."

Jacob looked at Gus as if he'd just sprouted horns.

"How do you know that?" Jacob asked.

"Simple," Gus replied. "I invited him."

While Jacob looked confused, Doyle was about to bust. "You mean we invited him. Gus mailed the letter but it was our idea."

"It was mostly my idea," Gus corrected.

"What idea?" Jacob fumed.

Folding his hands over his belly, Gus said, "Me and Doyle intercepted a letter from the kidnappers that was bound for Thomas Swann. I put in a letter of my own telling him to keep watch on this town for his daughter to arrive."

"So you knew about this place?"

"Sure!" Doyle replied. "Little holes like this are perfect for lying low. This one's real close to Prescott and there ain't even any law here to speak of. At least, there wasn't any the last time we were here. Hopefully, Swann knows where to find it. When did you tell him to get here?"

"I told him to start looking for us as soon as he got the letter. With the mail being as slow as it is, plus however long it took for Swann to get the letter, open it, read it and do something about it, he should have scouts in place by now."

"That's why you were in such a damn hurry to get here!" Jacob said. "That's a hell of a plan! Why didn't you tell me about that before?"

"You're still on borrowed time," Gus said.

Jacob winced. "You still think I got a reason to mess this up?"

"Why not ask him?" Gus replied as he waved toward Doyle. "He's the one you need to impress."

Rather than pose the question to Doyle, Jacob looked in a completely different direction. After a second, he asked, "Do you see what I see?"

Doyle followed the other man's line of sight to discover a pair of stooped-back old-timers dragging what looked to be a huge, dented bucket across the dusty street. "Well, what have we here?" he chuckled.

Gus couldn't help but be amused by the sight of the two old men struggling to move an empty container that was nearly big enough to fit both of them inside. "Reminds me of two turtles pulling one shell. My guess is that's supposed to be the bathtub Abigail ordered."

Doyle laughed at that, but Jacob wasn't amused.

"Not that," the bounty hunter said as he pointed a bit farther down the street. "I was talking about them."

Both Gus and Doyle were still laughing at the sight of the old turtles when they found what had caught the bounty hunter's attention. Four men walked toward the hotel, bringing a quick stop to the laughter and causing Gus to jump to his feet.

Smythe's glasses reflected the fading sunlight like the eyes of a cat staring at him from where it was about to pounce. Bennett stood to Smythe's left and Dan stood to his right. The fourth was a tall, lanky fellow Gus didn't recognize from Benson or Fort Verde. The stranger carried a rifle that was almost as tall as he was, and came to a stop as he brought it up to his shoulder, allowing the other three to keep walking ahead of him.

"I see you two found each other," Smythe called out. "That's very touching. Now just as long as you found Abigail Swann, we can leave you to your reunion."

"Don't do anything foolish," Gus snarled.

Knowing the comment was addressed to him, Doyle replied, "I didn't live this long bein' foolish." With that, he placed his hand upon his holstered .45 and stepped onto the edge of the porch.

Gus hopped down from the porch. When he took a quick glance over his shoulder, he saw Jacob had put his back to the hotel so he could get a better look at the other side of the street.

"There's more coming from that direction," the bounty hunter said.

"And a few more on the roof of the stable," Gus added. He'd seen a pair of heads poke up from behind the sign on top of the long, sagging building that was across the street and down a ways from the hotel. Either those two knew they'd been spotted or they were responding to a signal from Smythe, because they straightened up just enough to make their presence known. Each of them propped a rifle upon their knees so it could be displayed as well.

Smythe and his men came to a stop directly in

front of the stable. That put them about thirty yards away from the hotel. Standing like a statue in the middle of the street, Smythe took a slow look around. The only way Gus knew the man's head was moving at all was because of the shifting reflection from Smythe's spectacles.

"Bring her out and hand her over," Smythe demanded. "Do it now and do it quick."

"What makes you think we even got her?" Doyle asked.

"Don't insult my intelligence."

"All right, then. You shoot us and you'll never know where she is."

Gus could see Smythe's grin from where he was standing. "Or," Smythe replied, "I can burn the lot of you off the face of the earth and tear this pathetic town apart to find her at my leisure."

Doyle turned to glance toward Gus and said, "I guess he's got us there."

This was Doyle's element. If Gus had learned one thing during his years of riding through storms of hellfire and flying lead with the man, he knew that Doyle only truly came alive when he rode on the edge of death. Plenty of men liked to talk about living that way, but not many of them could back it up. Doyle, on the other hand, simply found it amusing to test the will of the Reaper.

"I fooled about with you men enough already," Smythe said. "Next time my man here fires his rifle, it'll be the death of you, Gus."

But Gus didn't need to be told the stranger with the rifle behind Bennett was the same one who had fired the shot to put the most recent wound in his shoulder. The stranger had a dangerous yet familiar glint in his eye that let him know he'd already gotten a taste for Gus's blood.

Smythe and Doyle swapped a few threats, but that just gave Gus the time he needed to get a look at the other batch of men approaching the hotel. That bunch rode down the western end of the street, which put the hotel and Smythe's men in front of them. Two men in the bunch rode on either side of a third. That third man sat tall in his saddle and was decked out in a suit that may have been even fancier than Smythe's. Those expensive clothes said a lot to Gus, but not as much as the horse the third man led by the reins. The horse was saddled up and ready for a rider, but wasn't bearing one just yet. Once the group got a little closer, Gus could see that the saddle was the broader, flatter kind made to be used by ladies.

"We have her, all right," Gus declared.

Jacob stepped forward to grab hold of Gus's arm. "What the hell are you doing?" he hissed.

Pulling his arm free, Gus raised his voice and said, "Abigail Swann. That's who you're after, right?"

"Abigail Swann?" asked the well-dressed fellow leading the riderless horse. He bellowed his next question loudly enough to be heard from one end of Killebrew to the other. "Where is she?"

"I've got her," Gus said. "But it seems these men have come to take her away from me. In fact, I believe they were the ones who took her in the first place."

The man who'd brought two partners and an extra horse along with him was refined, but not soft around the edges. His hair and beard were more silver than gray, which was a quality that seemed to come naturally to rich folks. From what Gus had heard, Thomas Swann was one of the richest folks around.

"Where's my daughter?" the silver-haired man asked, as if to confirm what Gus had already pieced together. "I was told I'd find her here."

"I sent the letter making that claim, sir," Gus replied. "I'm glad to see you brought along some extra help. Looks like we're gonna need it."

So far, the day was one of the few that actually spooled out exactly as Gus had planned. He'd arrived at the meeting place outside of Prescott, Abigail was still in one piece and her father had arrived to take her. Even Gus's guess that Thomas Swann would bring extra guns with him had panned out, but the day wasn't over yet.

At the other end of the street, Smythe wore the amused expression of a man taking in a stage show. "I hope you brought the ransom money, Mr. Swann. I trust you remember the original amount? Seeing as how you arrived in such a timely manner, I won't even charge interest for the inconvenience I've been forced to endure thus far."

"To hell with your inconvenience," Swann blustered. "If one of you men doesn't produce my little girl right quick, I'll have my men earn their pay by cleaning out every last greasy one of you from this town!"

Smythe remained in his spot, but Bennett and Dan shifted anxiously on either side of him. Calming the other two with subtle motions of his hands, Smythe said, "The arrangement is the same, Mr. Swann. Hand over the sum we agreed upon or your daughter dies. I have more than enough men here to finish the job."

"And I got men of my own," Swann replied. "There'll be plenty more on the way if need be."

Gus was keeping an eye on those men Swann referred to. Both looked more like ranch hands than gunmen. They dressed like cowboys and had the lean, eager faces of rowdy kids who'd gotten into a fight or two. Their hands were on their guns, but hadn't brought them up to bear just yet. That kind of hesitance could make them even worse than useless.

"All that matters is who's here right now," Smythe said. "Are you willing to bet the men I brought won't be able to pick your boys off? For that matter, do you think I can't kill your daughter in front of you if I don't receive my money?"

"You harm a hair on her head and I'll skin you alive!" Swann shouted.

Always ready to add more kindling to the fire, Doyle added, "And I'll help! I didn't come all this way just to talk."

Just then, one of the windows on the second floor of the hotel was opened and Abigail leaned outside. "Daddy!" she hollered. "Is that really you?"

Swann's eyes widened and he looked up to the window where his daughter was waving. Snapping his fingers at the men on either side of him, he barked, "Get her out of there!"

Both of the men with Thomas Swann drew their pistols and then pointed them at the silver-haired man.

"Now," Smythe said, "about that money you owe."

Chapter 25

"Doyle, can you get those two with Mr. Swann?" Gus asked under his breath.

"Sure."

"Jacob, fire all you got at that roof across the street."

"But I only got one gun," the bounty hunter protested.

"Then make the best of it." With that, Gus jumped into the street, drew the Army model .44 from his holster and fired at Smythe.

Doyle let out a wild howl as he took up a gun in each hand and sent a storm of lead toward the men on either side of Abigail's father. The men on either side of Swann opened fire. Even after one of them was hit, he kept pulling his trigger until another round spun him to one side and sent him flying to the ground.

Fortunately, Mr. Swann had the sense to duck. The silver-haired man's good fortune continued when the men who'd so recently betrayed him shifted their focus onto Doyle. All Swann could do from there was wrap his arms around his horse's neck and pray he lived through the next couple of seconds.

Jacob may not have sounded too confident a moment ago, but he held his end up well enough. Gus figured he'd either hear shots from behind him or feel one drill through his back. Either way, he'd know where he stood with the bounty hunter. So far, it seemed that his instinct to take Jacob at his word was holding up.

Smythe was caught in midsentence and looked positively appalled that Gus wasn't behaving according to his plan. It took a moment for Smythe to wrap his mind around Gus and Doyle's inexplicable call to arms, but in that moment a bullet caught Dan in the chest to knock him straight down. Dan landed in a heap and groaned in agony. It was clear he wasn't about to get up anytime soon.

Jacob pulled his trigger in a deliberate manner that seemed to go in time to a heartbeat. As he burned through the rounds in his .32, he hopped down from the porch and ran across the street. That way, he was out of the riflemen's line of fire.

Swearing under his breath as he watched the bounty hunter run away, Gus planted his feet and gritted his teeth. Although Smythe and Bennett were still in front of him, he was more concerned with the rifleman who'd taken up a position behind and to the right of those men. More gunshots ripped through the stables, where Jacob had scurried for cover. At least the bounty hunter was getting paid back for his cowardice while also keeping those riflemen occupied. Gus couldn't worry about any of that, however. He had plenty on his plate and only a pair of bullets left to clear it off.

Smythe fired a shot that whipped through the air within inches of Gus's left ear. Bennett was shooting up a storm, but his horse was too concerned with running for cover to take proper aim. Dropping to one knee, Gus took a split second to aim, fired his last two shots and sent Bennett to the ground.

Now that he had a moment to breathe, Gus ran for the closest water trough, which happened to be in front of the hotel. By the time his backside hit the dirt and his shoulder hit the back of the trough, Gus was already emptying the .44's cylinder and fishing fresh rounds from his gun belt. In a matter of seconds, hot lead from Smythe's pistol began punching through the wood on either side of him.

Gus turned to check on Doyle and instead saw Mr. Swann riding straight toward him. The rich man's panicked horse veered just before stampeding through the trough and wound up stomping onto the porch of the hotel. Amid the sound of hooves pounding against the porch, the rider dove behind the trough and scrambled to sit beside Gus.

"What the hell's the meaning of this?" Thomas Swann growled as he pointed a gun directly at Gus's face.

"I'm the one that sent the letter, you idiot," Gus replied.

"You set up an ambush?"

"No! Those men who held you at gunpoint are to blame. Them and the dandy at the other end of the street."

More gunfire picked away at the trough, which

did nothing at all to diminish the fire in Swann's eyes. "Those men are on my payroll and you're just some gunman who opened fire when we came to talk."

"You mean those nice fellas who pointed their guns at you? I'll bet they insisted on coming along with you and nobody else?"

After a pause, Swann replied, "Yes."

"And I bet they know about everything else you've done where getting your daughter back is concerned."

Slowly, Swann lowered his gun. "Damn it, they set me up! Those two weaseled their way into everything where this kidnapping business is concerned and I thought they were just trying to help me put an end to it."

Gus muttered something else, but his words were wiped out by the crack of the stranger's rifle and the knocking of a fresh hole getting blasted through the trough. Another couple of shots were fired, but these came from directly across the street and up a bit from ground level. Gus chanced a look over the trough and spotted one man on the roof of the stable instead of the two who had been there before. Jacob was that man and he waved like a madman to catch Gus's attention.

"I got 'em, Gus!" Jacob shouted. "I got 'em both!"

Suddenly, Jacob was pulled down beneath the sign on top of the stable by a pair of hands that seemed to come up from the building itself. When the bounty hunter struggled to stand up again, he raised a rifle over his head and brought it down like a spear. The stock cracked against something to make a jarring noise that could be heard all the way down on the street. Jacob stood up again and shouted, "*Now* I got 'em both!"

Thanking the bounty hunter just didn't seem good enough. Actually, Gus wanted to take the younger man as his own son for clearing that rooftop. Rather than stand around and wait for Gus's accolades, Jacob put the rifle to his shoulder and fired down at the street. Bennett was the first to stand up from cover and he was the first to drop when two of Jacob's shots found their target. Jacob shifted his aim to the stranger at that end of the street, but was only able to force the rifleman to a better spot behind some barrels.

The moment Gus saw Smythe running across the street, he fired a shot at him. Smythe kept his head down and moved fast enough to duck behind a post that supported the awning of a building next to the stable.

Doyle had his hands full as well. Having already put down one of Mr. Swann's turncoats, Doyle was wrestling with the other. Both men must have either burned through their ammunition or lost their guns, because they were both down to fighting with knives. Fortunately, Doyle was just as dangerous with a blade as he was with a firearm.

Doyle swung the hunting knife he kept strapped to his boot, causing the gunman to hop backward. The gunman drove forward just as quickly and lunged with a bowie knife. The gunman took one swing after another as his arm snapped out again and again to slice at Doyle. When one of his swings was blocked, Doyle was forced to duck under the bowie knife before losing his head to it. While he was down, Doyle flicked his arm upward and opened a wide gash across the gunman's belly.

"That's right!" Doyle hollered as he got to his feet and flipped his knife from one hand to another. "You just don't got what it takes to get through me!" With that, Doyle cocked his arm back so he could swing the knife with as much force as possible. He would have buried the blade into his opponent if not for the rifle shot that sent him spinning like a top.

"Doyle!" Gus shouted as he watched his partner wobble on his feet and then fall over. Gus looked down the other end of the street and spotted Smythe's rifleman kneeling behind a barrel so only a sliver of him poked out from behind cover. Before he could do anything, Gus had to fall back. He barely got behind the trough before the stranger sent a round screaming toward him.

"Let's put an end to this," Swann said as he pulled open his vest to reveal a row of guns that had been tucked under his belt. Before he could draw any of the firearms, Gus pushed Swann down with one hand flat against his chest.

Keeping the silver-haired man pinned while he plucked two of the guns from Swann's belt, Gus said, "You're gonna go into that hotel and get your daughter."

"But I can—"

"You can do what I told you to do!" Gus snapped. "You came here for her, so go!"

There was no denying the ferocity in Gus's eyes as he gave the order and it was doubtful the devil himself could have gotten Gus to change his mind.

Rather than draw any more of that ire, Swann took up his gun with a trembling hand and nodded anxiously. Gus was already on the move.

The moment Gus stood up, he was under fire. Dan was still alive, but he was unwilling or unable to get to his feet. He fired at Gus from where he'd managed to drag himself after falling and was promptly put down for good by a shot from above. Gus didn't bother waving his thanks to Jacob and he didn't count on the bounty hunter to save him again. On the contrary, there wasn't much Jacob could do from his perch since both Smythe and the rifleman were directly under him.

Gus no longer felt any pain from the wound in his shoulder. He merely adjusted to the lack of mobility he had on that side and fired from the hip. Luckily, his trigger finger wasn't affected in the least and he sent a torrent of lead into the barrel where the rifleman had been hiding. His shots were wild, but many of them managed to send pieces of the barrel flying off in different directions. Although he would have been happy to put the rifleman down then and there, Gus really wasn't expecting to get that lucky.

The rifleman rolled away from the barrel as the upper ring broke loose and fell away. The moment he came to a stop, the stranger brought his weapon up and took aim. His finger was just tensing upon the trigger when Gus fired the gun in his left hand. Knowing better than to completely trust his aim on that side, Gus fired again and again until the rifleman hit the dirt.

Gus wasn't about to rest on his laurels just yet. He

swung both guns to the left, which was the direction he'd last seen Smythe slither off to when the shooting had started. The gun in Gus's right hand was emptied first, so he pulled that arm away from his body to reveal the other pistol he'd taken from Swann. The gun had been tucked under that arm and now dropped into Gus's waiting hand. All he needed was a target.

Smythe must have ducked around the stable, so Gus took a moment to shout over his shoulder, "You still with me, Doyle?" When he didn't get an answer, Gus turned to look at that end of the street. All he could see was a pile of bodies lying near a few very nervous horses. One of those bodies straightened up to raise a knife over his head to prepare for what had to be a finishing blow.

The figure that had pulled itself up was too big to be Doyle. Still holding the bowie knife over his head, the man let out a grunt and fell backward. Although he couldn't see every last detail from where he was, Gus could make out something protruding from the man's chest. Another figure propped himself up and shouted, "To your right!"

That voice was Doyle's, marking yet another instance where he had saved Gus's life.

Gus turned and reflexively pulled his trigger when he saw the shape of a man walking out of the stable. That shot hissed through the air without hitting anything, but managed to make Smythe think twice before firing a shot of his own. When Gus turned to face Smythe head-on, he was able to survey the carnage on that end of the street.

Dan and Bennett lay in the dirt no more than a

few yards from each other. Folks peeked out from windows and doors on both sides of the street, but didn't seem anxious to do any more than that.

"All right, Smythe," Gus wheezed. "You like to talk so much. What have you got to say now?"

Smythe held his gun at the ready, but Gus had one in each hand.

Smythe had all of his men with him, but most were lying motionless in the dirt or out of sight altogether.

All things considered, there wasn't much else for Smythe to say and there was only one thing left for him to do. Glaring defiantly through his spectacles, Smythe raised his gun and pulled his trigger.

Both of Gus's pistols barked a heartbeat before Smythe's hammer could drop. Lead burned through Smythe's body, snuffing him out before his back could slam against the outside of the stable.

Gus kept his pistols at the ready, blinking in surprise when it became clear that Smythe wasn't going to get up.

Panting like a tired dog as he staggered out of the stable, Jacob asked, "Is it over?"

"Yeah," Gus said, "looks that way. You all right?"

Jacob was favoring one leg and bleeding from enough places that his shirt was pasted to his torso. "I'll live." When Gus reached out to help him, Jacob reflexively twitched. Even when he saw the grateful smile on Gus's face, he still didn't know quite what to make of it.

"You did real good," Gus said. "I'm real glad I didn't have to kill you."

"Me too," Jacob replied. His eyes were drawn to a

sudden burst of motion across the street as Abigail rushed out of the hotel with her father in tow. Although the elder Swann tried his best to rein his daughter in, he wasn't having much success.

Abigail ran over to Jacob and wrapped her arms around him. She buried her face against his chest and started speaking in a current of words that were all too muffled to be heard. When she pulled herself away from the bounty hunter, she gave Gus the same treatment. This time, however, the recipient wasn't quite as grateful.

"Aww, son of a . . ." Gus snarled before his words were choked off.

"What's the matter?" Abigail asked. "Are you hurt?" When she looked down at his, she pulled in a quick breath.

"Looks like that fancy pants got a shot off after all," Gus mumbled. He lifted his arm and touched the bloody spot on his ribs. A deep gash had ripped through his shirt as well as the side of his body. It hurt like nobody's business, but he'd had worse. "Where's Doyle?"

"Last I saw him, he was over by my horses," Thomas Swann said from his daughter's side.

Gus looked over there and still saw the crumpled forms that hadn't moved since the last time he'd checked. Gripping his side, he rushed over there as quickly as he could. At that moment, he didn't even take time to wonder if Smythe had any more gunmen stashed somewhere waiting to take a shot at him. He didn't waste any time looking about or trying to figure any angles. All Gus wanted to do was get to his friend's side.

Dropping to one knee beside Doyle, Gus said, "You must be slipping, Doyle. I thought you could handle two men without me looking after you."

Doyle lay with one leg folded beneath him. He'd managed to prop himself up on one elbow, but couldn't get any farther. His face was bruised and his mouth was bleeding, but what worried Gus the most was the deep slashes in his arms and sides. There were smaller stab wounds in his chest, which looked a whole lot deeper. "That big fella thought he could take me," Doyle rasped.

The big fellow in question lay on the ground with his back arched and a look of pain etched on his face. Doyle's good-luck piece protruded from his chest like a post that had been driven into a patch of open ground.

"He was mistaken about that," Gus said. "Can you stand up?"

"Nah. I won't be goin' anywhere."

"You got to. This may be a small town, but we can't just stay here after all of this."

"I ain't tellin' you to stay," Doyle said. "I'm tellin' you to leave me here. Better yet," he added with a chuckle that also made him wince, "have the kid cash me in. At least it'll be some way for me to pay him back for not skinnin' out on us when the shooting started."

Gus stuck his arm under Doyle's back and started to lift. "Come on. You been hurt worse than this. All we need to do is get you patched up."

Although he wanted to keep laughing at whatever had struck a chord with him, Doyle let out a sudden hacking cough and swatted at Gus. "Put me down! It's too late for me, so just get out of here before some law dog comes along."

"Shut your mouth and stop fighting."

Suddenly, Doyle grabbed onto the front of Gus's shirt and hung on with more strength than any man in his condition should have been able to muster. "Stop it, Gus! I mean it. That big fella managed to sink that bowie knife into my back sometime during the fight."

Gus rolled Doyle over a bit to get a look for himself. Sure enough, there was enough blood seeping through the back of Doyle's shirt to create a puddle beneath him. "Aw, Lord." Gus sighed. "That's pretty bad."

"I told ya so." As he let out his next breath, Doyle started to shake. Soon, his shaking turned into broken laughter.

"What's so funny?" Gus asked.

"One death too many. You went through all of this to avoid it and I got it instead."

Shaking his head, Gus tried to look away so his friend couldn't see the guilt etched into his face. Doyle's eyes were so vacant and clouded over, however, that he probably didn't see much of anything at all.

"I didn't mean for this to happen, Doyle. Not to you."

"Eh, it was bound to happen . . . sooner or later. Just don't waste your . . ."

"I know, Doyle," Gus said. "Save your breath."

"Don't waste your time on Abigail," Doyle continued. "She's sweet on that damn bounty hunter."

Gus nodded and held Doyle up until his friend's

body became heavy and slack. He gritted his teeth and laid Doyle down. From there, Gus stood up and walked back to where Abigail was speaking excitedly to her father.

"You find Doyle?" Jacob asked.

Gus nodded. "Yeah."

"Is he all right?"

After a pause, Gus replied, "No. Come help me load him onto a wagon. I ain't leaving him here."

Abigail picked up immediately on the change in Gus's tone and looked over to where Doyle was stretched out on the ground. She threw a flurry of questions at Gus, followed by a few panicked pleas before finally breaking into tears. Gus ignored all of that, along with the stern words spoken by Thomas Swann. He and Jacob collected a horse and draped Doyle over the back of it. From there, Gus led the way out of town.

Sometime during the ride to Prescott, Swann started talking again. The silver-haired man's smooth baritone managed to cut through the fog in Gus's head and hold his attention for a moment. When Gus realized his ears had picked up on the mention of a reward, he felt sick to his stomach.

"... anything at all," was the last part of what Swann had been saying. "You brought my daughter back and dealt with all the ones who took her. Just name your price and it's yours."

"I don't want no reward," Gus told him. "Just a favor."

Chapter 26

The months that followed were busy ones for all who'd survived the gunfight at Killebrew. Thomas Swann fired everyone on his payroll who wasn't related to him by blood. When he wasn't scouting for new help, he was searching for any last remnant of Smythe's kidnapping ring. While it eventually came to light that Smythe and his men had been responsible for several other similar instances over the years, there wasn't a trace to be found of any surviving kidnappers. Swann would never give up the hunt, however, and funded several posses to track down folks that went missing throughout all of the Arizona Territories.

After spending some more time with Jacob, Abigail was soon given the task of planning her wedding. There were arrangements to be made and a dress to stitch together, all of which she did with bright eyes and excited hands. Once the preacher declared them man and wife several months later, Jacob gave up hunting wanted men and rode shotgun for Thomas's shipping company in Prescott. Now that Gus McCord and Doyle Hill were no longer about, stagecoaches tended to arrive at their destinations at a much more reliable rate.

As per Doyle's wishes, Jacob was given the chance to bring in his body to claim a substantial reward. Jacob refused and buried Doyle in a shady spot that wasn't far from a rowdy saloon.

Gus McCord rode away from Killebrew and wasn't heard from again. Not long after the shoot-out, Thomas Swann was commissioned to drive a shipment of trapping supplies and mining equipment north of the border into Canada. Somewhere just north of the border, the wagon and its battered old driver with the bad eye and foul temper went missing. Considering the harsh terrain and unfriendly natives of that area, it wasn't a wholly surprising outcome. When Thomas Swann's associates thought to ask why he'd decided to risk such a treacherous journey for such a menial shipment, the answer was always the same.

"It was a favor for a friend."

"A writer in the tradition of Louis L'Amour
and Zane Grey!"
—*Huntsville Times*

National Bestselling Author
RALPH COMPTON

**Available wherever books are sold or at
penguin.com**

No other series packs this much heat!

THE TRAILSMAN

**Follow the trail of the gun-slinging heroes of
Penguin's Action Westerns at
penguin.com/actionwesterns**